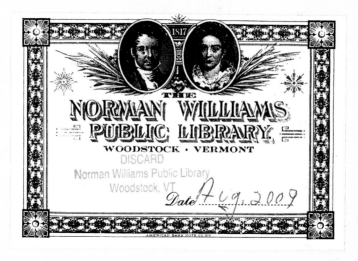

The Lie

Also by O. H. Bennett
The Colored Garden

The Lie by O. H. Bennett

ALGONQUIN BOOKS OF CHAPEL HILL 2009

Published by
ALGONQUIN BOOKS OF CHAPEL HILL
Post Office Box 2225
Chapel Hill, North Carolina 27515-2225

a division of
WORKMAN PUBLISHING
225 Varick Street
New York, New York 10014

This is a work of fiction. While, as in all fiction, the literary perceptions and insights are based on experience, all names, characters, places, and incidents either are products of the author's imagination or are used fictitiously.

LIBRARY OF CONGRESS CATALOGING-IN-PUBLICATION DATA
Bennett, O. H. (Oscar H.), 1957–
    The lie / by O. H. Bennett.—1st ed.
        p. cm.
    ISBN 978-1-56512-573-5
    1. African Americans—Fiction.   2. Race relations—Indiana—
Fiction.   3. Truthfulness and falsehood—Fiction.   4. Guilt—
Fiction.   5. Indiana—Social conditions—20th century—Fiction.
    6. Evansville (Ind.)—Fiction.   I. Title.
    PS3552.E54747L54 2009
    813'.54—dc22   2009011241

10 9 8 7 6 5 4 3 2 1
First Edition

for Pamela and Lillian

The Lie

one

HIS BROTHER LAY on the front porch, on the old, warped boards, eyes fixed on the bare bulb that hung above him. He was exposed lying there as if he were naked, because that is how it must feel when people can stare at you and you can't stare back.

Lawrence had been lying out there for a long time, and Terrell wondered if his brother would still be out there when their mom and dad came home. Lawrence had been out there when no one else had been. Terrell had checked. Standing over him, he had looked both directions on Gum Street and then he'd scanned each porch within view. He saw no one. Now, as if by magic, the entire neighborhood had turned out to see the body on the porch of the Matheus place. Children craned their necks and shoved one another. Some darted away to spread the word. Some neighbors whispered; others talked loudly. Old women caught their breaths and held the name of Jesus on their lips.

Lawrence's eyes stared straight at the dangling porch light. His mouth was partly opened, and that, along with his eyes, gave him a quizzical expression as if he were puzzled by the swarm of strangers around him. A photographer moved from his head to his feet and to one side then the other. Still Lawrence lay in his soaked T-shirt, wondering at it all.

Terrell could see the abrupt flashes of light from the camera through the front window blinds. The police had made no move to take Lawrence away or to cover him. They were more interested in Terrell, and his answers to their rapid spray of questions.

He could hear his answers as if he were just another person in the room. The questions kept coming. It was clear they wanted him to speed up his answers, to speak without thinking.

This is the story Terrell Matheus told the police:

"I was in the kitchen getting some punch.

"It was about three thirty or so, I don't know. Sometime after school.

"I was looking around for a clean glass, and I heard Lawrence's voice from outside and it sounded like he was cussing somebody.

"No. Don't remember him saying any names. He didn't know these guys. I told you that. So I went up front to see what was going on. The front door was open. The screen door was closed. Lawrence stood right in front of the door but was looking down the street.

"I didn't see the truck the first time it came around. There's a lot of cars parked on the street and trees along the sidewalk. I think I heard it, though, one of those busted muffler–sounding engines.

"Yeah, I asked him what was going on. He said some white boys in a white pickup truck stopped in front of the house just as he was coming up the stairs and asked him directions to the courthouse.

"Yes, he said he was just getting home when they honked at him. They said, Hey, bro, do you know the way to the county courthouse?

"He said they called him bro.

"No, I didn't hear the honk. I guess he said they honked, or maybe they just said hey or something. Lawrence, he say, he told them how to get there, and then they waited till he was halfway up the steps and asked if he knew the way to Africa 'cause he should get his black monkey ass on home. Then they cut outta there, squealing their tires.

"He said something like, You better burn rubber, you fucking country crackers. Yeah, that's what he said.

"No. I didn't hear that. That's what he told me he said. I just heard him cussing.

"Yeah. I think I did hear the tires peeling.

"Yeah, nah, I'm sure. Sure.

"He was pretty pissed off. Who wouldn't be? I was pissed just hearing him tell it.

"There were three of them in the front of the truck.

"No. He didn't tell me that.

"No. I didn't ask. I saw when they came back around.

"While we was talking. While he was telling me what happened.

"No, I was still in the house behind the screen door.

"About a couple of feet from the door . . . I don't know. I guess he walked to the edge of the porch.

"Like I said, they came back around and we could hear that loud engine and the gears switching. And Lawrence says, Oh, they want to fuck with me. I made to come out and he waved me back in. He said something like, They can't come on our street and talk shit. I don't think he thought they were going to get out and fight or anything. I don't know. I don't know. They didn't slow down much. He took one step down, I think, although I'm not sure—and they fired. It hit him all up in his chest and all. Around here. And then he fell backward. And it was so sudden I wasn't sure what happened. Like I saw it, but it didn't make any sense. He was standing there and then he wasn't, like that. Lawrence . . . he, Lawrence . . .

"I saw an arm pulled back in the pickup's window. The closest guy fired the shot. He had a black cap and blond hair, long, and there was another guy leaning over to see. And somebody driving—there were three of them. And they drove off.

"Nah, I don't know guns.

"Didn't think to look at the plates.

"Teenagers, I guess. Maybe older. Probably older.

"Chevy. I saw the Chevy sign on it. I don't know the year . . . old and beat up.

"When I went to open the door. It slipped from my hand. I forgot I had it. I kneeled down by him. Blood was all over his front and behind him on the walls too. His shirt was just soaked, just soaked. And he says, Oh. He says oh a couple of times, and I went to call emergency and I slipped and that's when I cut my hand on the glass.

"Then I called nine-one-one, and then I came back out.

"I wanted to get my brother to the damn hospital! What I want to talk about them crackers and their damn truck for on the phone?

"No, I didn't notice anybody else around. I was looking at Lawrence. I shouted at him. I patted his face 'cause I didn't want him to go to sleep. I wanted to keep him awake. I thought if I could keep him awake . . . but, I guess, he was dead already.

"No. That's all."

THE HARDEST PART for Terry wasn't the police officer. The hardest part was facing his parents. They arrived separately. Since the shooting, he'd felt each minute layered onto his life like brushstrokes, but later the minutes, like brushstrokes, blended together and he couldn't recall even the hours or the sequence of events. His father had come home. Terry sat in the front room on the sofa next to a police officer. He knew Lawrence was still out there, lying there.

Red and blue lights, chasing each other, circled the walls. He could hear the ambulance's idling engine.

His father still held his lunch bucket in his hand. He had stumbled into the living room and then ran out of momentum. He wore expressions Terry had not seen before on his father's face. Preston Matheus's round and wide-opened eyes questioned Terry. They pleaded with Terry to tell him that what had happened had not happened at all. The muscles of his face quivered and they seemed on the verge of shattering. Here was a pitiable, vulnerable father he'd never seen before.

Terry did not like seeing him that way and so he looked down at his left palm, wrapped with a cloth stained pink.

But the delicate wavering could be heard in his father's voice too. "Terry? Terry?"

Terry shook his head. He couldn't say it, not again, not to him.

"Terry, what happened? What happened to your brother?" His father's voice caught and choked.

Terry did not want to hear it.

The policeman patted Terry's back and Terry shrugged the hand away.

The stabbing light of flash cameras came through the front windows. Others came in the house. They walked by the scene in the middle of the living room, his father unable to advance another foot, and the son on the very edge of the couch unable to say another word. They spoke in hard, direct, and emotionless voices.

". . . only immediate family."

". . . spray pattern."

"Have Taylor dig it out of the siding only after he measures the entry angle."

". . . a list of friends and acquaintances before we leave."

Terry wasn't sure when they were speaking to him or to each other. Once he trusted himself, Terry managed a deep breath, and said, "Some white boys just drove by and shot him, Dad." It was all he could say. All he ever wanted to say. He could feel his father still hovering there.

His mother's scream, just like the shot itself, he would carry with him always. It would fill up silences and knife in at unexpected moments, through music or movie dialogue. She screamed and called God.

Terry looked toward the door. There were competing shouts coming from a cluster of people.

Only then did his father move. Hearing his wife's shriek brought Preston back to reality just enough to act and he went to the door just as his wife was being trussed through.

"Oh, my good Lord." Terry's mother's hands shook as she held them in front of her, her body bent and trembling. "Oh! My Lord. Ah, sweet Jesus! No!"

They collided into one another, husband and wife, and remained in an awkward embrace. He barely held her up.

"No. No. No. No. No, my Lord, no. Not my baby . . ."

Policemen hovered nearby, waiting for them both to collapse. One cop eased the lunch bucket from his father's hand. It looked to Terry as if his mother did not see his father, and didn't see Terry either, although her face was turned toward him. Her lips were stretched in an anguished, silent scream too full of pain to be heard by human ears.

"Mama!" Terry called. "No," he cried, and buried his face in his hands.

He looked up to see two of the officers help his parents up the stairs.

Later someone told him the family could use only the side and back doors until the initial part of the investigation was over.

It was late evening when Terry's uncle, Cap Porter, arrived at the house. Terry heard his familiar, heavy voice distinguishable from the babble on the porch. Terry looked out the living room window and was astonished to see the sidewalks and streets packed with people from the neighborhood standing shoulder to shoulder. The porches across the street were full as well. The old lady across the street who baked sugar cookies for them at Christmas stood on her porch with her hand over her mouth. Terry could see her white hair turn blue and red in the rotating lights from the squad cars. Officers strung yellow tape. Nearer the corner, four houses down, a channel 14 news truck was setting up floodlights.

He heard his uncle entering by the side kitchen door. Until then, Terry had not seriously considered going upstairs. Even the one time when he heard his mother call his name and the police officer had nodded assent to him, Terry had held his place.

Cap Porter had not been in this house in three years, since brother and sister had a falling out, over what, neither of them would say, although Terry believed it was over the way Cap lived. Yet here he was: the first of the family to arrive.

Cap's face was broader than Terry remembered, and his mustache was speckled with gray. He stood over Terry, arms crossed high on his chest. "What the hell happened?" he asked.

Terry pressed his hands over his eyes. God, he thought, how many times will I have to say it? Everyone will have to hear it from him. The police could tell them, but it wouldn't be the same. He uncovered his eyes and inhaled through the tent of his fingers. He felt vomit rise in his throat and he swallowed it back down. Talking behind his hands, he said, "Some white boys drove by. They shot him while he was out on the porch."

"Look up at me," Cap said. "Look up here. Did you know these boys?"

Terry shook his head.

"Terrell, look at me. What was—" Cap stopped, glanced sidelong at the nearby officer. "Come here." He grabbed his nephew by the upper arm and pulled him from the couch. Not relaxing his grip, he hurried Terry into the kitchen. "Where's your mama?"

"Upstairs with Dad."

"Okay. Now, what was you involved in? You and Lawrence?"

"Why you think it's like that, Cap?"

"'Cause I know you boys as good as your Daddy does, but I ain't your daddy. Means I can see some things better."

"Let go," Terry said, and pulled his arm free.

The kitchen was as Lawrence and Terry had left it that morning, dishes on the table, dishes piled in the sink, cabinet doors open. Only the light over the sink shone and Terry was glad it was dim in there.

"Tell me something, boy," Cap said. His face was set in a half snarl, his brow pushed over his eyes. He was shorter than Terry's father by half a head, but heftier, maybe forty pounds heavier. Terry had always hoped he'd grow into a physique more like that of his uncle than his father, but now that he was seventeen he knew it wasn't going to turn out that way. Terry had the weight but not the build, and his body was soft all over.

"What do you know about it?" Terry asked. "You ain't been around here in years. You think you know people you ain't seen for—"

"All right. All right. I got to go see your mama. God, poor Judy. My poor sis," he said. "I'm going to make some phone calls. I know some people. If these boys are anywhere around, I'm going to find them before the cops do."

Terry watched his uncle stride down the hall. He hesitated at the stairs but only for a second and then leaped up them. Terry sat down at the kitchen table, his elbow against a plate that held the dried corners of a piece of toast. It was Lawrence who always left the crusty corners of his toast. Lawrence.

Terry listened for the voices of his parents and uncle a floor above him. He could visualize that reunion. There would be that moment of awkwardness when they laid eyes on each other for the first time in three years, and then Cap would hug his sister and there would be nothing to say, no acknowledgment of the three years of silence, just the knowledge that blood comes home to blood at times like these.

The voices that Terry heard, however, were those of the cops and photographer out front. He heard what he suspected was a gurney bumping the steps. They were finally taking Lawrence away. Strange hands would grab at his brother's legs and arms and head, invading Lawrence's space. The thought tugged at him, and he stood. Lawrence would not know these hands lifting him. Now the crowd might be rewarded for their patience. Maybe the sheet covering him might slip off and they just might get a peek at Lawrence Matheus, who could not peek back at them, who would be still and bloody and different now.

Terry imagined he could feel Lawrence receding from him as the coroner's wagon eased through the press of people packing Gum Street. He felt his brother's presence diminishing like the light from the TV when its turned off, shrinking rapidly to blankness, leaving only the small, glowing dot that slowly dwindles to a point.

In a heavy haze, Terry numbly crossed the kitchen to the sink. The faucet dripped; he shut it off. He stood over the sink filled with plates and glasses. They had finally taken his brother away.

Lawrence had looked directly into Terry's eyes in his last moment. Remembering, Terry brought a hand up to cover his mouth. Maybe Lawrence knew everything in that moment: who had shot him, what had happened, and what it meant. Or maybe he knew nothing past the pain and helplessness, saw nothing beyond the little dot on the television screen as it slowly faded.

• • •

Cap returned to the kitchen, his hands jammed in his pockets. He looked at Terry as though seeing him for the first time. "Your ma wants to see you," he said, "Do you think you can be strong for her? You're seventeen, right? Time like this is when being a man counts for something. And being a part of a family counts for everything."

Terry nodded, but he felt a hollowness in his heart.

"Wait a bit before you go up, though," Cap was saying. "Tell me everything you remember about this truck." An accusing tone lined his words again.

Terry wanted to please Cap, hoping that if he could, Cap would go away. "It was dirty," Terry said. "Like they'd been running it in mud."

"Splashed up against it."

"Yeah, rooster tails. From the wheel wells and across the door." Terry supplied details he hadn't given the police. "And I saw trash in the back. Beer cans and McDonald's wrappers. And it looked dented up and a bit rusty too, along the bottom."

Cap waited.

Terry couldn't think of anything else to say. He had no more details to offer. He kept his eyes on the breakfast dishes, on the remnants of eggs and grits dried on them. If only Cap and the police would go away, he thought.

At breakfast, the two brothers usually ate in silence, although that morning they had talked. During truces between them, which became rarer as they grew older, they made breakfast with practiced teamwork. Terry fried the eggs, Lawrence boiled the grits, one handing the other a spoon or the butter in response to a pointing finger. Lawrence was as familiar as a shadow, except he was taller and much leaner.

Shoveling grits into his mouth that morning, Lawrence had said, "Tamara Groves graduates this week, a semester ahead of everybody else.

"And two years behind her age group," Terry had said. "Why can't you leave her alone?"

Lawrence shot him a look. "Fuck you, little brother," he said.

"Yup. You too." Terry considered letting the issue die there, but instead said, "Man, she's living with somebody. You don't want to mess with Bread. Besides, who wants to date a girl that actually likes Bread Williams? Yuck."

Lawrence pushed his chair away with the back of his legs. He smiled. "I got something for Bread," he'd said.

Terry hadn't known then what he'd meant. But now he did.

From the corner of his eye, Terry saw Cap's hand coming toward him. He flinched, and his palms came up reflexively.

The big man's arms encircled him and pulled him to his chest. "It's going to be okay, somehow. This is a strong family. We're gonna see our way through this. It's going to be okay."

Terry could smell cigarette smoke in his uncle's clothes, and the smoke of reefer too. He felt Cap's heavy hands patting his back, and finally he allowed himself to cry.

Still in his uncle's embrace, Terry heard a man's voice from just outside the kitchen saying, "We've wrapped up things for tonight, but there will be people back here in the morning. And patrol cars will be by frequently. We taped off the area so we ask no entry or exits by the front door."

Cap must've nodded.

"Again, sorry for your loss."

Terry felt instantly awkward and pushed gently away from his uncle's chest.

"Don't go see your ma with that shirt on," Cap said.

Terry looked down at the large brown-red splotch that covered half his stomach. He almost said to Cap, I don't want to go up there, but instead he pulled the shirt over his head and balled it up. The T-shirt beneath showed a smaller splotch.

"Change upstairs," his uncle instructed.

As Terry mounted the stairs he heard kids outside shrieking and laughing. He heard a car drive by at normal speed. The crowd had dispersed.

Upstairs, he went to the left, to his room, and pulled off his stained T-shirt. He crammed it and his shirt in his wastebasket, then sat down on his bed. He remained there for a long time as tears rolled over his cheeks and onto his bare chest and stomach. He asked himself what else could he have done. No answer that didn't frighten him came to mind and so he tried not to think at all. But he couldn't shut out the images. They were all there in the front of his mind: the gunshot, the blood, Lawrence's face.

A noise, a creak from somewhere in the house reminded him his mother wanted to see him. He grabbed a sweatshirt and tugged it on.

He tried to breathe in as he got to his feet and headed down the hallway to his parent's room. The door was half closed; he put his head and shoulder through.

His mother lay facedown on the bed, still dressed in her navy blue business suit. His father sat on the edge of the mattress next to her with the upper part of him lying over her as if protecting her. Their faces were together, buried in a pillow, and his hands covered both of hers. Only her shoes were off. The seam of her stockings ran across her toes. She had always complained how standing all day at the bank caused her feet to swell.

Terry eased himself out of the doorway. Now was a good time, he thought, and he hurried back downstairs to the kitchen. Cap was gone, as were the police and the crowds. They'd all be home and talking. In a city where murder was rare, they would be asking their neighbors, "Did you hear what happened to Lawrence Matheus?"

He opened the cabinet door under the kitchen sink and reached back past the cans of ant and roach spray and Lysol and Top Job until his fingers closed around the gun he had wedged under the sink's pipe where it disappeared into the drywall. There was a bit of blood on the barrel, and again on the trigger and trigger guard, and he held it under the faucet and ran water over it until it was clean. Then he took a dish towel and wiped it for fingerprints. At the back of the kitchen pantry door, his mother saved grocery sacks. Holding the gun by the towel, Terry took one of the sacks and dropped the .38 into it. He wrapped the sack around the gun the way the man at the market wrapped paper around fish.

Very carefully, he opened the back door, easing it open to avoid making any noise. Then he put a hand over the screen door's spring so that it would not squeak. Leaving the back door open, he looked to either side at his neighbor's dark windows and empty back stoops. Seeing no one, he ran across the backyard and stepped over the low back gate to the alleyway. He trotted down the alleyway behind the brick fire pits and garages of several of his neighbors until he found a garbage can that was full to over flowing. The lid sat as if it had failed to contain an explosion of trash. He lifted the lid and pushed the wrapped gun deep into the smelly waste.

When he got back to the kitchen, he washed the arm he had immersed in garbage and then scrubbed his face. No sounds came from his parent's room as he tiptoed upstairs. Back in his room, he lay across his bed. It was past two in the morning. He wasn't sleepy at all.

HE WORE GRIEF like a mask. Grief explained why he didn't want to talk, why he was brusque with visiting relatives, and why he stayed to himself.

Judith Matheus came into his room early the next morning. She sat next to him on the edge of his bed. She had taken off her jacket but still wore the same navy blue skirt. Her eyes were red and her hair stiff and pushed to one side.

"I know it must have been awful for you, baby," she said. She put an arm about him and her hand squeezed him in the spot between his neck and shoulder.

"Mama," he said with impatience.

"I know," she said. "Oh, we're going to miss him."

But she didn't know. This was familiar territory, where she thought she knew what was bothering him, but she missed it by a mile. Like when he didn't make the basketball team in middle school and she thought he was crushed at not getting a chance to play. He didn't give a damn about basketball and only wanted to show off for a girl who was a cheerleader. Or another time when Lawrence had just gotten a car. Terry had caught Lawrence's enthusiasm, but his big brother had refused to take him with him when he went out for a drive. Terry had been furious. "I know you want to be with your big brother," his mother had said, clinging to him as she did now. Actually, he was envious of Lawrence's new freedom, his newfound ability to come and go as he pleased. Terry had just wanted to get out of the house, to not be left behind.

"Sweetie," she was saying, "I know you saw something no one should ever have to see."

He felt himself tense. She was here to trip him up.

"I know there must be terrible pictures in your head right now."

You don't know anything. Go away, he thought but couldn't say.

"But good memories outlast bad ones," she said, and started crying again.

Her forehead pressed the side of his head. Her breath was stale.

"I don't know why they do. Maybe because we don't want the bad ones in the first place. I don't know."

Terry looked at his fists in his lap.

"Lawrence is going to always be——"

"Mama," Terry said, and stood up so quickly that his shoulder struck her under her chin.

She gasped. She must have bit her tongue or cheek because she checked her mouth with two fingers and came away with blood.

Terry wanted to say he was sorry but feared if he apologized for the bump, then everything he was holding inside would start rushing out. One "I'm sorry" would lead to another.

Instead, it was his mother who said, "I'm sorry for what you had to see, baby. There's devils in this world." She stood. "I'd better see to this," she said. At the doorway, she turned back. "But, why? Lawrence never had any trouble with any white people. Why would they want to take my baby?" She went down the hall to the bathroom. He heard the sink running and then her loud sobs.

He envied her because all she had to do was grieve.

Shortly after, family began to appear, and his witless second cousin, Tony, his junior by four years, came into the room and sat on the floor.

"Lawrence was the coolest," the boy said. After Terry didn't respond, he said, "I saw it all on the news."

It used to be, when Terry and Tony were both boys, Tony would get all of Terry's used toys. When Terry tired of a toy, it would be passed down to his cousin, who was always eager to get his hands on it. Terry believed it got so that Tony would scout about the house whenever he came over to see what he might hold claim to next. That was years ago, but it was the first thing Terry always thought of when he saw his cousin.

"They showed Lawrence's junior picture from the yearbook. He really had a big natural then."

It was a Wednesday. In the middle of a weekday, the neighborhood streets were usually cleared of cars. Directly across and just eight feet away from Terry's window was that of their neighbor, a window to a room, he figured, they never used, because Terry could not recall ever seeing the brown-stained blind lifted. The two houses were extremely close together, but Terry could still see some of whatever happened in the front street by standing at the edge of his window and gazing at an acute angle, which he did now while Tony continued to talk.

"Pop said unless they seen the truck for themselves or it been proved in court, they had to use the word *alleged*. The white people say *alleged*. Everything was alleged—"

"You can shut up now."

Tony's mouth opened to respond, but he shrugged and said nothing.

There were several familiar cars lining the sidewalks in both directions. "Who's all down there?" Terry asked.

"Everybody," Tony said. Then he proceeded to prove he could name "everybody." "Phyllis and her boyfriend, Walter, Floyd and Aunt Nancy . . ."

"Okay," Terry said.

"Tyrone and Betty and—"

"All right."

"And I saw your uncle Cap, his latest girlfriend, and some—"

"Okay. Shut up. Get out of here."

"I don't want to go down there either," Tony said.

"Fly." When Terry said it, he remembered Lawrence saying it to him, as he had on many occasions to which Terry would respond with a dismissive wave.

"Let me hang out here. I can bring us up some eats. My mom brought leftover ham. She said your mom ain't gonna have no thoughts to cooking or eating." Tony could see he wasn't getting anywhere with Terry. "I'll tell you what the ten o'clock news said," he offered.

"I don't want to know what the ten o'clock news said, and I don't want any fucking ham." Terry grabbed the boy by the front of his shirt and upper arm and dragged him to the doorway.

"Hey!" Tony cried but offered little resistance.

Someone was climbing the stairs. Terry said, "Get him out of here. I don't feel like playing!" He slammed his bedroom door.

Terry leaned against the door, listening, waiting for a relative to come asking what was going on. No one did. They thought they knew.

Terry went back to his window and considered his neighbor's house, so close by. What could they have seen or heard? The police would be talking to them soon if they hadn't already. They were not close to the Matheuses, but Terry knew three adults lived there and were all usually gone during the day. Had he heard something about one of them getting laid off from Whirlpool recently?

He had gotten up early that morning and washed his right hand. Scrubbed it almost violently so that now it was sore and wrinkled. Somewhere he'd heard that firing a pistol left residue on the shooter's hands and that the police could tell if the fine gunpowder was still there. Fingers spread, he slowly rotated the hand in the light from the window.

His heart was still racing from having thrown Tony out of his room. Lawrence had shoved Terry around like that plenty of times.

All the time. The biggest fight he and Lawrence ever got into was over a letter jacket with black leather sleeves.

Thinking of it now, Terry stepped out of his room, looked to his left and right, then hurried across the hall to Lawrence's room. The bed was unmade. Clothes were scattered on the floor. A picture of Chaka Khan sporting animal skins and feathers was taped to the opposite wall. Terry went to the closet and scooted the hangers back and forth. He finally found the jacket lying on the floor on the far side of Lawrence's bed.

Cap Porter had given it to Lawrence. Someone probably had paid a debt to Cap with the clothes off his back. "Don't fit me," Cap had said, "and since you're the oldest . . ."

Terry remembered thinking that "since you're the oldest" didn't sound like a good reason at all, though he'd heard it plenty of times. And it wasn't fair because Lawrence already had a letter jacket he'd earned in track.

The day of the fight he had gone into Lawrence's room, believing his brother was still at school.

"There's two things wrong with this picture," Lawrence had said entering his room and startling Terry, who had the jacket on and was standing in front of Lawrence's dresser mirror.

"You're in my room, one. And you're wearing my jacket, two."

"Cool it. I just wanted—"

"Take it off and get the fuck out. Don't say nothin' just do it."

Terry was going to comply. He was. He knew he didn't have a leg to stand on because long ago house rules had been established by their father that they stay out of each other's room. Terry was just going to take his time. He turned back to the mirror. The jacket was a little large for him, but he loved it.

Lawrence moved to get Terry out of the jacket, grabbing it by the back collar to pull it down and off. Terry tried to shrug him away and the fight was on. Terry had swung and hit first, though later he maintained Lawrence had. Lawrence's return punch had staggered him, but he swung again. It had felt as if Lawrence was flinging rocks at him at close range. But Terry took them. At some point their mother had screamed from the doorway for them to stop, but they would not, could not. And their wildly swinging arms prevented her from getting between them. Terry had gotten in a few good licks that day, but Lawrence had been relentless. The fight had wrecked the room, breaking a glass lamp and a mirror and caving in the closet door. Lawrence's pummeling finally forced Terry to turn and cover his head, and their mother finally got Lawrence to stop. Terry remembered looking up from the floor and seeing the cut over Lawrence's left eye and his split lip.

He tasted blood in his mouth. Terry stood. The brothers eyed each other. Their mother still shouted. Terry pulled off the jacket and threw it to the floor.

"No. Come back and hand it to him," his mother had said. But Terry had crossed the hall and slammed his bedroom door shut.

His mother had asked him once, "Why can't y'all show each other as much tolerance as you give classmates or friends?"

"'Cause he's no friend of mine," Terry had said.

"Aw, Terrell," she had said.

She stepped into the room now as Terry held the jacket.

He quickly put it down on the bed. "I just . . ."

"What happened with Tony," she asked.

"Nothing. He was just being a pest."

She glanced around Lawrence's room without coming in. "Get something to eat," she said before walking away.

• • •

TERRY EVENTUALLY DID go down to find some food. Friends and relatives kept dropping by, some for mere minutes, others seemingly to begin a vigil. There would be no avoiding them. Before he did go down to the kitchen, he hovered on the stairs and listened in on the conversations.

"You see, the thing is, Cap, deep down they still think they can do this to a nigger and get away with it. They think the law ain't gonna come after them."

Next to Cap was his new girlfriend. Terry didn't remember her name though he had met her once before. She was taller than Cap and had hair dyed auburn, straightened, and then curled out just above her shoulders. She wore platform sandals, and her black dress was very short. Even while the other men spoke, she did not relinquish her hold on Cap's upper arm.

"Least not as hard."

"That's what I'm saying. It's a perception. A perception," he said again, as if fond of the word. "As long as they think that, then some of 'em gonna try to get away with it."

"They think they can get away with it, because they can," a neighbor said. "Simple. You don't wanna know how many niggers get dragged away from in back of dey own home. Happened to my second cousin. He lived in Arkansas. He heard something gettin after his chickens. That's what he said to his wife. She said she just rolled over and went back to sleep, but he climbed on out with his scatter gun. He got off one shot. She said she sat up and waited for him. Knew something was wrong, you know. Said she was too scared to get out of the bed, waited petrified like that the entire night. They found him the next morning with wire wrapped around his neck."

"Hung him?"

"Nah, they wrapped him in the wire of his back fence and beat him with clubs. Never caught nobody for that one to this very day."

"They're going to catch someone for this one."

"Said it was because he signed a petition."

"Who?"

"My cousin. He signed some petition over crop prices. The black farmers weren't getting market value—"

"Melvin . . . ," the neighbor's wife said, her tone cautionary.

"I'm just telling it like it is," Melvin said.

When Terry came down the stairs, he could feel them looking at him. The conversations stopped. Terry couldn't look up.

His mother's cousin, a big woman, wrapped an arm about his shoulders. "I know it's hard, baby," she said. "We are all here. All together."

Terry nodded and stepped out of her embrace.

Someone else patted him on the back.

He didn't trust himself to say anything. He didn't trust himself to return their gazes. Quietly, he made himself a sandwich.

They figured his grief was different because Lawrence and he were brothers. They believed his grief was different because Lawrence had been killed right in front of him. All around him, he felt the pity and the compassion he did not deserve and he wanted to scream. Without ever speaking, he ran upstairs with his sandwich and shut himself in his room.

He didn't come out until someone knocked softly and said, "Terrell, the police are downstairs. They want to talk to you."

THE DETECTIVE HAD droopy blue eyes and a large nose, flushed pink from the cold outside. He wore a dark gray suit. He looked uncomfortable in his clothes.

He was speaking with Preston when Terry came down. Cap and some of the other men stood behind Terry's father.

"Hello, Terrell," the detective said. "I'm Bill Carson." There were dark bags under his eyes.

Terry absently rubbed a thumb over his cut palm.

"Why don't we go back upstairs? That way we can talk in private. Is that okay, Mr. Matheus?"

Terry's father nodded, then said, "I would like to talk to you after, Officer."

"Certainly. Terrell."

Terry looked from the detective to his father to Cap. He went up the stairs slowly with the detective following close behind. For a moment, all he could think of was how quickly Lawrence's T-shirt had absorbed the blood. Terry looked at his cut palm.

"That's the cut from your glass?" the detective asked.

Terry hurried up the last couple of steps and turned into his room, but the detective did not follow him in.

"Is that your brother's room?" He pointed with a thumb over his shoulder.

"Yeah."

"May I take a quick look?"

Terry did not want him in there. He didn't reply.

The detective went right in.

Terry watched him from the entrance of his own room for a half a minute, then felt compelled to follow the detective.

"It's okay, actually," Bill Carson said. He had a heavy voice. "I asked your father if I could look around."

The jacket lay on the bed exactly as Terry had left it.

Carson stood in one spot and rotated slowly. "Yeah. I wish I could let you be at a time like this. But . . ." When his rotation brought him face to face with Terry, he stopped. He didn't look so smart, but Terry had to fight to hold his ground. He wanted to retreat to his room and slam the door behind him.

"Remember anything else about the truck or about your brother's assailants, Terrell?"

Terry thought to tell him the extra details he'd told Cap Porter, but to his alarm, he couldn't remember what they had been. The detective had been talking to his father and uncle when Terry came downstairs. What if he already knew the additional details? "Um . . ."

"What's wrong?"

"Nothing. And I don't remember nothing else either."

"Okay." The detective exhaled as if tired. "How old are you?"

Terry knew the detective must already know this, and he suddenly felt that Carson was only circling the ring at this point, before pouncing. He answered, "Seventeen."

"Juvenile," Carson said. "And you are a junior at Bosse High."

You lied, Terry thought. You don't mind being here at all.

"What I need today are the names of Lawrence's friends. His running buddies. Oh, and any girlfriends too. I'm sure he had some girlfriends, right?"

Who else had seen the gun? Terry tried to think. Who was it he shouldn't mention?

"How's your hand?"

"What?"

"How's the hand? The cut?"

"Fine."

"Good. Good. Those names?" The detective produced a small, spiral notebook from his inner coat pocket. His pen had been clipped inside the spiral.

Terry looked again at the three-inch cut that ran from the meaty part behind his thumb to the tender middle of his palm. He had really given it no thought at the time. He wasn't thinking about it now, only using it as something to put his eyes on. He did not want to look at Lawrence's things and he did not want to look at the detective. He wondered if he'd said that black boys shot Lawrence, that it was a black arm he saw aiming the gun and three fluffy afros in the cab of the truck, would that have been more believable? He said, "I don't hang out with Lawrence or his friends." Cap might know their names, though, he thought. Even though Cap hadn't been speaking to their mother, he still kept in touch with Lawrence enough to know a few of Lawrence's friends. His mama knew most of them too. She'd fed them on occasion. He could get the names from her. Just because Lawrence had shown them a gun didn't mean anything and if the police found out about it and asked him, all he'd need to do is shrug and shake his head. He said, "Jimmy Toland on Mulberry. Numie Carter. That ain't his real first name. He lives over on the eight-hundred block of Chandler. Bobby Morris . . ."

"Spell Numie?"

Terry spelled it out. "He was tightest with Jimmy and Numie."

"Okay. You said Bobby Morris?"

"Yeah. And sometime his brother Carl goes 'round with them too. They live on Lincoln, in the projects."

"Lincoln Gardens. Got it."

Terry wanted this over. He wanted out of this room and this man out of the house.

"What about Jamal Teal?"

"Um, yes, they hang sometime, I think." He already knows all this, Terry thought. "Is that all?" Terry took a step back.

Carson didn't take his eyes off him. "Just a few minutes. It's going to be a great help to the investigation. Now, what about girlfriends?"

"I don't know."

"You guys were brothers. Brothers always talk about girls. Sure you did."

There was Tam, of course, and the girl last summer Lawrence took out once or twice, trying to forget Tam. Lawrence had complained she talked too much. "He liked a girl named Tamara. I don't think they dated anymore, though. I don't know. But I guess he still liked her."

"No one else?"

"Nah."

He waited. He kept looking at Terry.

"What's Tamara's last name?"

"Groves."

"So who are the guys he did not get along with?"

That's easy, Terry thought. Friends had told Lawrence to let go of Tamara Groves. But his nose was so wide open when it came to that one girl. Lots of girls had wanted to date his brother. Lawrence smiled at all of them and they smiled back. He couldn't smile at Tam, though, and she would not smile back. She was pretty, but her problem was her boyfriend, whom she lived with. Bread Williams was one hard brother and everyone knew that. He was too much for Lawrence. Bread was the street thug he bought the gun for in the first place. Terry had not thought about it this way before, but if not for Bread Williams there would have been no gun. Lawrence would be alive. And given the things he'd heard about Bread—the fights, drugs, you name it—he probably had killed somebody, or tried. Terry said, "I don't know."

Carson and his sad sack eyes waited.

Maybe he could turn those eyes to somebody else, Terry thought. And besides, I ain't accusing him; I'm answering the question truthfully. "Bread. Bread Williams. Think his real first name is Clay."

Carson did not jot the name in his book right away as he had the other names.

"And what was the dispute, what was the bad blood between them?"

"They didn't like each other."

"Got that. I'm asking why."

"Maybe they both liked the same girl?" Terry began to realize then he had said too much. He had warned himself to say nothing that he had not already thought out.

"A girl, huh? Tamara Groves?"

"Yeah."

"Is this girl, Tam, white or black?"

"Black."

"Got it. All these friends you mentioned — are they black?"

"Yeah."

"No whites in Lawrence's circle?"

"Not the ones in the truck. He didn't know those guys. I told you. They were just driving by."

"I remember. Looking for the courthouse. They must have been from out of town. I mean, driving around a residential section like this looking for the courthouse. Could be they were country hicks, huh?"

Terry pretended to study the cut on his hand. If some of his blood hadn't been on the porch, he would have been tempted to say he knew nothing about what happened to Lawrence. He would have said that he hung around school after classes.

"We checked to see if anyone matching your description of these guys had business at the courthouse that day — traffic fines, what have you. So far no one."

More than ever, Terry wanted to leave. "Is this over? I want to go lie down." He needed for the detective to leave so he could think about what he'd just said. If he could just think for a minute.

"Just about. Have you seen Bread Williams talking to any white guys?"

"No, not really. I never see Bread except maybe driving away in his Cadillac."

"Let's say you and your brother went out somewhere. Can you think of an incident where there might have been a little trouble? Maybe these guys were pissed. Followed you back here. A few days later, they bring a gun. That type of thing go down?"

"I didn't hang out with Lawrence. He did his own thing. I did mine."

"You two weren't so close?"

Terry felt himself tremble. "I'm going now, all right?"

"Well, I've got to canvas the neighbors again. Usually, we can find someone who saw something. You know Groves's address?"

"No."

Terry went to his room, knowing those droopy eyes were still on him. He shut the door and leaned against it and stayed like that for a while. Then he went into his closet and shut the door. It was pitch black inside and a little cool. He lowered himself to his knees just as his eyes adjusted and he could discern the thin line of light beneath the door. He swept his shoes out of his way and dropped to all fours. The tails of his shirts brushed his back. He pushed his face into a corner of the closet, so far that it was hard to breathe. Briefly, his tears were trapped on the top of his cheeks before trickling down over his nose.

THAT NIGHT HE watched the television downstairs. His mother had been given sleeping pills and was upstairs. His father was out with Cap Porter, Terry thought, but he wasn't sure.

"We are very concerned. Very concerned," a pastor, his mouth hidden by the reporters' sponge-covered microphones, was saying.

"More so than to show black people that they can expect equal justice under the law, authorities must show certain elements of our population that we refuse, defiantly refuse, to return to the kluxerism of our lynching past."

". . . a leading spokesman, who had a lot of support down here today. The black community is not going to allow this crime to go unpunished or let young Lawrence Matheus be forgotten. Back to you in the studio, David."

Terry could feel his heart like it was beating against bone.

THURSDAY MORNING, HE heard his mother crying across the hall in Lawrence's room. He heard her in his sleep. Her relentless sobs became part of his dream. In the dream, the next-door neighbors had come slowly down the sidewalk as if they were sleep walking. When they stood in front of the Matheuses' house, they handed something to Detective Carson. Terry feared it was the gun. Someone asked him if he'd wiped the gun and he nodded, then wished he hadn't. Could that be construed as an admission of guilt? But it wasn't the gun the neighbors handed the detective anyway. It was Lawrence's blood-soaked T-shirt. Blood still dripped from it. The blood fell everywhere, a spotted trail on the sidewalk, down the neighbor's legs, down Carson's legs, on the porch steps, on the front of the house. He heard Lawrence say, "Oh." Oh, like he knew something. His mom said, "Lawrence, why don't you take Terry for a ride in your new car?" And then she started sobbing. Terry tried to tell her he didn't want a ride in that rusty rattle anyway.

Terry woke in a stupor. It had been a fitful sleep. At first, he didn't recall the dream, but then he heard sobbing down the hall, and the dream images returned. He put his pillow over his head.

He saw his mother later that day as she exited the bathroom. She wore sweatpants and a bra. She had never walked around in just a bra before. Her hair was bristle dry and stuck out all over her head. She walked past him. She did not see him.

He whispered, "Mom?" though he did not want to talk to her.

She must not have heard him because she didn't stop.

The Evansville police returned that afternoon. Terry watched them from the living room window. One stood in the street and pointed his finger as if it was a gun. They were using the blood splatter and the position in which Lawrence had fallen to determine the angle of the shot. Bill Carson played Lawrence. He kept falling back. He'd throw his arms in the air. He tried falling from the porch and falling from the top step and from the one before that.

The detective with the finger for a gun was standing in the middle of the street, in front of the next-door neighbor's house. He said, "He must have been pulling away when he fired."

"Good shot, this guy," Terry heard Carson reply.

He was certain they would come in now. They would have more questions, and they'd also ask the same questions. Terry hurried from the room and leaped up the stairs to the landing. He waited there. No knock came. He heard their car start.

Around the time school would normally let out, three of Terry's classmates came by. Two were friends, and the other, a girl, was someone he really knew only by name. They gave him a card the entire class had signed.

They were awkward, not knowing what to say.

"Man," George Henderson said.

The girl, Cindy, said, "Everybody signed it."

"Kevin didn't want none of the white kids to sign it," George said.

"Might be one of them that did it," Kevin said with mock seriousness.

They could look at each other but had trouble looking at Terry.

Terry wanted them to go away. He stood near the door so that they would not go into the living room.

"Everybody's looking for them, man. They show their heads and they are gonna get fucked."

Cindy said, "We're sorry for your loss, Terry." She went outside.

The friends stood there. George and Kevin wanted to say more.

"Well," George said.

Then they finally left too. Terry decided right then that he would drop out of school.

ON SATURDAY, THE garbage truck rolled down the alleyway. Terry sat in his room, listening. He could picture everything. The two men riding the back would leap down, grab up cans, and tip them upside down over the truck's mammoth back end. They did not inspect the garbage; maybe they didn't even smell it anymore. The truck's engine idled loudly. The garbagemen would give one shrill whistle to the driver, who then set the truck rumbling down the cinder alley.

two

SHE SHOULD NOT have come. If they looked too hard at her, they might see what she had done; they might spot her guilt, like something stuck in her teeth, or a roller left in her hair. They might smell on her complicity in the death of Lawrence Matheus.

She glanced about. She did not know many of these people, and most did not know her. Still, she avoided eye contact with them, and though she realized that they were walled in booths of their own grief, Tamara Groves feared detection.

The church was packed and stuffy. People stood in the side aisles and leaned against the walls and shifted their weight from leg to leg. Folding chairs had been added to each end of every pew, and except for the front pew, the mourners were squeezed shoulder to shoulder and thigh to thigh into their spaces. There was even a sprinkling of white people in attendance. Pastors and priests from other churches and denominations sat like a council in a semicircle behind the pulpit.

A television station crew was there too, including a cameraman and a sound man dressed in suits and appearing uncomfortable. They worked silently, and Tamara did not notice when they left.

She sat in the second pew, directly behind the immediate family and slightly to the right of Cap Porter, a big-framed man in a too-tight suit, whom she had met once before. To his right sat Terrell Matheus, Lawrence's younger brother, and on Cap's left sat a woman with too-red-to-be-real hair, either a wig or a bad dye job, and Tamara spent a few moments trying to figure out which it was.

The man she assumed was Lawrence's father sat at the far end of the row. He had one of his wife's hands in his, but her face was buried against the breast of another woman. Her sobs stood out over the sniffs and prayerful whispers. The woman who held Lawrence's mother was whispering in her ear, and Tamara wondered what soothing words she might have found at a time such as this.

Lawrence's brother, whom she thought she may have spoken to once at school, kept his head down and appeared guarded. Physically, he did not remind her of Lawrence. He was shorter, not as broad shouldered and a bit pudgy, not as handsome.

Earlier, she had watched the kids from high school file into the church, a few of whom she recognized. They wore that scrubbed and brushed look usually reserved for senior class pictures. The boys had put aside their tie-dyes for suits and ties, but a few still had cake cutters in their bushes. The girls wore skirts and heels instead of boots and hot pants. She found something endearing in this apparent transformation, this effort to show respect for the Matheuses.

Tamara was not much older than they were, but in many ways she felt a world apart. They respected the situation but did not fear it. You could see lips turned up furtively to one-corner smiles, or flashes of teeth, or an elbow nudge. Mortality had not yet threatened these kids; Lawrence's death was a fluke.

She eyed the glossy coffin in disbelief and trembled. Lawrence had been her secret. She had seen him just a couple of days ago.

"Damn. Damn. Damn," Cap Porter said softly.

Tamara could see a bit of the side of his face, craggy with shaving bumps. She caught Terrell looking at her and told herself again she should not have come.

YOUTH KILLED IN DRIVE-BY SHOOTING. That headline on the newspaper that lay at her downstairs neighbor's door drew her to it. She caught her breath when the name Lawrence Matheus jumped off the page. Immediately, she knew who had killed him.

A WOMAN GOT up to sing "Do Not Pass Me By," accompanied by the organist.

Directly behind Tamara, a woman broke down in a loud, racking cry. Tamara did not turn around, but she heard the woman's neighbor saying, "There, there. It's okay. It's all okay."

Everyone around her stood. Startled, she did likewise.

The pastor was saying, ". . . forty-five in your hymnals."

Tamara smoothed down the front of her skirt, then adjusted her hat. She wanted to verify that no one watched her, but looking around might draw attention. She didn't know the hymn so didn't try to sing, and she noticed Cap Porter was also not singing. When he rubbed at his eyes, Tamara pulled a tissue from her purse and handed it up to the big man. He took it without looking behind him or acknowledging her. But when the singing stopped, he turned and said, "Thanks, little sister."

THE MORNING AFTER Lawrence's death, before she had crept down the long rickety stairs and spotted Mrs. Dorsey's newspaper, Tamara had lain in bed listening to Bread's uneven breathing and thinking of Lawrence Matheus, waiting for her, five blocks away.

Tamara and Lawrence were going to meet. He had promised to

drive her around to places where she wanted to submit an employment application. "What's in it for you?" she had asked the boy, but she already knew.

"Just the pleasure of your company. Does someone need ulterior motives to do a favor?" he said, smiling and showing his white teeth.

He was a good boy, a broad-shouldered track star, who did well in school, was popular, and, Tamara was sure, pleased his parents to no end. And he had the jones for Tamara Groves.

"Oh, sure," she said feigning skepticism.

"Bread Williams has a 1974 Cadillac El Dorado. If you'd rather borrow his?"

"Okay, smartie, watch your mouth," Tam said with a laugh.

"I didn't mean anything by it," he said quickly.

She wished he wouldn't do that, show timidity that made him take back anything sharp.

He was not her kind of guy anyway. He wore his afro close, which along with his letterman jacket, made him seem too clean cut. He looked as if the seventies had driven by and forgotten to pick him up. When she commented on his haircut, he said it was for track and added something about wind resistance.

Back when Tamara was trying to finish high school, he was one of a handful of puppies who used to follow her down school hallways and stare after her as she walked by. The difference between Lawrence and the other hounds was that he had actually approached her.

That morning, Tam had felt giddy about meeting Lawrence. It had little to do with Lawrence Matheus, however, and everything to do with defying Bread.

She quietly slipped from the bed and the softly snoring heap of her boyfriend, and tiptoed away after grabbing a neatly folded stack of clothes from under the bed. It wouldn't do to be scooting hangers in the closet. She dressed in the bathroom, careful not to make noise.

She knew Bread would ask her where she had been when she returned at the end of the day, but that did not scare her. Only the preemptive question, "Where are you creeping off to?" scared her, because if he asked it, she might change her mind. She might chicken out. She might not go.

The week before, she had gotten one of Bread's boys, Carl the Rabbit, as she called him, to take her on an errand. That trip had called for courage or cowardice, and as she washed her face she tried to decide just which it was. She applied makeup sparingly, some strategically placed cover and mascara. She teased her hair into life and turned off the light, removed the towel she had placed underneath the door before turning on the light, and holding her shoes in one hand, she tiptoed out of the apartment onto the steep, wooden exterior staircase. There were no good steps; they all squeaked so she had to hope Bread was deep enough in sleep not to hear the notes as she stepped on the various keys. It was that kind of care she had always taken, so how the hell had Bread found out? she wondered.

She must have put on her shoes then but did not remember having done so. She walked up Garvin Street, past houses that dated from the early part of the century. There was an old stone bench at Lincoln High School, the only all-black high school in town, placed there by the class of 1950. Lincoln was no longer a high school, having been converted to a grade school years ago. The bench was lopsided now because the roots of a huge oak had pushed part of it up. Tamara sat on the bench and looked up into the tree. She still had the newspaper in her hands. Five blocks from where she lived with Bread, this was where she and Lawrence had arranged to meet that morning.

"If you get a job, will you move out of Bread's joint?" he had asked.

The newspaper had said the killer was a white boy. Allegedly, a truck full of them had pulled over to ask for directions and then shot Lawrence. It would be like him to try and help somebody. Tamara wouldn't let her mind picture the scene. He was too full of energy, that track runner's body, lean and uncontained.

"Can I kiss you?" he had asked the first time, making him seem even younger than he was.

"If you have to ask," she had said, "then no, you can't."

They were supposed to meet here. She had chosen this spot because she could wait hidden from traffic by the great tree trunk until she heard that loud, smelly car of his. She had imagined that he would be the one waiting. He would get there first, eager as the family dog, music coming from his eight-track player, watching her walk toward him. She would have found his fascination with her amusing, also a bit unsettling. Now, Tamara was the one waiting. While she sat on that cool stone, she thought, wouldn't it be something else to learn that there are two Lawrence Matheuses in this city and then hear that noisy, rattling Dodge of his come lurching around the corner. He would apologize for being late, and she would pretend to be put out because he expected that reaction.

Tamara Groves took a deep breath. This time it was her turn to wait. And she did. She waited quite some time for Lawrence to appear.

When she returned home, Mrs. Dorsey shot from her door, "Is that my newspaper?"

"Oh, it sure is, Mrs. Dorsey. I carried it off without thinking." Tamara held it out to her.

"Naw. I done already sent Shevette to get me a new one. Plus I done called up the paperboy and cussed him for forgetting me."

"I'm sor—"

"You owe me fifteen cents," the woman said.

"I sure do. I'll go up and bring it right down." She turned to hurry up the staircase, and there was Bread, bare chested in his pajama bottoms.

"Where you been?" he asked.

THEY LIFTED THE coffin lid and Tamara could see Lawrence's dark head cushioned on a white pillow. He had on a gray suit.

The people at the pulpit had not known Lawrence; Tamara could tell by what they said. They did not know him even as well as she did and she had only known him a little, really. Actually, no, she had not known him at all.

". . . a young man full of life."

"His potential wasted . . ."

". . . a loving and dutiful son . . ."

They spoke in clichés, like advertisements, but then Tamara thought of the media and all the strangers present, and she realized they were trying to sell Lawrence.

"I don't want to do this again," a pastor said.

Tamara hoped all the robed men behind the pulpit weren't planning to speak.

"I don't want to hear another mother cry. I don't want to see another family in shock as the fruit of their love and the hopes of their future lies bloody on their own doorstep." He waited. Looking about, he wiped his lips with a handkerchief. "On their own doorstep . . ."

The truth, Tamara thought, is that they are not here because of how he lived but because of how he died.

"We must never permit the lynch mentality of the thirties and forties to return. We will not do this again. There must not be other Lawrence Matheuses."

He'd just used Lawrence's name as a synonym for victim.

Tamara looked down the pew to see how this eulogy was being received. Lawrence's mother remained huddled with the woman. The father stared at the casket. Terrell stared downward at his hands. This man's words were just noise to the people who knew Lawrence.

A tear fell from Tamara's eye and she wiped it off with her free hand. YOUTH KILLED IN DRIVE-BY SHOOTING. Tamara, with her shoes in one hand and her neighbor's newspaper in the other, had stared up the gray stairs. She had read the entire article twice while standing there.

People rose to join a reviewing queue.

Cap Porter stood. Terrell stood.

"Now's the time we say good-bye," someone said.

Tamara shook her head.

THE LAST TIME she had said good-bye to Lawrence was less than a week ago.

"I'm not afraid of Bread Williams," Lawrence had said. He opened the passenger-side door, which creaked so loudly Tamara thought it might fall off.

Lawrence gave her a mock bow.

In fairness to Bread, he had told Tam he might not be able to pick her up from school that day, but she had waited anyway. She really did not like walking, not in her platform heels. Also, she did not like to be seen walking by the other students, all of them much younger than she.

"What are you doing around here anyway?"

"Waiting for you," he'd replied.

Tam quickly surveyed the area for available witnesses. This could get back to Bread. "I thought you were going to be more careful."

He had flashed that widemouthed grin again. And Tam recalled thinking that he considered this as a game.

He repeated, "I am not sweating over Bread Williams."

She got quickly into the car. If Bread had come for her now then there might be a bad scene; it was better to get moving and not be there. Besides, she did not want to walk in those platforms.

It was a short ride, though Lawrence appeared to be taking the longest route possible, and was driving very slowly.

Lawrence talked about a track meet or a race with a teammate, but she had not been listening. She watched traffic, watched oncoming cars. Bread had friends.

Lawrence turned to her as if waiting for a response. The eight-track clicked over in the middle of a song. She knew he had said something about winning a race. "That's great, Lawrence," she said. "I'm proud of you."

He smiled and looked away, throwing a wrist casually over the steering wheel.

She knew she owed him more attention than this. But then she had given him too much attention already. Way too much.

He mentioned something about his car, about getting some work done on it, and then he talked about his younger brother, Terrell, about teaching him to drive. He said he was going to surprise him by giving him some time behind the wheel. Then he slipped in, "Cap, um, my uncle Cap said we could use his apartment again."

"We've already talked about that, Lawrence. Stop the car. This is close enough."

"So now you're pissed?"

He pulled the car to the curb and killed the engine.

Tamara grabbed the door handle but just held it. "I'm not pissed." She had been thinking about looking for a job for a long time now. Right then, the notion hit her forcefully. She felt stupid having to stop someone from giving her a ride to her doorstep. She was embarrassed, but Lawrence couldn't see anything beyond his own awkwardness and heated hormones. "Middle of next week, I want to go job hunting. Mostly, some places on the west side and at Mead Johnson."

"Cap works there. He can give you a reference. I'll talk to him."

She looked at him. He looked so young right then, younger than her, though they were nearly the same age. Maybe it was his life, which was so unlike hers. It had not required overnight maturing. He had not walked down a strange street in the middle of the night with all his clothes in a grocery sack. He did not sneak out of his house. It's the deals you get and the shots you take, she thought. His face said no truly bad hands had been dealt to him. And he was cute: he had puppy-dog eyes and a sexy mouth, which she tried to ignore.

He leaned toward her then, and she let him kiss her. She had to put a hand to his shoulder to slow him down a bit. Just a few seconds ought to do it, she thought. She kissed back, brushed his lower lip with her tongue, then pushed away, pressing her back against the passenger door.

"Lawrence, can I borrow your car? I need to go a few places next week after I get my résumé typed up."

"You're really going to go for it this time, huh?"

"Yeah, so can I use the car?"

He hesitated, which surprised her. "The car," he finally said. "I have that work on it to get done, like I was saying about putting it in the shop. It can be cantankerous. I wouldn't want it to quit on you. I'll do you one better. I'll drive you around, okay? I'll take you where you want to go."

"It's bound to take a while. I don't want to take up all your time." She was so tired of having to owe guys, first Bread and now Lawrence . . .

But in the end they had agreed to meet at Lincoln School at the bench beside the old oak tree where they had met a couple of times before.

"I'll be there," he had promised.

That was the last time she saw him.

CAP PORTER OFFERED Tamara a ride to the cemetery, finally recognizing her. She had not planned to go but changed her mind. Cap introduced her to the red-haired woman, whose name was Lynn.

Lynn said, "I remember you."

Tamara, though, was certain they had never met.

Six people wedged themselves into Cap's car. Tamara was in the back between Cap's girlfriend and an old man, who did not seem to know what was going on.

Lynn asked, "Are they going to put a purple flag on our car?" No one answered her. She said, "Remember to run your headlights, Porter."

Tamara had instantly regretted accepting the ride. The slow drive out to the cemetery was going to take forever. Token penance. She hated cemeteries, and the thought of seeing that boy put in the ground made her shiver.

Lynn looked at her and patted her wrist.

Outside someone wearing a black suit and white gloves placed a flag on the hood of the car, and motorcycle cops sped by with their lights flashing.

Tamara did not know what to do. She wanted to tell someone what she knew. The old man beside her gazed out the window, almost imperceptibly shaking his head. They had not introduced him, and she wondered how he was related to Lawrence.

She did not walk out to the burial site with the family and friends but stayed by the car. Cap and Lynn put the old man between them and did not even glance back at her.

She had been to more than her share of funerals in her young life. "They're dumb," she said in a whisper. "All of this." She crossed her arms, impatient for it to be over.

AFTERWARD, FAMILY, THEIR closest friends, and Tamara Groves returned to the Matheuses' home. People dressed in black crowded the living room and kitchen. They ate, and they talked in hushed tones, murmured conversations that had an eerie quality.

Tamara's eyes followed Judith Matheus as she walked in and out of the kitchen, carrying nothing each time. She finally wilted into an easy chair in the living room and other women bent over her from time to time.

Tamara yearned to go up to her, wanted to say, Mrs. Matheus . . . Judith, we haven't met, but your son and I went around together . . . and she would have to explain about Bread. She had never seen Mrs. Matheus before today. She wondered what she looked like before a mother's greatest nightmare happened to her. She looked breakable.

Tamara pushed off from the piece of wall she had claimed. An old woman bent over Judith, patted her hand. The outrageously wide brim of her hat came within fractions of an inch of Judith's face. Licking her lips, Tamara took a step forward, suddenly feeling an uncommon weight pressing on her chest, making it hard to breathe in the crowded room. She swallowed, thinking of what to say: "Mrs. Matheus, I knew your son . . . I know it's not a good time, but I thought you'd want to know. See, I know who killed your son." She skirted a circle of people in the middle of the living room and approached the chair.

The elderly woman in the hat was squeezing Judith's hand, but she appeared oblivious.

I know it's not a good time, Mrs. Matheus. I just thought you'd want to know . . . what.

A man nearly backed into her and stepped on her foot. "Oh, I'm sorry, Miss."

Tamara tried to smile.

The old woman had moved away and Judith was momentarily unattended.

"Are you okay?"

It took Tamara a second to realize someone spoke to her. Preston Matheus stood at her side. Could she say it to Lawrence's father? It might be easier saying it to a man. If she could just open her mouth.

"I . . . Lawrence," she said.

He waited.

She looked away from his pink eyes and saw Terrell Matheus looking at her. He did not break his hard gaze even when her eyes met his. Then he turned and ran upstairs. Tamara took a breath. "He was a sweet boy to me, Mr. Matheus," she said. "We had a good time together, you know? He made me laugh and he made . . . He was fun and nice. And he was a gentleman too. I mean, when I was out with him, he looked after me."

Preston smiled. "Did he?"

"He . . ."

"That's good. That's good to hear. What's your name again, dear?"

She told him her name, and he repeated it as if committing it to memory, which she suddenly hoped he wouldn't do.

Tamara backed away and watched as Preston Matheus walked over to his wife. Tamara imagined him telling Judith what a gentleman their boy had been to his girlfriend.

She needed to get out of there. The front door was blocked with people newly arriving. She turned, saw the stairs, and walked quickly up them. By the time she was on the second floor, she couldn't remember exactly what she'd said to Mr. Matheus. What she couldn't believe was what she had almost said.

"Your decision, your burden. Your decision, your burden. Your decision, your burden," Tamara repeated as she went into the bathroom and locked the door. She sat on the toilet and thought about what she should say. "Mrs. Matheus, it's just that I didn't know . . ." She took squares of toilet tissue and dabbed her eyes. She touched her stomach. Maybe I should have given it a chance, she thought. The last bit of Lawrence left in the world. But then, there were a lot of maybes.

Someone knocked at the bathroom door.

"Just a minute, please," Tamara said.

But she took a lot longer than a minute, and the person did not knock again.

She rinsed her face and dried it on the nearest hand towel. She pulled a stream of sheets from the toilet-paper roll and stuffed it in her purse. She examined herself in the mirror, sucking her lower lip into her mouth. She would just walk out and not trouble these people anymore. She rolled her eyes at the pitiful, red-eyed girl she saw in the mirror. She tried to chide herself. Bread would be looking for her to come home anytime now. He might get sullen.

She stepped from the bathroom. No one waited in the hall, and she headed to the stairs.

At the top step, she heard her name mentioned below. The voice sounded like Preston Matheuses', and she thought she heard Cap

Porter reply. She didn't want to face them again, afraid of what she might say.

She knew they would surely look for her in the bathroom, and all the doors to the other rooms upstairs were closed. She tapped lightly on the door just steps from the bathroom. When no reply came, she pushed the door open about halfway and leaned her head and shoulders in.

Terrell Matheus sat on the edge of his bed, one shoe on and one shoe off. He glanced up.

"Hey, Terrell." As far as she knew, he knew nothing about her and Lawrence, but young men like to brag and share their exploits so she wasn't sure. In fact, he probably knew everything, she decided.

She stepped into the room. "May I hide in here?"

He bent over and began unlacing the remaining shoe. He looked up at her. "That's the only thing allowed in here," he said.

Tamara closed the door behind her and sat on the floor, using the door for a back rest. She folded her legs beneath her and tucked her skirt between them.

Terrell kicked off his remaining shoe and leaned back on the bed.

To Tamara, he did not look anything like Lawrence. He was chunkier than his brother had been, a bit heavyset. She estimated his height to be about five eight, five eleven if you counted his afro. And his eyes were very dark, whereas Lawrence's had been a medium brown.

Lawrence had not spoken of Terrell except to say he had a younger brother, so she knew virtually nothing about the boy.

Tamara wanted to get out of this house and hoped that maybe Terrell could sneak her out the back way. "Would you like to go for a walk?" she asked.

He shook his head. "People," he said.

Tamara wasn't sure what he meant, but she said, "Yeah," in agreement, then blurted out, "I didn't like the funeral."

"I hated it," he replied so quickly, he startled her. "They didn't even know him. Six people talked and only one, Reverend Saunders, even knew him a little bit. None of his supposed friends, his pothead friends or his jock teammates, said shit."

Tamara sat forward. "All those people looking at the family like it was on display. They couldn't have all been friend's of Lawrence's."

"Not even half."

He was studying her.

"What?" she said.

His animated face became still. "I didn't think you cared. Is your boyfriend downstairs?"

She could see that he did not like her. Maybe she should tell him about her suspicions. She could hint it and then he could go to the police. "I bet Lawrence had lots of friends."

"People say they're your friend, but how do you know?"

"I don't deserve the vibe I'm getting . . ."

"He liked you."

"I know."

A tear ran down Terrell's cheek. He didn't move to wipe it away. "I didn't think you'd come here or be at the funeral."

Tamara thought about the spectacle that had been made of Lawrence's funeral. Part of her coming today had been to learn more about the boy, but in this she had failed. He was a good athlete and student and son—even she knew more than that. "That funeral," she said. "I think most of the pastors there were just showing off, you know. All those cameras."

"Lawrence got cheated. It should have been about him. They should have kept it real. That was false."

"No. He didn't get cheated. We were cheated. Everyone who wanted it to be about him were the ones cheated."

"He was cheated."

Tamara pressed the back of her head against the door. She wanted to go see what Lawrence's room looked like. She'd been hoping to find it when she poked her head in what turned out to be Terrell's room. Now she didn't want to risk leaving and being found by the people downstairs. The day had sapped her energy. Her body felt weighted.

Terry unbuttoned his vest and the first couple of buttons to his shirt, then let his upper body flop back on the bed.

Tam wondered what Terrell knew about her and Lawrence, suspecting he did not know much. So maybe she could have trusted Lawrence with her secrets. She had told him a few things. And he had confided a thing or two to her.

An idea lit in her mind and flew out of her mouth in one swoop before she had time to think about it or wonder how it would be received. "We could give him a better funeral. Right now, we could," she said.

Exhaling loudly, Terrell rolled to his side. He frowned. "How?"

"Well," Tamara began. "First, we would make it about how he lived, not about how he died."

"Right on."

She tapped the index finger against two from the other hand. "And, second, sorry, but anyone who didn't know him could not attend."

"I don't want anybody else."

"Okay, yeah. It could be just you and me . . ."

"What would we do?" Terrell sat up.

"Something simple, with dignity," she said, looking at his expectant face. "We both tell one good story about him. You know, something we remember that the other person might not know. That'll be easy for you; I didn't know him too long."

He nodded, "I don't want to go back out to the cemetery."

"No. This will be about his life, not his death. He didn't live in a cemetery. We could go to his room."

Terrell buttoned up his shirt and vest. "Where's my tie?" he said to himself.

She hopped up and went to his mirror. She fussed with her hair and moistened her lips by running her tongue over them.

"What happened to my shoe?"

She pointed to the floor near his closet door.

A person's room was the best place for his funeral, Tamara thought. In his bedroom, where he probably spent more hours of his life than any other single place, there would be clues and traces to his life everywhere you looked. Pictures or posters on the wall would make statements. What sat on his dresser or draped over the headboard of his bed would carry his vibe, his essence. In Tamara's estimation, it would serve better than a church ceremony with TV cameras and pastors mimicking politicians. And if not in their bedrooms, then funerals should be held in the place where the deceased defined himself, like a boat for a fisherman, a classroom for a teacher, the court for a basketball player. Yes. And there should be no bodies. The presence of a body, Tamara thought, was an admission that the survivors believed that the body was all that was really left of their loved one. Why exalt the decaying body when it was the spirit—whatever people believed that to be—that was the important, enduring, and true part of the person? All the reverence given the body, the beautiful coffin, the white gloves of the pallbearers, the inscribed headstones of the graveyard all disputed the belief in the soul.

Tamara shivered.

At the funeral of her mother, they had kept the coffin closed. Her body was too wasted away, she had heard them say. The closed box had made it hard for the young girl to believe the whole thing was real. Of course, her mother was not in there; she was hiding.

Terrell grimaced as he tugged on his shoe. Then he mumbled something Tamara did not catch and opened the door. She followed him across the hall.

The air inside the room was stale. He must have noticed too because he went to a window and cracked it open three or four inches.

Tamara closed the door. So this was where her track star had lived. She looked around. The room had been straightened or else Lawrence was neater than she would have thought, judging by the Burger Chef wrappers and stinky sweat clothes that littered his car. The bed was made up with a white spread. A black jacket lay folded on it. Next to the bed was a nightstand with a ceramic lamp topped with an old, yellowing shade. There was change, just pennies, in a green glass ashtray. The floor had a large square of indoor/outdoor carpeting of a dark blue-green color that came short of the walls and corners by a foot and a half. Tamara figured the furniture and the rug were not chosen by Lawrence and would tell her nothing of him.

On top of the tall chest of drawers across from the bed stood a small hand mirror and three bottles of cologne forming the points of a triangle around it. A comb and a pick were aligned next to a box of Kleenex tissues. There was also what looked like three or four check stubs and a jar of Afro Sheen.

A Chaka Khan poster was on the wall, and two shiny track trophy ribbons were tacked next to it. Against the far wall was a ragged, worn chair, and a table with a compact stereo that could play either records or eight-tracks. Above the stereo, thumb tacked to the wall was a poster of the Bar-Kays, and next to that poster, also held in place with red thumbtacks, was an Earth, Wind & Fire album cover.

A stack of albums leaned against the wall next to the stereo. The album in front was the Brothers Johnson, and the picture showed two guys with guitars, one with an afro so huge it obscured his face.

Tamara walked around the bed. Between the bed and the closet on the floor was a row of books with bricks at either end for bookends. Tamara squatted down in front of the books and read the titles: *A Survey of American Literature; An Introduction to Geometry;* various workbooks; paperbacks of *Go Tell It on the Mountain, Lord of the Flies,* and *Black Boy; Foundation* by Isaac Asimov; *Black Like Me* by John Howard Griffin; *History of the American Continent 1400–1750.*

"Did he read these on his own, or were they for school?" she asked.

"I don't know. Most of those are from school. But he read some," Terry replied after a moment. "He wanted his own place. He was saving up." Terry sat in the chair. "You ready?"

Tamara stood and nodded, watching Terry.

He said, "You go first. I have to think about what I'm going to say."

"Um, well, don't think about it while I'm talking. I'll wait as long as you need after I'm done."

"I'll listen."

"Okay."

"Do we have to stand?" he asked.

"No. I just want to."

Terry sat up in the chair and propped his elbows on his knees. His left hand was a fist, and the right hand massaged it.

Tamara had not thought about what she would say. The first story that came to mind, perhaps the best Lawrence story she had, was about the cornfield, the night they were being chased. But she looked at Terry and figured that would not be the right story to tell.

"Well, this was your idea," he said.

"Hold on. I have a story. The first time I really said anything to Lawrence was when he offered me a ride. I'd seen him around, you know, checking me out." She smiled at Terry, but he did not look up.

"I finally let him give me a ride, although his car was embarrassing. Not that I really cared what people think. Anyway, I was walking across the parking lot with a load of books and he—"

"So you allowed him to do you a favor."

Their eyes met. He didn't look as if he wanted a response anymore than she felt like giving one. She thought she should leave.

"Go on."

She kept her eyes on him.

"Go on."

"He was just a boy jonesing after a girl. I don't have a lot of friends at Bosse. I keep to myself. I didn't know Lawrence except he'd said hello a few times. Anyway, he pulls up and offers me a ride and I thought about how heavy those books were, so I got in. I told him where I lived and he started driving and talking"—Tamara mimicked a mouth with her thumb and fingers—"and talking, which surprised me because I had an impression, don't know why, that he was shy, but he wasn't. I think he talked about track and football. He might have been asking me to a game, but his car was so smelly, I really only wanted the ride to be over with."

"Smelled bad," Terrell said.

"So, of course, I told myself this was the last time I'd ever get in that damn thing. We were going down Bayard Park past Stanley Hall grade school, and he saw this boy on the sidewalk crying and stops the car. 'I know him,' he said. I'm thinking, Oh, man, what is this? He's gotten out of the car and is talking to this little boy, a fourth-grader, it turns out. He's squatting so that he's even with the boy. I'm calling out to him and telling him I don't want to stay in this car any longer than I have to.

"He tells me to hold on and jogs back over. 'This girl I knew— that's her little brother,' he says. 'He's afraid of being beat up by some guy in his class. Said the guy was waiting for him after school, some-place on his way home.'

"I told him to give him a ride, if you can find room back there with all the trash, but drop me off first.

"Lawrence laughed and said, 'There's the problem. His mama told him he can't get into cars with strangers.' Lawrence was leaning in the window, scratching his head. You could tell he was amused at the whole thing, not just that the boy wouldn't accept a ride that could save his little black hide, but at me for being impatient and wanting to get out of his stinky car and at himself for wanting to be alone with me and for whatever made him stop in the first place. I asked, for no reason, if he and the kid's big sister were tight, and he gave me this slow, wide smile.

"He runs back over to the kid, talks with him again, and pats him on the head. Then he gets back behind the wheel and says, 'This won't take too long, okay? And don't laugh, when I was in fourth grade, my teacher, Mrs. Wooten, did the same thing for me.'

"So off we go, at something like five miles an hour . . . no not even. Following this boy all the way to his house. We followed that mama's boy all the way home! Lawrence couldn't even put his feet on the gas, just took it off the brake and rolled from Stanley Hall school up to Mulberry Street off Lincoln Avenue. Little boy walking, trying to look brave and peeking around every alleyway he come to. And Lawrence and me in the car trying to stop ourselves from laughing so he wouldn't hear us. Cars driving around us, honking . . . Lawrence had to put his arm out and wave cars around.

"After we saw the boy home he waved at us and he has this big, silly grin on his face; he was relieved, you can bet, to be home. No bullies showed. And he didn't get into a car with strangers either."

"I could have walked home already in the time it took." Tamara shrugged. "But it was okay."

That was the first good look at Lawrence Matheus, him trying not to laugh while shepherding a friend's little brother home. His eyes were bright and vulnerable and danced. "Anyway, that was the first ride I ever got from him."

"Did you guys see the boy who was waiting for the kid?"

Tam shook her head. "No. I already said." She sat down on the corner of the foot of Lawrence's bed opposite Terry. She tugged on her skirt. "I'm tired of funerals," she said.

"It doesn't take many."

"No."

She waited for Terry to begin his story, but he sat quietly with head down.

"That's your story?" he said finally.

She nodded.

"When we first moved here. Lawrence and me used to ride our bikes together investigating the new neighborhood," Terry began. He pushed air out of his mouth loudly. He said, "God," and rubbed his hands over his face. "There was this dog I found. Its snout was taped—" Terrell jumped up so quickly, Tamara flinched. "Screw this. That story you told wasn't about Lawrence anyway. Hell, that just shows you didn't even know him." He yanked the door open and was gone. She heard his door across the hall slam.

Tamara picked up the letterman's jacket and held it to her face. She was tired all of a sudden, and wanted to get out of her dress and panty hose.

three

PRESTON SQUEEZED TERRY'S shoulder. Terry resisted the urge to pull away, but his father must have felt him tense up and took his hand away.

"This shouldn't take long," he said to his son.

They were in a lumberyard on South Kentucky Avenue, the busy highway connecting Evansville, Indiana, to Henderson, Kentucky, on the other side of the Ohio River. The air smelled of cut wood and sawdust, and nearby a saw whined as it buzzed through wide timbers.

Preston had selected the boards he wanted and was waiting for someone to take them away and cut them to the size he needed. They would be used to replace the boards on the front porch into which so much of Lawrence's blood had soaked.

Terry watched the man they were waiting for, a bald white man wearing a denim apron like the ones Terry had worn in eighth-grade shop class. He was a busy man with a lot of customers waiting for him. Thinking of shop class reminded Terry of school and filled him with a nauseous dread. The idea of facing all those faces was overwhelming. Everyone knew. They had gone to the funeral. They had seen it all over the television. All eyes would be on him.

"Wait a minute here," his father said as he crossed the lumberyard headed toward the man in the apron.

"Oh, man," Terry whispered.

"Excuse me, but my son and I have been here for at least a half hour and you haven't waited on us. We were here before him," he said pointing at another customer.

The other customer threw up his hands.

"Sir, wait your turn. I'm the only one on the saw today," the bald man said.

"I've waited my turn and his."

Terry thought the other customer had been there before them, but he wasn't sure. He didn't think his father could be certain either.

"I'm not putting up with this. I'm in no mood. Where's the manager?"

"The manager is not here now."

"Oh, that figures."

"Look, buddy . . ."

Preston took another step forward, standing just inches from the man. "Do you honestly think I'm your buddy?"

Terry saw his father's hands turn to fists, still dangling the little piece of paper on which he had scribbled his measurements.

"You better back down," the man said.

"I'm not takin' this shit anymore."

Terry ran across the yard. "Dad!"

The customer, who looked at first as if he was going to walk away, now seemed to be siding with the lumberyard man.

Terry grabbed his father's arm. "Let's go, Dad," he said.

The men glared at each other.

"C'mon." Terry pulled on his father's arm. "Mom's at home alone," he said.

Preston resisted and then relented.

"You see how they treat you if you let them?" Preston said when they were in the car. "I'm going to tell everybody I know not to buy there. I am." Then he said, "Shit," and hammered his steering wheel. "Damn crackers . . ."

WHEN THEY GOT home, neither of them talked to Judith Matheus. In fact, since the funeral, she had not talked to either her husband or son. She took to her room after the funeral and had stayed there. She had a small black-and-white portable TV in there and it was on constantly, even late into the night when the stations were no longer broadcasting and only white sand could be heard.

USING LUMBER PURCHASED at another yard, Terry's father replaced the blood-soaked boards on the porch, creating a lane of unfinished, raw wood approximately four feet wide from the porch steps to the front door. His father had done the work quickly but then lost steam when it came time to paint them, so the untreated wood glared like a strip of wounded skin in contrast to the chipped gray-painted, weathered boards of the rest of the porch.

While he worked, Preston talked to Terry about a visit the day before from Reverend Saunders. "He talked for an hour, I swear I don't know what he wanted. I'm not full of the milk of forgiveness, Terrell. I told him that much. I hate those boys. I don't think I ever really hated anybody my whole life. Not when Louis Naylor fired me to make way for his inept brother-in-law and said it was because I didn't work fast enough . . . not even then." He looked Terry in the eyes: "But I hate now.

"Hold it. Don't let it move."

The saw sliced through the board. The vibration traveled up Terry's arms.

The work with the boards was finished and Terry stood.

"A man works hard to get his family a decent house in a good neighborhood. Not the best neighborhood, but still, a working-people neighborhood. People who have to get up each day and carry a lunch pail. And you think, Okay, everybody's safe. Safe at least when they is home. You worry about them when they at school, 'cause you hear all sorts of things these days what with all this marijuana and psychedelic nonsense—and you especially worry when they go out. I know what boys do. I know they drink. I know they can be careless when they drive. Then Lawrence . . . they say some other boy liked his girl. You know anything about that? She seem like a nice enough girl. Your mom wants to talk to her some more. Lawrence was well over eighteen and a man, he know not to get into anything too messy. He's got sense; I taught you boys that." He stood, holding his hammer tightly. "You just worry. Parents do. When your child is in the crib, you worry about that SIDS or if they too cold, or will he smother himself with that blanket. And then they grow up and they's out riding their bikes and finding mischief and you try not to worry, but you still feel this little light trickle of relief every time the door squeaks and they's home. And then they get him right here . . . right here on his own doorstep."

Terry opened the screen door. "I gotta go," he said.

Preston was shaking the hammer. "We're going to get those bastards. I feel it. And I swear I'll crush the life from them myself if given half a chance. I told Saunders that's what I want the Lord to do for me: give me half a chance."

• • •

TERRELL WENT BACK to school because he had to get away from his mother and father, even though he wasn't really ready to face his teachers or the other students.

He hoped though that his return to school would begin the road back to routine. He wanted everything and everyone to be and to behave as close as possible to the way they had before the shooting. He wanted his parents back at work. He wanted the family friends to stop calling and coming over. He wanted the police cars to quit their slow, useless roll down his street. The murderers would not be found. When would they all forget?

After getting dressed for school, he sat in his closet with the door closed and the light off, and he tried to figure a way of leaving this trifling, suffocating town that he'd always hated anyway. He wished he had money, but Terry had only forty-seven dollars and that wouldn't take him far.

It was early and frosty when he went out the back door. Lawrence's Dodge Dart sat in the driveway. It was a pale green car with a black vinyl roof and rust-spotted chrome bumpers. Terry had once asked to drive it. "Yeah, right," Lawrence had said at first, then, to Terry's surprise, had actually said, "Okay, I'll let you take it cruising one of these days." But one of these days never came. Terry peeked into the car. A couple of eight-tracks were on the front seat. The floor of the back seat was littered with newspapers and burger wrappers.

Terry walked to school slowly, wanting to be late. He wanted everybody to be in class and at their desk and unable to say anything to him.

"Oh," Lawrence had said. He had not screamed. He had just looked surprised, like he couldn't believe what had just happened. Terry walked slowly over the uneven sidewalk of Chandler Avenue and turned left on Evans, which was a busy street. Cars rumbled by in both directions. He kept his head down. He did not have to look where he was going. It was a route of two miles he had walked five days a week for over two years.

If he went to school, maybe his parents would go back to work. And his dad would paint the new boards on the porch. And people would stop calling. And his mother would turn off the television. And somebody could assure him that Lawrence was okay in heaven and that everything was not nearly as bad as he knew it was.

He wondered if Lawrence was in heaven. The last big thing Lawrence had done was buy a gun to shoot a rival but only if Bread messed with Lawrence first. Lawrence never looked for trouble; he just didn't step away from it.

Tamara Groves going to the funeral and then coming by the house was hard for Terry to figure. And she talked a lot more than he would have expected. He could tell she was sorry about Lawrence. She also seemed a little weird.

All of this was Lawrence's fault. He had bought the gun and brought it into the house. The gun, the weight of the metal, cool, heavy. "Why did I touch it?" Terry whispered, feeling the tears yet again, but he fought against them. He didn't want to look all weepy in school. He did not want the attention. Damn, Lawrence. He could have kept the gun in his car. He caused all this but will get no blame. They all think he's innocent, when he was the fuckup. "Ah, Jesus!"

Terry stopped and looked about to see if he were being watched, but the rest of the world appeared to be moving normally, oblivious to him or his turmoil. He wiped his eyes with the palm of his hand. All I had to do is not touch it, he thought. I could have threatened to tell Dad: "Dad's gonna kill you, fool. He's going to go up side your head so fast you'll be on the floor before you hear the smack." I could have said that or I could have said nothing and shrugged and left and gone upstairs. No, I could have said, "You're going to get yourself killed." I did say that. "Lawrence, you're going to get into trouble big-time."

"Oh, Lawrence," he said out loud.

Terry stopped. Maybe he couldn't manage school after all. Sometimes things would not stay inside. He tried to swallow, and it took effort as if he were trying to swallow everything he had done and everything that had happened.

Mama had said, "You can't always be with Lawrence. He's getting to be a man, and that calls for going without little brothers sometimes. The ones who are barely men fear hanging with boys will make them backslide into boyhood themselves."

"Stupid Lawrence," Terry said. If I hadn't touched the gun . . . How do you go back and not touch it?

He cut across Bayard Park. He walked between the two iron dogs guarding the park's entrance. He felt safer under the trees, under the shadows of the maples and sycamores. The swings and the slide weren't the same ones he'd played on ten years ago, but they stood in the same spot, in a clearing where the sidewalks and trails converged. His mother used to take Lawrence and him here.

Lawrence. He tilted his head up in an attempt to cut off the tears. He wondered again if Lawrence was in heaven—if there could possibly be a heaven.

That girl probably thought so. She probably thought Lawrence was looking down on her. Tamara, with the black stockings and short skirt, who thought she was Lawrence's girlfriend. Mom and Dad had talked to her on the way out. Terry had watched from the top of the stairs. They were whispering like they were still in church, and Tamara had nodded. How would she have reacted if Terry had said the first thing that had come to mind: Here's my Lawrence story. Lawrence was crazy about you, a girl who couldn't give a damn about him, but he had it bad for you. One night he thought he had a date. He had showered and dressed the whole damn day—the whole day. I passed his room and he was in the mirror patting his afro so it would be perfectly round. He caught me watching, gave me the finger, and shut his door. I laughed. He heard me and laughed from the other side of the door. Least he knew he was crazed. He had smiled the entire day too and joked with me and Mom. He gave me five dollars to wash his car for him. "I want it looking like a divine chariot," he said. I said something like, Maybe if I wash it in holy water. But I pulled out the stops, cleaned it spotless as that heap could get, inside and out, an effort worth way more than five dollars.

Lawrence left for his date but then returned in less than two hours, stalked right past us straight to his room, and slammed the door behind him. I heard him kicking stuff around. "You'd stood him up, Miss Groves. So there's your Lawrence story. How's that for a better funeral?" No one asked her to come upstairs anyway.

"Never really hated before," his father had said. "I hate now."

Again, he saw his mother's face, quivering lips stretched in a great, silent scream that came from so far back her voice could not reach it.

"Oh, this is too heavy, too much," Terry said aloud again.

Ahead walked two girls Terry did not know but recognized from the corridors of the high school. They were talking loudly and Terry could catch a few words and the laughter that finished each statement.

"But I hate now." He heard the saw screaming through the wood.

Terry slowed his steps to maintain his distance from the girls. He didn't want to get to school until first period had started. He wanted to walk right into Ms. Britton's social studies class, late with no time for visiting and no opportunity to talk to anyone and no opportunity to be talked to.

When he arrived in front of the old school building, it looked abandoned. Two or three tardy students raced past him and were swallowed by the building. It was either this or go back home or go sit in the park all day.

He walked in. The big doors closed behind him. The smell of waxed floors reminded him this was a familiar place. He almost relaxed and then he saw two huge banners.

In the front hallway, over the trophy case, someone had hung a banner, and another strung over the door leading to the auditorium.

The first read DON'T FORGET LAWRENCE MATHEUS. The writer had run out of room, and the *e*, *u*, and *s* of Matheus dribbled down the far edge of the banner, making the slogan look like a dying plea. Another read, JUSTICE FOR LAWRENCE in fat, balloonlike letters. It was adorned with peace signs, and blue and pink daisies, and black fists.

He knew then he had to leave.

"Mr. Matheus, Terry." It was Mr. Winfield, his biology teacher.

Terry waited hesitated, tempted to run, but anxious not to create a scene.

Mr. Winfield, a tall white man with a bald shine ringed by white hair, said he was personally sorry for what had happened. He was. Terry did not let his eyes rise above the man's chest. Mr. Winfield said everyone in the school felt Terry's loss keenly. He said he had taught Lawrence three years ago.

Terry waited for him to finish.

"Mr. Lipscomb will want to see you before you go back to class. Are you sure you're up for it? Oh, it'll be fine. It's good to get back to class and homework. I'm glad you're back." Mr. Winfield looked as if he was going to put a hand to Terry's back, but Terry stepped away quickly to avoid it.

They walked by classrooms with open doors, and Terry avoided looking in, hoping no one would see him.

The secretaries in the principal's office greeted him with sympathetic eyes. Vicki Stover and Valerie Allen, two classmates, were waiting to see the principal, seated in a row of chairs typically reserved for the condemned. Vicki gave a shy wave, but Valerie said, "Hey, Terry, glad you're back. Have you talked to Larry yet?"

Terry only had time to shake his head, as Winfield ushered him quickly into the principal's office.

"Mr. Lipscomb, look who I found in the hallway."

Mr. Lipscomb looked something like Edgar Allen Poe with a broad forehead and wild black hair. He was short, but didn't act it. He came around his desk quickly and shook Terry's limp hand.

He made a variation of Winfield's speech: "This is an incredibly terrible event. How are your parents, son?"

It took Terry a moment to realize a question had been asked. He had been waiting until Lipscomb was finished so that he could say he just wanted to get back to his classes. Winfield stood too close behind him. Terry said, "They're okay."

"Good. Good," Lipscomb said, then gestured Terry into a seat. "Of course, all this terrible incident is a matter for the police, and from what I've read in the papers they are sparing no expense or manpower to locate the perpetrators. What I mean, Terry, is it has become a high-profile case. These cowards will be caught."

The bell rang. Homeroom was over. Out in the hall, kids were walking to first period.

Lipscomb wore the shoes all old men wore, the heavy black shoes with the dot design on the toes. Terry hated the man's shoes. He had tuned Lipscomb out, though he remained aware of the principal's voice droning on.

". . . those same passions more constructively directed."

Terry looked from Lipscomb to Winfield, who stood guard at the door with his arms crossed.

"Follow me, Terry. Your priority is healing and getting your education. Mine is making certain all the students here at Bosse have the opportunity of getting their education. The disruptions serve no purpose here."

Terry nodded because he felt Lipscomb wanted him to.

"There is no need to be confrontational just because it is in vogue."

"I want to go to class now."

"All right then. That's the spirit."

Terry got up. Mr. Winfield still wore an irritating, sympathetic smile that Terry wanted to get away from.

Terry had the door opened when Lipscomb added, "Work hard, Terry. I don't know why, but it always seems to help."

Terry only tried to make sense of what the principal had told him as he made his way down the hall. Work hard? He had not listened to enough of it to be sure what the man had meant.

Terry had been late to classes before. He knew that every face would turn his way the moment the door opened. His friends would smile. And the teacher would either shoot him a warning look or send him to the principal for a tardy admittance slip. But it wasn't like that this time. The faces looked up, but many immediately looked back down. There were no smiles or suppressed giggles, only silence.

Ms. Britton, a pale, thirtyish woman, who always wore dark skirts and flat shoes, nodded to Terry and used an open hand to indicate he should take his seat. He was already edging along the side of the classroom toward it.

The class discussion continued. From outside a hotel in San Francisco, another woman had tried to kill President Ford. Someone wanted to know if she was a member of the Manson family, like the girl a couple of weeks ago. Ms. Britton said she didn't think so.

Terry had not gone to his locker before class, so he did not have a pencil or paper. His fingers fluttered on his desk in frustration. The little white girl seated next to him, Beth something, to whom he'd rarely spoken, tore two sheets of paper from her spiral notebook. She passed them to him along with a pencil.

"Here, make some doodles or something," Beth whispered.

"Thanks," Terry said, and felt obligated to return her smile.

"Beth, we all missed Terry," Ms. Britton said. "We can talk with him after class."

Beth took cover behind the student in front of her. She turned her face just enough to whisper, "Geez, what a tight butt!"

Terry almost laughed. His amusement surprised him. He grinned with his tongue poking out between his teeth.

After class, Ms. Britton called him over. She told him which chapters they'd covered while he was away. As Beth walked by them on her way out, Terry returned her pencil. She waved bye with a couple of fingers.

"She was just loaning me a pencil before," Terry said. "So don't give her a conduct mark or anything."

"Okay, Terry," Ms. Britton said.

Kids were waiting for Terry in the hallway.

The teacher said, "Maybe you should go see Mr. Lipscomb before you go to your next class."

"I already did."

"You did?"

Someone shouted from the hallway, "Terrell, man, get yourself out here, bro."

Ms. Britton was speaking to him. When he sensed she was done, he said okay to whatever she had been saying and walked into the waiting circle of schoolmates. The kids closed around him. They knocked fists with him. The girls smiled at him. Gabe Portis, he knew, and Moon, but Larry Dingham, and Cynthia Dortch, Yolanda Mitchell were all upperclassmen who'd never shown him any attention before. Kevin Dawson, his dark face greasy and animate, Denise Geary, a junior, who Terry had always thought was cute, all fell into step with him as he walked to his next class, and they were joined by others. Terry had white friends as well as black, but only blacks ringed him now.

Larry Dingham, a guy with a huge afro that he wore like a crown, was the leader of the group. He had never spoken to Terry before.

"Glad you're back, my man," he said. "We've been hoping you'd show soon."

Terry knew they had all been at the funeral, though he had not spoken to them then.

Moon asked, "Did you dig the banners?"

They were back in front of the trophy cases.

Terry managed to look up at them again. The warm feeling of returning to something, of having pulled himself from mud, of coming back to himself that had briefly embraced him with his circle of friends, faded like a light turned out.

Someone's hand rested on Terry's shoulder.

"I just want to get to class," Terry said.

"Denise, let's show Terrell what's in your locker."

"They are in the trunk of my car, Larry," she said. "They wouldn't fit in no locker."

"That's cool. That's better, actually," Larry said. "Hey, y'all, let me and the brother rap for a moment." He grabbed Terry's wrist and led him down the hall and through the battered doors of the school's auditorium.

It was dark in the auditorium and the rows of seats looked to Terry like the silhouettes of headstones.

Larry stood so close to him that Terry could feel heat coming from him. "Listen, little brother. Lawrence was a good friend to a lot of people here. He was more than just a football star."

"Track. He ran track."

The bell rang to begin second period.

"Terrell, these are dangerous times. Malcolm and Martin have been removed. Politicians we might have gotten a decent break from have been assassinated. The civil rights movement is dead. With it, the campaign of subservience and appeasement has been swept away too. The Negro accommodators need to be elbowed out of the way too. We are black, we are proud, and we are not going to bend our knees ever again. Our history changes right here and now. Terrell can you dig this?"

"Sure." Terry was thankful of the darkness, glad they could not see his terror.

"Terrell, we are not a bunch of jungle bunnies they can lynch at will. We want justice. It's our right. We demand it. Terrell, have you been watching the news? I know you have, my brother. They ain't got no leads on Lawrence's murder. Imagine that. Not a one. The police department has no comment. No comment on leads. No comment on suspects. No comment on getting the FBI's help.

"The previous generations put up with this crap from the man, but we are not going to kowtow.

"Hell, in Boston they are fighting busing tooth and nail. Those white folks don't want us in their schools. They want to send things back the way they were before. But we are not going to let them sweep the killing of Lawrence Matheus under the rug of their indifference."

Larry paused, waiting for Terry to speak.

The upperclassman leaned in. "We're not going to let Lawrence down. Or you or your family. Or ourselves, Terrell. Or ourselves."

Terry nodded in the darkness.

"Are you with us? We need you. It don't work without you."

"Sure."

"Cool, Terrell. Talking is through. Now we act." Larry shook Terry's hand, led the way into the bright light of the hallway. The group that had congregated around Terry still waited, despite the fact second period had begun. The gathering had, in fact, grown larger.

Larry said to them, "He's with us."

They cheered and clapped.

Something twisted in Terry's stomach. People patted him on the back.

"See?" Larry said to Terry as if something had just been proved. "Okay. We're going to do this . . ." He swallowed. "Get the word to every classroom. Don't be disruptive. Just poke your head in. Give the sign"—Larry gave a peace sign that turned into a defiant fist—"and say, 'now!' They don't follow, then to hell with them."

"Kevin, call channel seven, then meet us outside. Denise, let's get the signs from your car."

In fifteen minutes, the school walkout was in full force. Kids came streaming out the front door as if the last bell of the day had sounded.

They congratulated each other. They told stories of their teachers' re-
actions to their gathering their books and walking out. They'd been
threatened with detention and expulsion. Not a black student was left
in the school building, and a scattering of white students had joined
them too. They massed around the flagpole in front of the school.

Larry kept Terry at his side. He had a picnic table brought over
and jumped on top of it. He tried to pull Terry up with him, but
Terry refused and turned away from the older boy's frown. The refusal
gave Larry only a momentary pause. He pivoted around as if trying
to see everyone who waited on him. He held his hands out, drawing
quiet from the crowd. "The murderers!" he shouted, and that got
the attention of the last few of the crowd still talking. The festive
atmosphere choked and died. Larry continued, "The murderers think
they've gotten away with something. They believe a black man's life
isn't worth two nickels and they set out to prove it. The Evansville
Police Department has not even brought in a suspect yet. They think
a lip-service investigation will satisfy us. They think we will tolerate
the lynch mentality that gripped this nation for the first half of this
century. The murder of Lawrence Matheus will not be ignored, will
not be filed away, will not be swept under the rug. Lawrence Matheus
will not be another lynching statistic. We want justice and we want it
now! What do we want?"

"JUSTICE!"

"When do we want it?"

"NOW!"

"What do we want?"

"JUSTICE!"

Terry could see the faces of teachers and white kids peering out from
the windows, gaping down in surprise and some with amusement at

the pool of black kids. The protesters filled the campus front yard. Nearly two hundred kids shouted responses to Larry Dingham.

"When do we want it?"

"NOW!"

"What?"

"JUSTICE!"

"When?"

"NOW!"

four

THE WHOLE THING started when she said, "Lawrence, don't take me home just yet." That's truly when it all started.

Her sin was in not really seeing him, not seeing the real Lawrence, at first. She could not get past the letterman's jacket, with the giant scarlet *B*. *B* is for boy, she had once said to him under her breath. He had not heard her, or more likely, he pretended not to have heard her. He was from someplace that she had only glimpsed long ago. Every time he would say something innocent: "My mom gets mad if she puts on supper and we're late to the table" or "Dad wants that front yard cut so I'd better get a move on," she would think of the letter *B*. So before, if she thought of him at all, what came to mind was a ratty car, a shiny afro, and the letter *B* for boy. He had asked her to come to his track meets. He said she could sit with his parents. She declined.

She was nearly two years older than he, but they were going to graduate the same year. She would be finished this winter, and he would graduate in the spring with everyone else. But she knew, based on life experiences, she was far older than the two years that separated them. She suspected that he sensed it too, because he was nervous around her. She already knew she could use him any time and any way she might want, and she didn't fight the compulsion to do so. It was just that she just didn't think he could be of any real use. But that afternoon, she felt restless and in a mood she sometimes got in when all the demons of her history came flitting around her. "Do you have some weed?" she asked him.

"No, do you want some?"

"No, I just asked to hear myself talk," she said. Was there anyone else she spoke to like a smart-ass except him?

She could have scored some grass easily, but that meant driving by the houses of people who would wonder who the jacket was and why was he with her. He came back to the car claiming all his contacts were having supply problems. She rolled her eyes. "Just get back in the car," she said.

"You hungry?" he asked.

They went to Una Pizza located in a tiny little stone building, at the corner of Kentucky Avenue and Washington Avenue. It had the best pizza in the city, they agreed. The few tables inside were occupied, so they ate in the car, the pizza between them on the front seat. There was no talk at first except his comment on how good the sausage was. But then suddenly Tamara found herself talking about her family. The one she had another life ago, the one that came complete with a loving mother and a hardworking father. She said being an only child was great up until the divorce, then you are truly alone, and that's when you could really use a sister or brother. She told him her mother had died of breast cancer years ago. He looked at her and did not let himself get distracted even when some kids came by laughing and goofing around. She didn't know why she talked so much; it was an unusual outlet for the demons. She had told Bread some of the same things she told Lawrence that day, but always she had the feeling he wasn't really listening, that he was thinking of his next hustle. Lawrence, though, was a good listener.

After the pizza, they drove around Bayard Park. Evening had fallen and the park looked denser with trees than it really was. The passenger window turned partly reflective with the darkness, but even without that image of him in the glass, she sensed him watching her as much as he did the street in front of them.

He had driven in a roundabout way, but finally they were on her street and near to where he always stopped to let her out, a spot two blocks from home, where she could walk the rest of the way. Tamara felt the peace she had just found begin to slip away. She put a hand on Lawrence's arm.

"What?"

That's when she said it. That's when the current story started, "Lawrence, don't take me home just yet."

He stepped on the gas, aiming his car between all the parked cars on either side of the street. As they drove past the second-story apartment she shared with Bread, she saw lights from the apartment shining down the staircase, and at the bottom of the stairs sat Angelo, one of Bread's boys.

Tamara ducked below the window. She could have sworn she saw Angelo's eyes following the car. "Did he see us?"

"Who?"

"Just drive."

Lawrence stepped on the gas again, and the tires squealed.

"No," she said, punching his arm, "don't announce us to the neighborhood."

"Sorry."

"Turn. Turn here." She swiveled about, peeking over the back of the seat. "Then turn again."

He drove one way and then another. "We're burning gas for no reason," he said.

Tam said nothing. She had not thought about his time, his plans, or his finances.

He slowed his car. They meandered down Washington Avenue to Riverside Drive. He took her to the levee at Sunset Park. He turned the key, yet the motor continued to run with a choking sound that finally died out.

"Is it all right?"

"Oh, yeah. It runs so well it doesn't like to stop."

"Why are we here?" she asked. This was the most popular make-out spot within the city limits, though it was empty at present.

"Tell me some more about you," he said.

But she was feeling cautious by now and had not really wanted him to stop driving the car. "I cannot believe you brought me here. Get this thing started."

"I didn't bring you here to make out."

"That's what people do here."

"Is it?" he asked with mock surprise.

Tamara did not give him a hint of a smile.

He waited. She guessed he waited for her not to be mad or to smile again or to tell him where to drive.

"Sometimes I wish you wouldn't look at me like that."

"Like what?"

"I don't know. Like who you see is . . . couldn't possibly be me. I'm not like you . . . mow the front yard, Mom, Dad, little brother, off to college . . . You won't see that here. I haven't been that since I was nine years old."

"I see. I'm trying to see you . . ."

"Like you're seeing somebody I wouldn't even recognize. Gives me the willies."

He looked away, peering through the front windshield at the twilight sky and the emerging stars.

"Don't be hurt," she said.

"I think I see you. I . . . it takes time, right? That why people get to know each other." He didn't look at her when he said this.

"Okay. You can look, but don't look look, okay?"

He started the car. "No look looking for now." He grinned.

When they drove out of the park, they passed an oncoming car she thought she recognized as Angelo's, which meant that it was actually Bread's car.

Trying to convince herself that she did or didn't see what she thought she saw, she said nothing to Lawrence for a long moment. "That's the shape of his headlights," she said, not meaning to.

"Whose—"

"The guy we saw at my place. I think that was him; he was following us." Lawrence still looked bewildered. "That car that was coming into the park when we drove out. I think it was one of Bread's brownnose corps."

"Does he pay all those guys?"

"Yeah."

"He does?"

"Lawrence, focus. We're being followed."

"That was a white dude in that car. The one that went past us. A Mercury Monarch, right?"

"It was a white guy? Angelo's light skinned. Did he have dark hair? Was anyone else in the car? They travel in packs."

Lawrence shrugged. "Is that the car?"

"Damn. Damn, Lawrence."

"Do you think Bread was in the car?"

"This could be bad." She sunk down in the seat.

Lawrence was looking in his rearview mirror. "'Cause that car is coming out of the park already."

Lawrence turned left on Riverside and followed the Ohio River west past town.

Tamara said she saw the car take the same left, but Lawrence wasn't sure. Her anxiousness fueled him, though, and he flew through the downtown streets. She lost the headlights amid the general traffic but felt certain the car was still just behind them. They turned onto Old Henderson Road, a narrow strip with the river and its wooded border on one side and farmland on the other. Away from the streetlamps, the darkness came right up to the car's windows.

"Do you see anybody?"

Under the deep shadows of overhanging trees, they rocketed down the isolated road.

Tamara peeked over the back of her seat. "I don't think so."

"See?"

"See what? You shouldn't have come out here. You should have stayed in the city and just driven around a few blocks or shot down an alleyway or something. We're out in nowhere land. If they see us out here—"

"They won't see—"

". . . where there are no witnesses."

"Hey, you're really scared."

She turned away from Lawrence. Maybe he would have been scared too if he knew as much as she did about Bread and his jealousies. Across a field she saw the lights of a farmhouse. Who would live out here, she wondered. It looked lonely, the light in the middle of a spread of darkness.

"Where does this road go?" she asked as they rounded a curve.

"Nowhere."

"Headlights. Behind us."

"Square ones?"

"Can't tell." Lawrence's eyes were lit by the light in his mirror. Lawrence stepped on the gas. Amazingly, his car accelerated smoothly.

"There are no turnoffs."

They zoomed under a railroad bridge. From between the trees they could see a scattering of lights from Henderson, Kentucky, across the Ohio.

"This is insane. You don't know where you're going."

"This will lose them!" he shouted, pumped a fist, and punched off his headlights.

They were surrounded by complete blackness. Tamara could see nothing. She screamed. "Lawrence!"

"Did you see that? Something just darted in front of the car."

The car bounced. The tires ground rocks. They careened blindly, insanely along, Lawrence laughing all the way and Tamara laughing too despite her fear. She heard limbs scraping along the side of the car and window. "Stop! Stop! You won't see the next turn in the road! Turn on the lights. Turn on—"

And suddenly they were airborne.

They were lifted out of their seats. Tamara felt her insides rise and her head hit the car ceiling. "Whoa!"

Lawrence's right arm shot out, restraining her. The car landed, still tunneling forward. Something beat the car with a thumping staccato repetition like the fists of a mob.

"What's that?" Lawrence shouted. He must have managed the headlight switch because waves of cornstalks suddenly appeared, cobs of corn flailing against the car.

"Stop! Stop!"

He brought the car to a rocking stop. "Jesus, they probably beat the hell out of the car." A green-black wall surrounded them. Cornstalks crowded the car.

"Turn off the lights. If anyone's behind us . . ."

He killed the lights and the engine.

A newly burrowed path lay behind them, bathed in red light.

Tam whispered, "Take your foot off the brakes."

The silence was as complete as the darkness. They both remained still. Breathing rapidly, Tamara experienced a dizzying sense of relief.

Lawrence began laughing. "You should have heard your screaming. 'Turn on the lights! Lawrence! Lawrence!'" he mimicked.

She slapped him and joined in on the laughter. "What if there'd been a fence or rocks."

"I had no idea what that thumping noise was."

"I told you the road made turns."

"It looked like it went straight for a bit. Shhh."

Above and several yards behind them, a car passed on the road.

Lawrence laughed as it passed. "Woo!" he said and imitated Tamara screaming his name. She joined in.

It was a while before the laughing died out and the silence returned, leaving only their breathing filling the space. It was eerie. It was a different kind of quiet, something Tamara had never experienced.

She could still feel her heart racing. She aimed a punch at where she thought Lawrence's shoulder was.

"Hey," he said.

His door latch clicked. The dome light came on.

Tamara used her left hand to shield herself from the light's glare, which was turned off immediately.

"I can't open the door with the stalks so close," Lawrence said. "Roll down your window. Follow me." She heard him clambering out and then heard him on the car's roof. "Come on up," he said. "What's that smell?"

She rolled down the window and climbed out, the leaves brushing against her legs. She could see Lawrence now. He lay on his back on the car roof. Everything in the darkness seemed frosted with silver light. There was no moon visible, but the sky was filled with stars.

"I was going to just climb up and look around," he whispered, "but then I saw them."

"Yeah. I love them or use to back when I was younger." An image of her with her mother, standing in the backyard flashed through her mind, her mother pointing to a particular star, and Tamara pretending she can follow the pointing finger. It's a planet her mother wants to show her, but Tamara can only see stars. Tears pebble from Tamara's eyes because she can't see Mommy's planet. "When is the last time I just looked at stars?" Tamara said. "Aren't you worried about how we're going to get out of here?"

He didn't say anything, which was unusual. Lawrence usually answered her immediately.

Tam took her shoes off and lay down next to him, her heels resting on the windshield. "Ohh, the roof is cool," she said, but still Lawrence said nothing. The stars glittered in random alignments.

He slipped his arm under her head.

The quiet did not feel at all awkward or eerie to her now. She could hear her breathing and his too. Lying next to this boy, she stared into the heavens and felt herself within this world and without it too. She felt the cool metal of the car warm under her back and the pulse from his arm through her neck. She felt the merest breeze touch her, and then she heard the sound, a sound she had missed in that first silence minutes ago, a sound she surely had heard before, yet never like tonight, a sound revealed through the gentle scratching of the communing stalks: the earth breathing.

They kissed. Later she would try to remember who initiated it, but she couldn't. It wasn't an aggressive kiss, but it was sure and gentle and seeking, and she allowed herself to look at his beautiful brown face all the while.

The boy she thought she had seen was gone.

She would not remember whose idea it was, but they reentered the car and then wiggled over the front seats to the back. She pulled his shirt over his head. He eased the straps of her dress from her shoulder. She tasted his sweaty skin the sticky night had given him, and her hands slipped along his body. Their lovemaking was gentle, although she had to slow him down to make it last. She said, "We have plenty of time, at least until corn harvest." She could feel his whole body bounce with laughter.

Afterward, they lay together in the backseat. He let the pads of his fingertips play over her tender breasts while kissing her forehead.

One foot was jammed against something near the door. She was stuck skin to skin with him. Their clothes were a jumble on the car floor amongst all his junk. Just outside, leaves and tassels of corn swayed. The absurdity of the moment was not lost to Tamara, but nonetheless, she felt a touched-inside feeling, like a pebble had been dropped in the middle of her soul, sending waves fanning out to every part of her.

"WHAT WAS THAT?"

"Shit, that was a car door. Get dressed!"

Footsteps crunching over broken cornstalks came closer and closer.

"Get up."

"Get off my leg."

"Shit! Where the hell's my—"

"Go without them!"

Lawrence was gazing out the back window as he struggled into his pants. "I think it's the farmer." He pushed on his sneakers without his socks.

Tam slipped into her dress, but the underclothes would have to wait.

There was a loud banging on the trunk. "Halloo. Y'all all right in there? Y'all all right?" A flashlight beam dance around the interior of the car.

"Oh, crap," Tam whispered.

They scrambled over the front seats. Lawrence was quickly out of the window. "Yes. Thanks. Sorry about your corn, sir."

Tamara found a way to squeeze out the door.

"Ain't my damn corn." The man was big and white and had big jowls. He wore a patched pair of coveralls, looking like a cliché from the Indiana farmland. Two kids were bouncing after him down the trail Lawrence had carved. He thumbed behind him. "We was by this way earlier and Patty, my oldest, said, the car in front of us done gone off the road. Well, we slowed and took a look but didn't see a thing, and then I had my sister's kids with me and had to drop them off, so I figured on the way back, hell, we'd take one more look and sure 'nough we spotted y'all the second time."

"Um, well, thanks for checking on us. We . . ."

"Ya stuck?"

"I don't . . . um." Lawrence looked to Tam.

Tam covered her face.

The two children, a boy and a girl, said, "Hi," in unison.

"Hello," Tamara replied.

"Well, ain't you tried to get her out?"

"Sure," Lawrence said. "But I flooded the engine. So we were waiting."

The flashlight played over Lawrence and then over Tam. "Well, let's get you kids out of here," he said. "Mitch, Patty, pick up any cobs you see. Only from the down stalks, you hear?"

The kids eagerly set about their task.

The car started immediately. Tamara stayed in the field while Lawrence backed the car toward the road. It was clear, though, that it could not climb the rise to the road itself, so the man, whose name was Danny, took rope from the bed of his pickup. Despite Lawrence's offering to be the one to crawl beneath the car, Danny dropped to the soft ground and tied the rope to the car's rear axle.

Tamara helped the kids gather the ears of corn. They each had armfuls, until adding to the load caused another ear to drop. The children grinned at her, clearly enjoying the darkness and each other.

Lawrence was thanking Danny for about the fifth time, when the girl asked Tamara, "Is he your boyfriend?"

five

JUDITH MATHEUS COULD not seem to find her feet. She could not string enough separate movements together to qualify as being in motion. She knew she was neglecting her son when he needed her the most. She knew her husband needed her too, though he was trying to project strength, in the process fooling no one except possibly himself. But at least he had managed to leave the house. He had been to the police station and to the hardware store, and he had cooked dinner and brought it up to her. Judith had no desire to be strong. She could see no advantage in it. Emotionally, she hovered between disbelief and sheer panic. She was that drowning person at the first intake of water; she felt only the overwhelming helplessness and saw only the frantic splashing.

She had imagined this horrible thing before. It was the kind of thing that happened when you let your guard down. When you forget to ask them questions, like where are you going? When will you be back?

It happened before when Judith and her mom were in the kitchen talking about the man next door, who had his girlfriend living with him and his wife. Mom can spin a story. The wife, apparently, had not caught on yet . . . And then Judith heard a sickening thump. She knew immediately. She saw her mother's questioning eyes, but Judith knew. Her mother asked, "Where is he?" But Judith was already running up the stairs. Running as fast as her legs had ever taken her. The thump had a hollow, metal drum sound that led her straight to the bathroom. And there was her fourteen-month-old lying perfectly still in the bottom of the white cast-iron tub. Her mother had screamed, "No, don't touch him, baby!" even as Judith had gathered him into her arms.

So she had imagined Lawrence being dead before. She had let herself go to that worst place and afterward become the most vigilant mother anyone knew. She had imagined the emptiness, the choking bitterness, the loss that stretches through you and through everything you'll ever do again. She had held her son and rocked him until his little eyes blinked open. But even then, imagination had fallen woefully short.

She hoped no one would come to visit today. She didn't want anyone to pat her hand, bring her a dish of greens and turnips, and tell her it's not for us to know God's plan or that God needed some of the good boys with him in heaven.

When she got out of bed, she was not surprised to see Preston already gone. She thought the first thing to do would be to look in on Terrell. She would fix him something to eat, make sure he's eating right. Preston too. She had not dusted and vacuumed in a while. She put her hand on the knob of her bedroom door, but she could not turn it. Her hand trembled. On the morning of Lawrence's first day of school, Preston had asked him if he were scared. He had not said a word. She had walked him to the school door, held it open. Preston had remained in the car with baby Terrell. Lawrence had looked up at her just before stepping into the building. "I'm not scared, am

I, Mommy?" "No, you're Mommy's big boy." She had seen he was scared, as had Preston, but he had climbed from the car and walked, back straight, into that school.

She saw that little boy make his way down the sidewalk and knew she would not have to worry about him. Lawrence made it a point not to be scared. He was braver than his little brother.

She pulled her hand from the knob. If someone else had come along to open the door, maybe then she could walk through, just as Lawrence had walked through when she opened the school house door for him.

Not too long ago, Preston and Judith had been at the front window of their Lincoln projects apartment, watching people gathered to see a spectacle. A woman, Judith had known just well enough to complain about the weather to, argued outside with a cop. Judith couldn't hear what she was saying. An ambulance arrived.

"Look at the kids playing," Judith had commented. "It's like it's a game to them, Preston." She was thankful that her boys were upstairs asleep. "No one is shocked. Look at them. It's a picnic out there. No one is outraged . . . we're not outraged."

It turned out that the friend had stabbed the woman's son and she had taken the same knife and chased the friend off with it.

"I should invite her to our church. Maybe in a day or two," Judith had said.

"What? No."

"Why not?"

"Meddling, I guess."

"And maybe she needs a friend."

Preston had simply said "Huh." Maybe he knew she would not ask the woman. Maybe he knew that Judith would no longer even offer the woman a comment on the weather.

"We have to move from here, Preston. Now."

He had not said anything. She looked up at him, the argument for moving ready to explode from her, but her husband's face was carved stone and he was nodding.

Tamara Groves—that was the name of the girl she had met after the funeral. She had been picturing the girl and trying to picture Lawrence with her. She seemed older than Lawrence, and Judith had wondered the girl's age while the girl introduced herself. She seemed older than her son, not necessarily in her face but in her eyes. So Lawrence had a steady girlfriend. Judith had not known that. Again, she had not been looking. Judith wanted to know more. The girl had not looked like someone she would have picked for Lawrence. Lawrence's girl would not be so . . . out there, with the short skirt and the too-deep neckline. She would have been a young student planning for college. Judith wondered if her boy had been in love. She wanted to know.

She opened her bedroom door. "Terrell," she called. She thought she had heard someone on the stairs. Terrell would know how to get a hold of the girl. After the funeral, they had been upstairs talking, Preston said. She could send Terrell to give the girl a message.

Terrell could tell her something about Tamara; the brothers probably talked about girls all the time. She hoped so, but she had not seen a lot of evidence of it. She had seen them working together in the kitchen or mowing the backyard, but they went their own way when it came to friends and playing. Time was they'd ride their bikes together up and down Gum Street. When the family first moved here the brothers went exploring together. They would be propelled from the house and she would shout after them to shut the door even as they were leaping over the porch steps.

"Lawrence," she whispered. "I should have been watching."

six

HER ASS WAS at eye level as the detective followed her up the stairs. Just when Tamara thought they would not be knocking on her door, here they were.

They had caught her on the sidewalk as she was going to the grocery store. Now they wanted to talk to her, and she didn't know what she would say.

"How long have you lived here, Tamara?" the older man asked.

Something about his sunken eyes told her he would not believe anything she might say. He never believes anyone, she thought. The younger detective in the plaid jacket didn't look too smart, and she all but dismissed him.

She unlocked the door and stepped in first. "Nearly a year. In a month or so."

The detectives stepped inside and immediately their heads swiveled. Tamara looked around quickly too, hoping no bags or roach clips or anything had been left in view.

They had not asked to see Bread, who was out anyway. Any of Lawrence's friends could have mentioned her to the police, but she figured it must have been Terrell Matheus, who dropped the dime on her.

"You live here with Clay 'Bread' Williams," the young detective said.

It had not sounded like a question so Tamara did not reply.

"You knew Lawrence Matheus? Tell me about that," the older detective, who had introduced himself as Bill Carson, said. "Tell me, did you two used to talk a lot? Go on dates? Tell me about that."

"We were—"

"And, please, don't say we were just friends, because everyone, everyone says that, you know, and that doesn't give us a good picture."

Tamara sat down on the edge of her couch. With a gesture, Bill Carson asked if he could sit on the other end, and Tamara nodded. The other detective seemed content to stand.

"He gave me rides. I don't have a car. He gave me rides home from school."

"You're still in school?" plaid detective asked.

"I missed a year or so due to family problems."

"Well, good for you. Making it up. So many never go back. Good intentions . . . So he gave you rides . . ."

"Yes."

"A couple of times? Every day?"

"Every now and then."

"What's that? Twice a week?"

Tamara shrugged.

"Did you ever go to any of his track meets?"

"A couple of times."

"He wasn't bad. I saw some of his times. I think he was going to make something of himself. Good in school. Tall, good-looking kid . . . Went to church . . . Yeah, I think he was going to make something of himself."

Tamara felt a tear escape and quickly wiped it away, tilting her head up. She crossed her arms.

"So he drove you straight home. You guys didn't go around? Go get a burger? Some pizza and talk?"

She didn't know what they already knew. She looked down at the stitched flowers on the bells of her jeans. "No. not really."

"You ever see Lawrence hanging out with white boys, some you didn't know, some that didn't go to Bosse?" He flipped the pages in a small steno pad.

"No."

"Guys with long blond hair."

"No."

"Maybe older . . ."

"No."

Plaid Jacket asked, "Where's your parents live? They know you living here?"

"They're dead," she said, and felt her throat filling.

"Long time?"

"Since I was ten."

"Guardians?"

"The state of Kentucky was."

"Yeah?"

Plaid jacket walked to the middle of the room. "Bill, I think she had two boyfriends."

"What do you want to tell us, Tammy?" Bill Carson placed his notebook in his lap.

Tamara thought, I'd like to tell you nobody calls me Tammy.

Bill Carson was studying her. She could not return the gaze of those tired eyes. "You got something to say? Anything about Bread Williams? Did he know about these rides you got from Lawrence?"

Tam hoped Bread would not come home before they left. She could feel them watching her, but she had nothing to say that was anyone's business. What she had done, she had done. In her mind, she had put finished on the whole thing.

"I think Lawrence was probably mostly a good boy. You agree, Rick? Yeah, we're getting that picture. You know what I think was the most screwed up thing in his life? That was you, Tammy. You're his fuckup, aren't you?"

Tamara started as if struck. She looked to Plaid Jacket, who quickly hid his surprise. "Wh—"

"Oh, yeah. I'm never too far off on these things. Good kid gets mixed up in mud and sinks." Carson stood. "Rick, give her a card."

Plaid Jacket dropped a business card on the couch next to Tamara.

She swiped at it, brushing it to the floor.

"Well," Carson said. "Pick it up before Bread gets home. You're going to want to call us later, honey. Just don't make it too late. That's when I get pissed off. Let's go, Rick."

She wiped her cheeks then jumped to her feet in time to slam the door behind them.

She rested her forehead against the wall next to the door, hearing the detectives' footfalls on the creaking stairs. She had said nothing, and now it was too late.

Silly Lawrence, liking her so much and no one had asked him to. Schoolboy. Tears rolled down her face. She had not told them. It had been a silly thing to think, but for a couple of days there she had convinced herself Bread was the killer. She lifted her head from the wall, rubbed her forehead, turned around, and there was Bread, standing in the shadows.

"What did they want? And what did you tell them?" he demanded.

"Where did you come from?"

Bread's eyes looked small. And she had seen his mouth set like this before.

Mrs. Dorsey, downstairs, was shouting something, threatening to call the landlord. Had she known the police were just outside she would have shouted for them. Bread must have come in through her apartment using the inside stairs. Had Mrs. Dorsey's daughter let Bread in? Tamara wondered. How had he unlocked the door at the top of the steps?

"'Fore you even start—"

"You think I'm stupid, don't you?"

"No, Bread. Those cops don't know what—"

He put a finger to his lips. "Shh."

She heard the doors of the cop car shutting. Before, she had wanted them gone. Now she wished she had followed them out.

Bread crossed the room and was peeking through the small glass in the door.

His cologne was strong, and Tamara wrinkled her nose. She thought to say something about it, something lighthearted.

The blow came just as she was about to speak. It was an elbow to her temple that put white flashes in front of her eyes and turned her head. He then grabbed a fistful of her hair and shoved her head down so that she was bent at the waist and left gasping for breath.

"Cop seems to think you have two boyfriends, 'Tammy.'"

He was pulling her hair. He steered her around him in a circle. She struggled to keep her feet. "Wonder who else besides . . . besides . . . Pick that up for me. That. Pick it the fuck up."

He tried slapping at her face with his free hand.

She managed to ward off the weight of the blows as she reached for the card and finally trapped it between two fingers. She held it above her. Blood rushed into her head.

Bread snatched the card. "Detective Richard Shoenfeldt of the Evansville Police Department, Homicide Division, and I know you have two boyfriends . . . had. Had! Punk's dead now, ain't he? Uh-huh. Sunk in the mud that is Tamara 'Even-my-own-daddy-done-left-me' Groves. You told them dear Daddy was dead? You lyin' left and right." He tried to slam her head into the door, but she managed to turn so that her side took the impact.

She grabbed at the wrist of the hand that held her head down.

"Wonder who else knows about you and me and him beside you, me, and Detective Shoenfeldt?"

"You're my only guy, Bread. You know that," Tam managed to say while trying to breathe.

"Oh, naw, don't even. I knew. I went to pick you up after school and that punk pulls his car, some rusty tin can, up right in front of you. But you had already seen me and walked right past his car. But he wasn't so swift on the uptake and opened his door. Then he must have seen me in his rearview and drove off.

"I asked you then who it was, and you said you didn't know. Now, if he was just a friend, you'd say, 'Oh, that just so-and-so, that's all. He always trying to get girls in that car of his.' But you didn't say anything like that. Naw. You said, 'I don't know.' But that was Lawrence Matheus. Punk. Guess I don't have to worry about him anymore."

Tamara quit trying to grab his arm. From the way he held her head, she could see the floor, Bread's pants, and his crotch. She made a fist. She would only have one chance.

Before she could swing, Bread pushed her away and she crashed into the bottom kitchen cabinets. Her knee banged hard on something.

"God damn it, Bread." She tried to get up.

"Don't move. Don't move a fuckin' muscle. And don't look at me like that. Don't you . . . Shit." Spit sprayed from his mouth. His face was contorted.

Tamara rubbed the side of her face. She could feel the skin already swelling.

"You hurt me way more than I ever hurt you. Way more, so don't even." He sat on the couch. He still had the cop's business card in his hand. One leg bounced up and down with unspent energy.

She knew he could explode off that couch. He could dive right at her. She weighed saying something versus staying quiet.

"You don't have to be a goddamn track star to get muddied up. I'm sinkin' too. I'm sinking up to my goddamn eyeballs."

He looked almost as if he would cry. But Tam could see his mind working. He glanced at the card. The police scared him and he was wondering what he should do. He was probably wondering if he should go out tonight or lay low. Should he tell his boys what happened? He fished cigarettes from his pocket, lit one up, and snapped off the lighter. He closed his eyes when he exhaled the first time. "You got the damn cops lookin' at me. I won't be able to breathe in this back water . . . Geez."

Tamara's knee hurt. She wanted to straighten it, but she did not move. "Every black kid in our class went to his funeral, Bread. I went and he did give me rides, so some people must have started saying we were going together or something. You know I hate to walk. They must have told the cops he and I were seeing each other. I didn't tell you about the rides 'cause I was afraid you'd get jealous. Guess I was wrong about that, huh?" She tried to sound more pissed off than scared.

He was going to make her wait, but then waiting was usually good when it came to Bread's temper. She reminded herself that if Bread had come up the usually locked inside stairs, then she had another escape route available to her. She leaned her head against the kitchen cabinet.

"I see. It's all my fault for not picking up your lazy ass. You always think I'm the bad guy. You always think the worst with me. You think I'm gonna do the worst thing you can think of," he said. "And that's what makes it come true. You make it come true."

The sun dipped behind some large maples in the backyard, making the room suddenly dark. Bread had gone through three cigarettes. She hoped he would go out because she knew there was no way he was going to allow her to go anywhere while he was there.

The heavy smell of Mrs. Dorsey's cooking filtered through the cracks in the old house.

seven

CAP PORTER'S BOSS moved as if he had no time to waste, as if he were being timed. He led Cap from the shop room down the hall to his office. Cap passed Cheryl at her desk and winked at her, but she kept punching the keys on her typewriter.

"I'm in a fight here, Porter," Douglass said as he slid behind his messy desk.

It took Cap a moment to realize the man was anxious, that his hands did not stop moving. "I got management questioning the need for the whole department. The VP is asking why pay benefits when we can outsource. Outsource!" He reached for a cigarette, then put the pack in a drawer. "I'm gonna shoot straight. We can't have this. You been late. That's documented in your file."

"What . . ."

"And, Porter, I've gotten reports. People have smelled the liquor on your breath . . ."

"Who has?"

"Never mind who. It just don't matter. Porter . . . Porter, we know you've been taking a nip at lunchtime too." He snapped his head to the side, then shook it. "Got to let you go. My hands are tied on this one." He held his hands out, palms up as if to show the binding ropes. "Completely tied. It's gone over my head."

"Douglass, what are you fuckin' talking about?"

"We gonna get that last check to you, but I need for you to get up any of your personal tools. I know a bunch of you boys bring in your own, and—"

"Wait a minute. Wait a minute, Douglass. Who said I been drinkin'?"

"I ain't about to name names for you. My hands are tied. I'm just doin' the dirty work. Hell they might ax the whole damned department before long. Outsourcing! We have to be above reproach." He raised his hand to indicate a level at least two feet over his head. "Above reproach. You tied my hands." He let both hands fall on the desk in resignation.

Cap sat stunned.

Douglass was working hard to maintain a poker face. Maybe his hands were tied. Cap suspected he enjoyed some part of this power trip, this chance to act as a real manager.

Outside, Cheryl, at her desk, lined up forms with carbon paper between them and coaxed them into her typewriter. One quick glance betrayed her: she knew what was going on in here and had not told him. His friend. He could see most of the shop from the office. Milt was sweeping behind the work benches. Bob was at his workstation fiddling with the elbow joint of a pipe with stupid Murray, who had to ask how to do something no matter how many times he had done it in the past. They knew what was going on and one of them had helped it along, had dropped the dime on Cap.

That knowledge hurt the worst. It overwhelmed Cap's rage at being fired with a hurt at being stabbed in the back by someone he trusted.

"Come on. We'll quietly get your tools." For a moment, Douglass quit his game and became nearly human. Cap thought he glimpsed a man, who may have stayed up late last night going over his outsourcing-hands-are-tied speech and still not gotten it to sound as it had in his head. "Cap, um, you can . . . I'm not going to tell them the reasons. I mean, you can tell them anything you want."

"Damn, Douglass."

"I'll walk you out, partner."

"What if I don't want you to walk me out, partner?"

Later, Cap would wish he had jumped in Douglass's face, told him off, and told him where to stick it. He would, in fact, say to his friends that he had made quite a scene before threatening to call his lawyer and the NAACP. But, in fact, he went to his locker with Douglass shadowing him and pulled down his Snap-on tools calendar, found his wrenches and a pair of vice grips that turned out not to be his, and put them in his toolbox. He looked at Cheryl on his way past her desk, but she refused to look his way, and he thought of how he had flirted with her the other day. She had laughed with him until two white men had walked by and saw the white secretary laughing with a member of the maintenance crew. Maybe they said something to her. Had that embarrassed her, he wondered, caused her to smell the liquor this time?

He latched his toolbox. He asked Douglass, "Do you need to look in it?"

Douglass shook his head.

Cap walked out of Mead Johnson into the harsh glare of a bright day. He looked at the long rows of cars on the company lot. He had two pocketknives with him—a small one with a mother-of-pearl finish that he used to clean under his fingernails and the larger elk-horn knife that he could open with a flick of his wrist. He look down the lines of cars searching for Douglass's. He wanted to slash all four of his tires. Cap smiled at the thought of that smug bastard coming out at the end of the day and seeing his car six inches lower than everyone else's. Cap had slashed someone's tires before, a long time ago, in high school. The car had belonged to a kid who liked the same girl Cap liked and Cap had stuck his tire on an impulse and felt bad about it for a long time. He saw Douglass's new Chrysler Cordoba and walked on by it.

The trunk of Cap's car was filled with all kinds of junk including two old wheels, and he had trouble fitting his toolbox in there. He would have to rearrange everything.

He looked back at the MeJo building. He had worked in Facilities there for eight years, and had enjoyed telling his friends he worked at Mead Johnson, second only to Whirlpool as the largest employer in the tristate. He knew that during the lunch break, a few of the people inside would be talking about him. He hoped someone might express anger that Porter was let go based on an unsubstantiated rumor. "For God's sake," someone might say, "he just lost a member of his family; that was his nephew got gunned down last week. So he took a nip or two. Who wouldn't?"

He thought of the moment he would tell Lynn. That look on her face would kill him. It would kill him because it would not be a look of surprise.

The trunk still wouldn't close. He'd have to shift the wheels farther back. They had been for Lawrence, part of the rehabilitation plan they had for his car. But his nephew had seemed lukewarm to the wheels—maybe he didn't like their styling or didn't think they could find two more to match. Cap remembered he had pulled one out of the trunk for Lawrence to inspect. Removing the wheel had uncovered something his nephew was keenly more interested in, a .38 revolver.

Cap had owned three guns. One he kept in the house, although he had shown it to Lynn and she might have thrown it away. Another was in the luggage compartment of his Harley, but that was just a .22. And one he had kept in the trunk of his car. It was that one he had let his nephew hold, instructing him on how to cradle it with both hands and how to sight along the barrel.

"Keep it pointed down and your finger outside the trigger guard. It's like your own personal atomic bomb. You ever notice that none of the countries that have the bomb get attacked?"

Lawrence was hardly paying attention. He weighed the gun in his hand. Finally, he looked into Cap's eyes. "I need this gun, Cap." And then he'd added quickly, "Not 'cause I want to hurt anyone; I don't. But there's this guy. He's bad news, man, and he hassles me and Tam. I'd just like to have something in case of the worst. Probably won't be nothing, but, you know . . ."

Cap was about to shake his head and say no.

"Mom and Dad would scream, of course. But they don't understand. They think I'm still a boy and should come running to them every time, every situation. This guy has friends . . ."

Cap used to be a favorite of his nephews, but that had changed when he and Judith had a serious falling out. "You can borrow it," Cap said. Here was a chance to be the cool uncle again and Cap had seized it.

When Cap drove from the Mead Johnson parking lot for the last time, two stacked mag wheels remained behind on the asphalt.

CAP PARKED HIS CAR in front of the house he rented with Lynn and went inside long enough to pee. Then he went to the garage and rolled out his new—and still not half paid for—Harley-Davidson Electra Glide. It was aquamarine, and he had a matching aquamarine and black helmet, which he wiggled onto his head and strapped under his chin. He used the kick-starter because he had not ridden in a while, maybe not since a week or so before Lawrence was killed. The big bike shuddered and burped and then roared to life, a bass sound that never failed to stir Cap Porter. He turned up Kentucky Avenue and headed to his sister's house on Gum Street.

He rode down Lincoln Avenue, but no one was out on the streets. The workday still had nearly two hours to go. A brother he did not recognize hung out in front of Doc's Liquors, looking desperate for one more dollar. The man's eyes followed after Cap's Harley.

He turned on Evans Avenue, passing the funeral home he had been in just a few days ago. He crossed Bellemeade Avenue at the baseball diamond where he used to play in pickup games. Then turned onto Gum Street and rode into the Matheus driveway. He had helped them move in. That was a day for sweating and laughing. The boys competed to see who could carry the most. Judith's face had beamed. They had a home of their own. For a while, Cap was a frequent visitor, but then there were problems, and all that changed.

Lawrence's car was in the back and Cap parked the big bike next to it and swung off the seat. Someone had thrown a blue tarp over the car, as if it too were dead. Cap pulled the tarp off. Seeing the car and its one thousand dings and dents brought back memories of Lawrence standing right there, under the hood, scratching his head. Cap immediately understood the tarp. Cap rummaged in the car's glove compartment, finding only papers, trash, and a box of Lemonheads. He searched under the seats. "Damn," he said, finding instead of the gun, some petrified french fries. He climbed into the back and rummaged through hamburger wrappers and school papers. Cap found a social studies exam on which Lawrence had gotten a C. One question had been, "If you were President Ford, what three reasons would you give for pardoning Richard Nixon?" Lawrence had written, "1. He gave me the job"—and as if that weren't clear enough he added in parentheses "I'd feel obliged"—2. Save the country money on a trial. 3. He might have something on me." Cap laughed and let the paper fall back to the floor.

"Hey, Cap."

Cap turned and saw Terry standing outside, peeking into the car. Cap waited a moment. "Hey, nephew. How's your mother?"

"She's . . ." He shrugged, and turned to inspect the motorcycle. "You know, all right."

"You lookin' out for her, right?"

"Yeah. Sure."

Cap scooted out of the car. "Where's the keys?"

"You takin' it somewhere?"

"Need to look in the trunk. Lawrence had borrowed some of my tools."

Terrell made no move to go in the house for the keys.

"You back in school?" The boy didn't reply so Cap repeated the question.

"Yeah. For now," Terry said.

They were silent for a while, standing apart. Cap looked at the eight-year-old Dodge; it had not been well taken care of. Terry seemed to be staring at the motorcycle or maybe at nothing at all. Cap wanted to say something. He felt guilty for having lied to the boy, but mostly he just wanted to find that gun. He wished his nephew had been carrying it when those white boys drove by for the second time. "Has the cops said anything to y'all 'bout them boys?"

Terry breathed out, an exasperated sound. "They don't tell me nothing."

If the gun wasn't in the trunk, it was probably squirreled away somewhere in Lawrence's room, Cap thought, and then flashed on what would happen if the police or Judith found it.

"I want to go someplace," Terry was saying. "I want to go far away for a while, where nobody knows nothing about me. Someplace new. You know? I wouldn't even have to ever get there, really. I just want to be on the road to it, just moving."

"I'll take you for a ride," Cap said. "We'll hop on the Harley and ride to Louisville or somewhere."

Terry shrugged. "That's not what I meant." Cap noticed he looked thinner, especially in the face.

"We used to go on rides, along the river . . . find some drift wood. Remember? Are you eating?" When Terry didn't respond, Cap said, "Really need that trunk key."

"Dad had them. I'll look." Terry went in the house.

Cap waited, wondering if he should go inside and say something to Judith. Not today, he decided. He did not want to risk it. All his life she could read him. Still, he moved toward the door and was standing there minutes later when Terrell came back out with the keys. Cap rummaged through the car trunk, which was easily as messy as his. The spare tire was flat. Cap lifted it. No gun.

"The only tool I see is a tire iron," Cap said, but he glanced over a shoulder to discover Terry had left. He closed his eyes for a minute and wished he was stretched out on his couch at home with a drink in hand. He hurried inside the house and dashed up the stairs to Lawrence's room. In two or three minutes he had turned over or poked his hand in every possible place a gun could be hidden. He should have taken the boy out for target practice, he thought in the middle of his search. If he was going to loan him a firearm, he owed him more than a few safety tips. Cap wondered if Lawrence had told

Terry about the gun and if Terry knew where it was. Terry's door was closed. On his way out, Cap heard the sound of television voices coming from Judith and Preston's room. He wanted to check in on her, just say hi, and ask if there was anything he could do. Instead, he crept down the stairs.

He let his Harley roll out into the street before starting it.

At Doc's, he bought a fifth of Jim Beam and put it in a saddlebag. He finished it while laid out on his couch and still he did not feel drunk. He didn't even feel the buzz. He heard the sound of a television, though, distant voices coming from behind a closed door in the middle of a workday.

eight

TERRELL MATHEUS RODE his bike to the Ohio River just to get away from home and his neighborhood and would have gone farther had he not been stopped by that wide stretch of brown water on the other side of the levee. It felt good to be out, and he liked laboring at the pedals. His momentum took him halfway up the levee, and when he could no longer push the pedals he hopped off the bike and walked it up the rest of the way. The river was high and choppy. He had smelled the earthy, spoiled muckiness from two blocks away and had heard the water surging and gurgling along the slope of the levee.

At the levee's top, he let his bike drop while he looked around. To his left was the Evansville Museum, which he'd visited several times on class trips.

Across the river lay Kentucky, first a fence of trees and beyond the trees an expanse of flat fields. In the summer, the full trees obscured the land behind them, making the far side look like an unexplored wilderness.

To the west was downtown Evansville, Indiana. He could see the one tall structure, the Old National Bank building, the green of the courthouse dome, and close to the river, the dark bricks of the old McCurdy Hotel. He had been told during the great flood of 1937, boats actually docked right at the hotel. That was before the concrete wall was constructed and the raised earthen levee was piled along its flanks to save the city from the river. Since they built the levee, only farmers gambling with corn seed had to fear the floodwater.

Terry sat down on the brown grass on the riverside slope. Twenty feet down, the earth met the water with a line of giant white rocks placed there, he presumed, to stop erosion. The wind caused his bike's back wheel to tick around slowly.

That bike had been stolen two summers ago when he had left it leaning against the brick trash pit that folks in his neighborhood once had used to burn trash.

Terrell was afraid to tell his father that the bicycle, a ten-speed bought for him at Sears, was gone.

His parents had told him to lock it on the porch, and instead he had left it at the trash pit.

He did tell a couple of the guys at school that someone had boosted his ten-speed, but it was not the boys he told that came knocking on the door late one evening. He only knew one of them, Dennis.

Terry went out on the porch with them.

"Hey, my man, heard your wheels got lifted."

They both smiled. Terry's radar was warning him that something was not right.

"Yeah. So?"

"Look, brother. We found it. A white ten-speed, am I right?"

"Where is it?" Terry looked from face to face. One had stopped smiling, but Dennis did not seem capable of holding his back.

"You want your ride back or not?"

Terry went back in the house for his sneakers. His father, seated in the living room, asked where he thought he was going so late, and

Terry said he was just going down to the corner to say hi to someone. "Ten minutes," his father had said.

"So where is it?" Terry again asked the boys.

They slipped between houses and into the alleyway. I should have told Lawrence, Terrell thought, because he did not believe these guys. But he followed them because he wanted his bike back before Dad or Lawrence or Mom realized it was gone.

"We have some guys down there now, keeping an eye on it for you."

"Bastard snatched your bike, man," one of the boys said.

"Who?"

"You know Carlton Teague?"

"No."

"Yes, you do. Went to our school last year. Don't know where he goes now."

"He thinks you're a punk, Terrell. He bragged he took your wheels."

"He don't think you'll come get it. He thinks you're a punk."

"He gonna keep pickin' on you, boy." Dennis laughed for no reason Terrell could see.

At the end of the alley, they turned right for a couple of blocks, then went down another alley.

"Hurry, man," one of them said. "You gonna have to teach him a lesson, Terrell."

"Hell, yes, he will," Dennis replied for Terry.

They crossed one more street then stopped at the backyard of the first house. There near the back door, leaning against the house, was a white Sears ten-speed.

"That's it, Terry."

Once again, Terry wished he had gotten Lawrence to go with him.

A boy stepped out from some bushes.

"Hey, Terrell," he said. "That's your bike, man."

Another boy came from behind the garage. Someone asked, "Is Matheus ready to kick ass?" But no one answered him.

He looked at the boys who had stepped from the shadows. He recognized some of them. They looked at him.

"Get up there and get it."

They crowded him as he walked through the dark backyard.

"Knock on the door," Dennis said.

Terry said, "I just want my bike back."

"He called you a punk, Terrell."

In the house, only one weak light shone from an upstairs window. Terry went to the bike. It caught what light there was and even in the shadow he could tell it was his bicycle.

"I'll hold it for you, bro," a boy said.

"Kick his damn door in, Terry," said another.

Terry hesitated.

"Here, I'll do it." One of the boys pulled the screen door open and hammered at the door. "That ought to wake up these bicycle thieves," he said, and the boys laughed.

"You gonna have to teach this nigger a lesson about your property rights. You hear?"

The hammering created a stir within the house. Terry could hear angry voices and footsteps. Lights came on. Someone pushed him forward. There must have been six boys behind him egging him on.

"Kick his ass, Terrell."

Terry hoped the boy's parents would be at the door, but when the door was jerked open, Carlton Teague was silhouetted in front of the light. He had on boxers and a T-shirt. "What the fuck is going on out here?"

"Hey, Carlton get out here."

"Don't let Terrell Matheus have to go in there and drag your sorry, bike-stealing ass out of your own house."

That got all the boys laughing except Carlton and Terry. Carlton was no bigger than Terry. In fact, they looked to be exactly the same size.

"Stroke on him right now, Terrell. Kick his ass."

Carlton was hanging in the doorway.

One of the boys stepped forward and grabbed him by the arm and tried to pull him out. He resisted and managed to pull away. "Leave me alone," he said.

Terry said, "That's my bicycle. It's mine."

Dennis said, "You got his bike, Teague. It's his. I seen him on it at school."

"I found it in the alleyway," Carlton said.

The same boy who'd grabbed Carlton before made for him again, but Carlton slapped his hand away.

At the same moment someone pushed Terry forward. "Fuck 'em up, Terrell. He called you a punk."

"They's both punks," someone said, and all the boys laughed.

"I found it."

Terry grabbed his bike by the handlebars. He tried not to look at the faces around him. He could feel them grinning. They were calling them both punks now. This must have been too much for Carlton Teague and he stepped from the relative safety of his back doorway.

"It's my bike," Terry said over his shoulder. He had to push his way through the circle of laughing boys. He took a couple of running steps, hopped on a pedal, and swung onto the bike. He heard more laughter behind him. "Fuck you guys," he said, and behind him the laughter grew louder.

When he got home he brought his ten-speed inside and carried it to the basement.

The next day after school, Lawrence was sitting in the front yard and Dennis and the other boy who had steered Terry to Carlton Teague's house stood on the sidewalk. Terrell knew what they were talking about. From the living room window, he could see them acting out the whole thing for Lawrence: Terry being pushed forward. Bobby having to do the knocking for Terry. The boys trying to push and pull the two combatants together. "I just want my bike!" They laughed with their hands in front of their mouths as if they were trying to contain their laughter, but they were just pretending to be holding back. Lawrence was not pretending. He rolled in the grass, laughing with them. He enjoyed their story.

TERRY WENT FROM thinking about how he got the bicycle back to thinking about the girl, Tamara Groves, because maybe he could have told her that story. After the funeral, he had been surprised to find her in the house let alone in his room. "May I hide in here?" He remembered exactly how she looked sitting on his bedroom floor, her skirt tucked between her legs. But in that story, Lawrence was only in it at the end, lying on his side in the front yard, laughing at him.

Terry could smell her, in his room that day after the funeral. He could smell her perfume or soap or whatever it was. It wasn't heavy;

it was like walking by flowers. He couldn't describe the smell, but his nose remembered it, just like his eyes remembered things, mostly things he wished to forget.

He had almost told her the story of the dog but hadn't because, like the bike story it was more about Terry than Lawrence. Nonetheless, those stories unwound themselves mostly in connection with his big brother.

The summer they had moved to Gum Street, Terry had found the dog, quiet as a ghost, ribs showing, and blood on his snout where the dog had been trying to rub off duct tape that sealed his mouth shut. The dog turned those eyes like glowing green-brown marbles on Terry and froze him. After a second that felt like thirty, the dog loped away looking over its shoulder at Terry, a plea in those round marble eyes.

Terry had called after the dog, tried to follow, but the dog must have slinked between fence boards, in and out of someone's back yard in a flash. He had lost him.

Later, eating his grilled cheese sandwich at the kitchen table, he told his mother what he had seen. "He can't eat or drink. He's starving."

"What are you going to do about it?" she asked.

He wolfed down the rest of his sandwich and bounded back outside. It had been a damp, gray morning, but now the sun was coming out. He rode up and down every nearby street, whistling and calling out to the dog. He went back home long enough to recruit Lawrence, who joined the search. Terry came across a group of younger kids from around the neighborhood, all with bicycles. He told them about the dog and they were eager to help. He assigned them streets to search. They would meet back at the big sycamore on the corner each hour to report any sighting.

Those large marble eyes haunted Terry, but none of the searchers found the dog. After dinner they resumed the search, which continued until the voices of mothers could be heard calling the kids in. Terry urged them to stay or to sneak out later, which he alone did, searching until his father, armed with a flashlight, found him and ordered him home.

Terry moped into Lawrence's room. He had hoped if they found the dog, they could keep him. "Don't worry about it. We'll look again tomorrow. It's probably rubbed the tape off by now on its own," Lawrence had told him.

All night, Terry saw the bloody snout and the heaving rib cage and could not sleep.

The search continued the next day, though the other kids, who were not haunted by the ghost dog as Terry was, got bored and did not stick with it. Lawrence continued to help, for which Terry was grateful. After dinner, their mom even drove him around the area slowly.

When Terry came in from the search, Lawrence was at the back door to greet him. "Hey, I saw the mutt. All white, longish hair, right?"

"Yeah, what! Where is he?"

"Yep, saw him. Man had already taken the tape off. Some guy was putting a leash on him. It was his dog, and they'd been looking for him all over."

"Why was his mouth . . ."

"Oh. I asked. He said they were giving him a shot and he always bites when he's getting a shot so they tape up his snout. But then he ran off."

"What was his name?"

"What?"

"What was the dog's name. I was gonna name him Ghost."

"Name?" Lawrence looked annoyed. "I don't know. Man didn't say."

Two days later, the dog was nearly forgotten when Terry was riding to see a friend. He was in the alley between Powell Avenue and Blackford Avenue just four blocks south of home, when he smelled a clingy, oily odor and pulled his bike up. He heard the flies buzzing. Behind a garage, amid vine entangled bushes, was the white dog, Ghost, curled in death. His eyes were shut, but flies pestered them. The persistent silver tape, frayed and bloody, still had its strangle hold.

Lawrence and their mother were in the kitchen watching the little portable TV. They heard him come in but did not look up.

"You're a liar!" Terry shouted. "I could have kept looking. I could've found him." He lowered his head and rammed Lawrence in the chest. Lawrence grabbed him and pinned his head with an arm while Terry tried in vain to punish his brother. He heard his mother shouting their names and finally Lawrence pushed him away.

Terry fell to the floor. "We could've kept looking," he said, almost crying now.

Their mother sent them both to their rooms.

Following Terry up the stairs, Lawrence said, "I found him dead. I was just trying to give you a happy ending, punk."

Terry slammed his door. Lawrence slammed his. His father shouted, "What the hell's going on in here?"

"If that's true," Terry said from behind his door, "tell me where you found him, huh?"

"Both of you shut up," their dad said.

"Where'd you find him?"

Lawrence did not answer.

It had taken Terry a long time to realize Lawrence's lie for what it was, so that might have been a good story to tell.

Long after the dog incident, even after the stolen bicycle, his mother came to Terry and asked why Lawrence and he never got along or joked around or played basketball together like they used to.

Terry had shrugged.

But she had waited for an answer.

"Are you going to ask Lawrence too?" Terry finally asked.

"Don't worry about Lawrence now. I'm asking you, Terry."

She waited a long time. Finally, she turned to leave. At the door she said, "He's your brother, Terrell. The only one you're going to have."

As Terry led his bike down the levee, a man stepped out of a Cadillac and headed toward him. There were others in the car, dark faces all turned in his direction. Terry angled his bike away from them, but the man called out, saying Terry's full name. Terry stopped. He recognized the man as a deacon at Liberty Baptist.

"I thought that was you," he said.

"Hi," Terry said, unable to think of the man's name.

"Deacon Wills, son." He put his hand out. The deacon had a big afro and long sideburns.

Terry's weak grasp brought a fleeting scowl to the deacon's face.

"I'm with my family," he said, indicating the car.

Terry let his eyes meet the deacon's.

"Well, I certainly do not wish to bother you, son. I just want to add my condolences to your family, to let you know we lift your family up to the Lord in prayer each night. Tell Sister Judith, won't you?"

"Okay," Terry said.

The deacon turned to leave, then turned back to Terry. "Son, they going to find those bastard crackers, you hear me? God's righteous wrath will rain down upon them." The man's sudden fury deepened the lines on his face and sharpened his nose. He seemed to be waiting on Terry to respond, to make a fist or growl back in some way.

Terry said, "My mom . . . I should be home by now."

nine

TERRELL SET OUT for school but did not get there. He had awakened that morning to the bumping noises of his father's moving about the house, then opening his door to ask if he were getting up. Terry had said yes but only got out of bed when he heard his father's car start.

When he passed his parent's room, he heard his name called.

He cracked the door open. "Yeah?" The room was dark. He could only make out the shape of his mother lying on the bed, under the sheets. The room had a stuffy smell.

"Hi, honey, do you need any lunch money?"

"No," he said, and almost closed the door. Then he asked, "Do you want me to bring you a cup of coffee?" She did not answer. "Mom?" When there was no response, he assumed she had fallen asleep and quietly closed the door.

Yesterday, he had heard locker talk at school of more planned protests in Lawrence's name. Kids looked at him. Some teachers looked at him, while others would not look at him. If not for his mother's presence there, he would have gone back home. He could not talk to her. He could not face anyone. Sometimes he felt like he could not breathe, could not swallow.

He walked without thought down the block, but stopped at the corner. He went to the East Branch Library, which was not yet open, and sat on the building's broad steps. When the librarians showed up, he moved on deciding to go over to his uncle's place, hoping he could hide there. Cap and his current girlfriend, Lynn, would be at work, but he knew where his uncle kept a spare key, nailed low on the inside of his garage door. And even if they were there it would be better than hanging around the house.

He walked slowly and mostly kept his eyes on the sidewalk. Cap lived on Judson Street, maybe two miles away from the library.

Last time Terry was over there, Cap's then girlfriend, Millie, told him about the night she and Cap laid out four rat traps. They suspected a rat was living with them. He put peanut butter on the traps, and he and Millie sat down to watch television. They heard the first snap in just five minutes. While they were removing the dead rat, two more traps snapped in rapid succession. Millie went from being grossed out to laughing. "We had to jump up from the couch every other minute! It was so gross! I thought we might run out of peanut butter!" Millie said when she and Cap told the story. Cap said, "I think we were pulling rats from the whole neighborhood. You serving Jif, word gets out." Millie had been the best girlfriend Cap had. They had only lasted a handful of months.

Terry took his time on the walk to Cap's. At Cap's, he was surprised to see his uncle's car and motorcycle. Before knocking on the door, he went to the tiny garage. It was one of those old, narrow garages designed for the little cars of long ago, or maybe even for a carriage. If you drove anything bigger than a Gremlin into it, you wouldn't be able to open the car doors to get out. Cap usually stored his motorcycle in there. Terry stooped, feeling for the key. It was still there. As he stood, he saw something amid the shadows and the dust wink at him, a crescent glint of light.

He left the key suspended on the nail and went to Cap's back door. He knocked and waited. Lynn answered. She was pulling on a sweater. "Hi, Terrell," she said. Her smile flattened. "Oh, so you're in on this with him, huh? Foolish—look that up in the dictionary. Foolish." She let him in as she went out. "Some of us can't skip work anytime we want to." And she said without turning back, "He's asleep. Maybe you can wake him. I couldn't."

Cap was on the couch, snoring loudly. His face had a slight frown. He was lying on his back, one arm across his chest, the other thrown over his head. He looked as if he'd been knocked unconscious rather than fallen asleep.

Cap's house smelled. Terry thought of the rat traps. "Cap . . ." Terry said softly.

The snoring continued. Terry sat down in an old easy chair. Terry's mother had told him her little brother had slept with pocketknives under his pillow when he was a kid. "He had quite a few of them, wood handles, mother-of-pearl . . ." Terry had thought that made Cap one tough kid, but now he wondered if maybe Cap had been afraid of something.

Except for the snoring, Cap appeared dead. Terry stood quickly and left the house, fleeing the sudden vision of Lawrence in Cap's place on the couch.

Lynn must have taken Cap's car.

Terry mounted his uncle's big Harley, grasped the handlebars, and made engine sounds as if working through the gears. He imagined being on the highway, crossing the bridge over the Ohio River. No one knew where he went and soon they would forget and go about their business. Wherever he ended up, there would be no one to tell him about God's wrath, and about how much they hate, or that they wanted justice now.

The imaginary flight ended abruptly. He was back in his uncle's driveway. He slipped off the Harley.

Besides keeping to alleyways as much as possible, he had no planned direction. He saw few people and hoped even fewer saw him. He fantasized that he was invisible or a ghost and that he was just moving through the world, but unattached to it, drifting like a leaf broken from the tree. In this way, he managed to kill the better part of a day. Evening came, the headlights on cars shone, heavy clouds moved in over the city. Finally, he reluctantly headed toward home. He stopped at a Stop-N-Go and used the restroom and bought a bag of chips and a Coke. He imagined that the white clerk did a double take when he made his purchases, but Terry's face had not been in the papers so no one could know who he was.

Back on Gum Street, he was grateful for the darkness because here everyone knew who he was and would stare at him, Lawrence's brother, the one who had seen the white boys in the white pick-up speeding away. They might even offer words of encouragement much like the deacon's. They would not let him be invisible for even a minute.

As he crossed the street, avoiding the streetlamp, he saw someone on his family's front porch. The porch light came on, and directly under it was Tamara Groves.

She did not see him and he considered letting her walk away. Instead, he called her name and saw her flinch.

"Jesus. Is that you, Terry Matheus? What are you doing skulking around?"

"I'm not skulking."

He was standing in the street and she was on the sidewalk. With the porch light behind her, it was hard to see her face. "Well, so where have you been not skulking to?" she asked.

He wanted to ask her about Lawrence, if she had liked his big brother as a boyfriend. It would be better if she had liked him. "Why are you skulking around our house?"

"I was talking to your mom. She called me. I don't know how she got my number, come to think of it."

"Maybe Lawrence had it written somewhere."

"Hmm."

"She was curious about you."

"No. She was curious about Lawrence."

Terry wanted to apologize for walking out on her during their private funeral service.

Down the block, car tires squealed. A pair of headlights raced toward them.

"Get out of the street," Tamara said.

A black Buick Wildcat squealed to a rocking stop right where Terry had been standing.

The driver's side window was down, but Terry did not recognize the driver. "Hey, Terrell, we got the ba—"

"Shut up." He recognized Cap's voice. The back door swung open. "I'm driving, Lee." Cap said jumping out. There were others in the car, one on the passenger side and another in the backseat.

Cap said, "Where the hell have you been?"

"Over your house."

"Get in the car, Terry. Lee."

Lee hesitated, rolled his eyes, then relinquished his hold on the steering wheel. "It's my car," he said, climbing out.

"Get in, Terry," Cap said.

"Where're you going?"

"Get in."

Cap had a hard expression on his face.

Tamara Groves had taken a couple of steps back.

Lee held the back door open for Terry. He folded himself into the backseat and Lee climbed in after him. In a second they were speeding off.

Lee had a wild look in his eyes that showed when the car slipped under a streetlamp. "We got them," he said to Terry. "We got the redneck bastards who killed Lawrence."

ten

"HELLO? TAMARA GROVES?"

For a long moment, her heart seemed to stop. Tamara thought the voice belonged to Mrs. Wilcox at the orphanage; they had found her after so many years.

"You're not going to be placed," Mrs. Wilcox had told her, bending to the girl's eye level. "You're going to have to become your own."

"Tamara?"

Even realizing it could not have been Mrs. Wilcox, she said nothing.

"This is Lawrence's mother. We met . . ."

"Oh yes, ma'am."

The invitation from Lawrence's mom had surprised Tamara, who figured Mrs. Matheus must have gotten her number from among Lawrence's things, because the apartment was listed under the name Clay Williams in the phone book.

"Everyone is out. So it'll just be us girls. I won't keep you long," she had said.

Tam had not known what to wear, so she put back on the same black dress she had worn to the funeral. Then, just as she was going out her door, she thought about what wearing that might say and quickly changed into jeans and a sweater.

She thought she might have to walk over there, but one of Bread's boys, Carl the Rabbit, who didn't mind giving her rides, showed up in time to take her to the Matheuses' place.

The compulsion to confess to Mrs. Matheus what she had done had long dissipated. Now Tamara believed it important not to say too much. In fact, there wasn't a lot to say, and she was sorry for that.

She knocked on the door and waited. The boards on the porch that ran straight from the door to the steps were new and raw, needing paint. At first she did not absorb their significance and when it did occur to her, she stepped off the boards quickly.

"I want to take you away from everything," Lawrence had once said with his trembling hands on either side of her face.

She was almost relieved when no one came to the door. She could say she had made the attempt and maybe they could talk some other time.

She walked to the end of the porch and peeked down the driveway. Lawrence's car was there. A pair of legs stretched from under it. Tapping and a bit of cussing came from under the car too.

"Hello. Hey," she called.

With loud grunting, Mr. Matheus wiggled from under the car. "Damn."

"I didn't mean to disturb you," Tamara said as she went down the side steps. She extended her hand to Mr. Matheus.

"No. No bother. Don't want to get you dirty, young lady." He showed his blackened hands. "How are you?"

"I'm fine, sir."

There was a pause and then Mr. Matheus said, "There was this horrible rattling. Turns out the exhaust pipe had got stove in and knocked loose. I got it hammered out and put a C-clamp on it. I think that did the job."

Tamara thought she knew how the pipe had gotten dented and smiled with the memory.

"What?" Preston Matheus asked, noticing her smile.

"Oh, nothing, sir. Lawrence was always wrestling with that car."

"Yeah. Yeah he was. I told him not to buy the worthless thing. I think we could have found something better . . ."

"No, he liked that car."

"Well."

Another pause and Tam began to regret having come over at all.

"So what brings you our way today?" Mr. Matheus asked.

"I came to see Mrs. Matheus," Tamara said. "Nobody came to the door. She called me."

His forehead crinkled. "Did she?" He wiped his hands with a rag from his pocket. "Well, she should be in. Let's see." He didn't take her in the side door, which was closer, but led her to the front.

"Judith," he called when he pushed the door open.

He let Tamara in first. The small foyer had a wooden bench. Last time she was here people and folding chairs had hidden much of the front room.

"Wait here," he said. He went upstairs.

This was a mistake, Tamara thought, and also wondered if Terrell were home.

Mrs. Matheus stopped at the top of the stairs, her husband hovering behind her. She was small and looked worn, but she made a gesture with her hands, open palms at her breasts, that said forgive me and welcome all at once, and instantly Tamara felt more at ease.

"I vacuumed the living room, but I think the kitchen table?"

Judith was shorter than Tamara, and as she led the way to the kitchen she saw the woman's hair had not been combed out well in back.

She thanked Tamara for coming and pulled out a seat for her.

Mr. Matheus said something from the hallway about being outside, and they heard the door shut.

"I have tea," she said. "Are you hungry?" Tall green glass tumblers were already sitting on the table.

Tamara shook her head.

After Judith poured the ice tea and put the sugar bowl and spoons on the table, she sat down. She lay her hands in front of her and then pulled them down to her lap. She looked embarrassed, but a smile leaked out and she said, "Marlene, an elder at Liberty Baptist, whispered in my ear at the funeral. I could hardly hear most of what she said, but she patted my shoulders and I heard her say that all her children had passed. She has grandchildren. I know they bring her to church. But all her children are gone. She said it doesn't get any better. I think she meant the grief. It doesn't get better, she said, but you, you, she said, get stronger. So far, I know she's right about the first part."

Tamara nodded, then sipped her tea, unsure of how to respond.

"Do you have family in town, Tamara?"

"No," she said. "I have an aunt in Virginia and my father, he's in Virginia too."

"Do you get out that way often?"

"No, ma'am, I don't."

"Sorry, Tamara, I don't . . . I didn't bring you here to pry. Well, not to pry too much." She grinned. "And you finished school?"

"Yes. Six years and four different high schools, but my diploma was the same size as everybody else's."

"Seems hardly fair. You sure?"

"I know! Well, I could've waited and graduated with everybody else. So I can't say what size their diplomas are. Maybe it is bigger. Maybe everyone else has these really small—"

"Good for you, young lady." Mrs. Matheus reached across the table and patted the back of Tamara's hand. "I'd give you extra credit for perseverance. And I'm gonna take it on myself to speak for your mother too. She's proud of you."

Tamara swallowed and looked away. "She . . . she made me promise. So . . . and she wanted me to go to college too, so that's the next big challenge."

"You must do it."

Tamara nodded. No one else had congratulated her for finishing school. She had simply finished and walked away. Bread had done nothing. And here was this sad woman patting her hand. Well, Tamara thought, she didn't call me here to talk about me. Tamara took an audible breath. "Mrs. Matheus—"

"Judith."

"Judith," she repeated. She pulled her ice tea nearer. "He always opened the car door for me." Then she told Judith about their rides and how they'd met and she again told about Lawrence seeing the scared little boy home. And how he waited for her after school, wearing his letterman's jacket, leaning against his car, or his head under the hood. And maybe she pushed the edges of things a bit here and there but not so much that anything she said was actually untrue. The ice in the tea melted and water pooled around the glasses. She even told an abbreviated version of how Lawrence had once driven off a country road into a cornfield. Mrs. Matheus laughed and kept repeating "He did that?"

MRS. MATHEUS WALKED Tamara to the door and both were surprised to see that it was dark out.

"I'll find Mr. Matheus and he can drive you home."

So he can see Bread waiting on Lawrence's girlfriend at the top of the stairs, Tam thought, shaking her head. She insisted that she would be all right and wanted the walk.

She was surprised when Judith Matheus gave her a long hug. She had not been hugged like this by a woman in a very long time. "He loved you, didn't he?" she whispered in Tamara's ear.

"We loved each other," Tamara said, telling her only real lie of the evening.

She stepped off the Matheuses' walk onto the sidewalk and spotted someone coming toward her. Her first instinct was to head back to the porch. But he called out her name. It was Lawrence's brother. "What are you skulking around for?" Tamara asked him.

"I'm not skulking. You're skulking around my house."

"I just had a talk with your mom. She called me. Come to think of it. How did she get my number?"

He shrugged and said something she didn't fully catch.

Just then, she heard tires squealing from down the street and a gunning engine heading toward them. Her first thought was it was Lawrence's killers returning. She took a step back, finding she couldn't move as quickly as she wanted to. "Get out of the street!" she shouted.

Everything happened in seconds. Cap Porter jumped from the back of the car and climbed in behind the wheel. Terry was pulled into the car.

"Terry, what's going on?" Tamara called out, but the car was already roaring away with the car door not completely shut. Tamara ran out to the middle of the street and watched as the car whipped around a corner and was gone from sight. She heard it for a little while longer and did not move until the engine sound was gone too.

She looked back at the Matheus place. Surely one of them had seen or heard what just happened, but the house was quiet.

She jogged up the short sidewalk to the Matheus porch but stopped before she reached the first step. She looked down the street again. The dark, still neighborhood seemed to have made no notice of Terry and his uncle.

She turned and started for home. The sidewalk was a straight line between parked cars and the bushes and trees in the stubby front yards of narrowly packed houses. Equally spaced streetlights made feeble ponds of light. Tamara kept to a steady pace through the shadows. There was a good chance Bread would be out by the time she got home.

eleven

THE CAR FISHTAILED as they skidded around a corner. Lee cursed under his breath. The lights of houses and streetlights blurred quickly behind them.

The man in the front passenger seat said, "Maybe we should just find a pay phone."

"Fuck that," Cap said.

They took another corner. Terry was hurled against Lee.

"Get pulled over for a ticket now . . ."

"I know," Cap said, but the car didn't slow down. They were on Lincoln heading toward downtown.

The man next to Terry, whom he didn't recognize, had a sheet on his lap and was trying to tear it. "I can't get this funky-assed sheet ripped," he said. "You pulled this right off your bed and now we got to put it around our faces . . ."

Terry asked, "Uncle Cap, where are we going?"

"You'll know when we get there, nephew."

"But . . ."

"Just be cool. You too, Lee."

"Fuck you."

"This sheet won't tear, goddamn it."

"You just ran a fucking stoplight," the passenger in front shouted.

Cap fished into his pockets and handed back a large pocketknife. Terry took it and the man next to him snatched it from his hands. Cap said, "Feel better?"

"Hey, no one's gonna identify me, and I know you don't want them to identify the boy here."

"Where we goin'?"

They skirted the downtown district and scrambled onto Diamond Avenue, the major road connecting the west side of town. The car bumped and bounced over railroad tracks. Lee cursed. From the Diamond Avenue overpass, Terry saw the dark waters of the Ohio River. Cap was driving crazy. Terry could see his uncle's eyes in the rearview mirror and tried to make eye contact, but Cap did not glance up.

They turned onto Franklin Avenue for a couple of blocks and Terry lost his way after that. It seemed Cap had lost his way too. They bounced over uneven payment, turning corner after corner.

"No. Left," the man up front said.

Cap cursed.

They drove down a dark, quiet block. He stopped and whipped the car into reverse. He turned in his seat and Cap's eyes met Terry's for a second. He reversed for a block, then turned down another small, gravelly road.

"Not here," the man shredding the sheet said.

"God damn, J. D., watch that knife."

Their headlights illumined what looked like a junkyard. Terry saw rusting washing machines, the old type with rollers on the top. A man in a bulky brown coat stepped into the headlight beams. He had a bottle in one hand and, with the other, shielded his eyes from the light. "What y'all wantin' here?" he croaked. "This is a private drive. What y'all wantin'? This is posted!" he repeated even as Cap reversed yet again, leaving the man in the shadows.

"Shit," Cap said.

He found room to turn about.

"You got it," Lee said as the back of the car came within inches of a hurricane fence.

Cap stepped on the gas, causing the tires to throw rocks.

"Cap . . ." Terry whispered, but then didn't know what to say. They had found a dark part of the city with streetlamps few and far between and streets of uneven concrete slaps and squat little boxes for houses.

"Right here. Then a left."

Cap turned hard enough to press Terry into the man on his right.

They went on for two or three more blocks. There were fewer houses here and more trees.

"Here?" Cap asked slowing the car to a crawl.

Terry could feel the men around him tense up.

"Maybe we should just find a pay phone," the man in front said again. "I saw a Amoco station a few blocks back."

"Did you? You're chickenshit, Payne. Now will you please shut up."

Lee whispered, "Kill the goddamn lights."

Cap did as ordered, and everything turned black. The men were still. On the curbside, the houses were set far back from the street and surrounded by trees and bushes. Small squares of light shone through the black shade under the trees. The house they were parked directly in front of was surrounded by a four-foot wooden fence, and Terry could see only its low roof. The house to the side was farther back and had a narrow gravel driveway leading to its side. Parked in the driveway, showing dully by light from the window that it was parked under, was a white pickup truck.

Terry felt his face heat up. Something caught in his throat and he began to gag. One of the men asked if he were okay.

Lee's face was at Terry's ear. "This is where your brother get his justice."

Cap said, "It's them. It's fucking them."

Terry looked up just as a fist rapped on the passenger-side window. He jumped as did Payne and Lee. "Shit!" Lee said. "What the . . ."

"It's Morris," J. D. said.

Payne rolled down his window.

Morris squatted beside the car. "What took you so goddamn long? You left me in those chigger-infested bushes out here in Redneckville, Indiana." Morris had a gun in his hand.

"Quit wavin' that shit around, Morris," Payne said.

Cap reached across Payne's chest and Morris handed him the gun. "How many of them is there?"

"How the hell am I supposed to know?" Morris said in a loud whisper.

"I thought there was three," Lee said.

A dog was barking somewhere behind them, but it looked as if there were only trees back there. "Cap . . ." Terry began.

"We had trouble finding Terrell," Cap said.

"Did you think we wasn't comin' back for you?" J. D. said. He laughed, but no one else did.

"Let's go," Cap said. "Terry, stay here. We gonna bring 'em to you."

Terry shook his head.

Payne said, "No we ain't. That's kidnapping if they ain't the right guys. Terry's gonna have to come up there with us and take a look."

Cap said, "No."

"We all agreed, now. Don't be changin' things up, God damn it. 'Sides, we don't want them to know we have an eyewitness. They read the papers. Everybody knows Terry was the only witness."

"That's right. Makes sense."

Lee said, "Let's just fuckin' go."

"Cap," Terry said. "These ain't the guys who . . ."

"How the hell do you know that already?"

"They were from out of town."

"That askin' for directions was just jive," Cap said.

"That's right," Lee said. "If they was really lookin' for the court-house like the paper said, then they'd at least be downtown."

"C'mon," Morris said, "before someone wonders what six niggers are doing out here in the middle of the night."

Payne turned to Lee. "My wife is going to kill me."

"She ain't gonna know."

J. D. said, "Maybe she'll just leave you. Wish mine would. Here." He was handing out the strips of cloth from the torn sheet.

Cap said, "Payne, you talk shit, my brother. You are free to ease on down the road. But I don't want to hear any more crap from you about how the black man ain't done nothin' since King was killed. No more from you."

"That ain't the same . . ."

"It's exactly the same," Cap said. "It is the fucking the same."

No one said anything for a moment. The vinyl seats creaked.

Outside, Morris whispered, "C'mon, y'all." He took a strip of cloth from J. D. "Y'all look lost. Let's go ask for some directions to the damn courthouse." And then he was gone, absorbed by the darkness under the trees.

"Wait, kill the dome light," Payne said.

"Yeah, I'll get it." Lee fussed with it a bit. "Damn." Finally, he wiggled the plastic cover off and pulled out the bulb. "All right."

"Terry, stick close to me." That was Cap's voice. The door hinges creaked loudly.

"Don't close the doors. No need."

They were out and across the sidewalk and under the trees. Terry followed the shadow in front of him that he thought was his uncle. "Cap," he whispered.

The ground was rough and all but invisible. He stepped on something and almost turned his ankle. They stopped. Terry ran into the back of someone.

The lights of the little house had grown bigger. He could see the white pickup truck clearly. It seemed to have a dull glow. It had rooster tails of mud along its side.

"We know they have at least one gun," Lee said.

"Put your masks on."

"And don't use no names around them, you hear?"

Cap's voice said, "None of this mask shit is gonna matter."

The men tied the strips around their heads, leaving ragged, uneven holes for eyes, making them look like spectral scare crows.

"This is role reversal." Terry thought it was Morris speaking. "All the way with the AAA."

"AAA?"

"Angry Afro-Americans."

"Shut up."

Someone took Terry's strip of cloth from his hand and tied it about his head. The vision in one eye was partially obscured and the cloth covered his nose too. It was tied too tightly and dug into his skin. He knew they had come to get him because they wanted him to confirm they had found the killers. They wanted him to point and say, "That's them. That's the sorry-ass crackers that gunned down Lawrence." The masks, maybe it was Payne's idea, were for the off chance they might have gotten this wrong.

Payne and Lee were assigned to the back door and they disappeared like phantoms. Terry wanted Payne to stay—he seemed the only one making any sense.

Cap pulled Terry down by his upper arm. Cap's face, covered with a white rag, looked as if it had large misshapen black eyes. "Okay nephew, we gonna look in the window and if we can see them, I want you to take a good long look, tell me what you think. Then we going in. The door has glass; we can bust it in."

"Cap . . . what . . . if it's not them? Aren't you going to call the police?"

"Maybe. Maybe fuck the police. We caught these boys, and the cops couldn't with all their manpower? Don't look like they was trying."

"I don't think that's the right truck," Terry said. "I don't think that's it, Cap."

"What? Why not?"

Terry shrugged but realized no one could see that gesture. "I don't know. It doesn't look right."

"We'll find out. I know you don't want to let Lawrence down. Stay low." He was off without making a sound. Morris and J. D. flanked him.

Terry followed. He could hear things crunching under their feet, their loud breathing, stuff jangling in their pockets. Any second, they would be found out.

They crouched at the truck. Terry wondered if everyone's breathing was as loud as his. The men looked at Terry as if to ask, Is this the right truck? The bed of the ratty truck looked a bit crooked on the frame. He shook his head, but they probably didn't see him. Cap snuck around the car while Morris went to the front door and crouched by the steps. Terry did not see J. D.

Cap was under the window, which had bent blinds hanging crookedly three quarters of the way down. Cap's head eased over the sill and then he was lit from his upper chest to the eyes as he peaked into the window. He signaled Terry to join him.

The first thing Terry saw was a confederate flag on the wall behind a sofa. The flag was as big as a bedsheet.

There were two men in the room. One was on the sofa below the flag. He had long blond hair and a spiky beard. The other guy had midlength brown hair and wore a black leather vest. His back was to Terry. He was on his knees watering plants, which were arranged in various trays and buckets along the opposite wall. Terry recognized the plants immediately, some of them were already two feet tall. The TV was on, but neither man paid much attention though it was loud. If there was a third man, Terry did not see him.

Apparently, Cap thought Terry was trying to identify the two men. "Well? Well?" he whispered.

Terry waited. In a moment, he would tell Cap that these are not the guys he saw, and they would all go home.

Cap pulled him down by the collar.

"Lawrence weren't mixed up in any pot dealing was he, nephew?"

"No."

"Did he smoke dope? Either of y'all?"

"No, Cap."

"They can't hear us over that TV. Do you recognize the one on the sofa?"

Terry shook his head.

"Damn, where's the third one? Wait for the other to turn this way."

They slowly eased back up. The black-vested guy had already turned around. He had a broad face with a lot of acne scars. His eyes went straight to Terry's. A second passed. "What the hell! Somebody's out there."

Terry and Cap ducked down.

"Stay here."

Cap ran around to the front of the house.

Terry crouched.

The window squealed as one of the pot growers jerked it open. Black Vest leaned out looking over the dark yard. Then looking down, he spotted Terry. "What the . . . Come here." He reached down and grabbed a handful of Terry's shirt. "Troy, I got him!" he shouted.

Terry and Black Vest both heard the breaking glass and a loud bang. Black Vest looked back into the room. Terry rolled away, breaking the man's grip, and collided into the back wheel of the pickup. There was shouting from within the house, followed by the sounds of things being overturned. Terry got to his feet. His first thought was to run for the car, and then he considered running to the next house and asking to use their phone to call his dad or the police. Hearing Cap's voice, however, he decided he did not want to be alone outside, so he ran around the little house to the front door, which was wide open. The door's glass was shattered. He stepped through the doorway onto shards of glass.

Lee, straightening his mask, appeared. "Close the door. Pull the shade," he said, and disappeared around a corner.

He heard J. D. say, "There's just the two of them."

"Search each room again." That was Cap. "The closets, under the beds. See if this shithole has a basement."

Terry pulled down the shade as he closed the door. His sneakers crunched glass shards. He pushed the shade to the side to peak at the yard in front of the house. There was no sign of movement. The noises had been so loud, he expected to see police cars and concerned neighbors rushing like a mob across the front yard. He could make out Lee's car sitting at the curb.

He walked through a tiny kitchen. Payne's back was toward Terry. In the living room, the blond man, who Black Vest had called Troy, was on the floor, chest down, with Morris kneeing him in the back and pushing a gun at his temple. Black Vest was trying to get to his feet. Blood arched over his left eye and streamed down his face and chest. Lee stood over him with both hands in tight fists. Lee's mask was askew so that he could probably see out of only one eye. Blood was on his hands and on his mask where he had tried and failed to straighten it.

All the blinds in the room had been lowered. Cap wasn't there. Payne crossed the room cursing under his breath. "Remember nobody use nobody's name," he said.

Sounds of furniture and lamps being thrown around came from the back rooms.

"Wait," Terry heard himself say. He was aware his voice was squeaky. "Just wait." Terry started to cross the room in the direction of the crashing noise, wanting to find Cap.

J. D. put his hand out. "You." He pointed at Terry. "Stay put."

"What the fuck do you guys want?" Black Vest asked. Red spit arced from his mouth. "Son of a . . ."

Morris said, "Punk, just keep talkin' and I will put a goddamn hole in your girlfriend over here. Find out if I mean it, please."

"Anybody else here?" J. D. asked. "Is there anybody else here with you two?"

They both said no.

"Sit your ass back down," Lee said to Black Vest.

Black Vest sat. He put his hand to his bleeding eyebrow and then inspected the bloody palm that came away.

Troy's eyes flitted about from mask to mask. He looked frightened and breathed loudly.

Cap and Payne returned. Cap looked at Terry. He had a gun,

which he kept by the side of his face, pointed up to the ceiling. "You saw three come in?" he asked Morris.

"Yeah," Morris said. The barrel of the gun was still pressed into the man's temple. "I think so."

"Think or know?"

"Look, I think so."

"God damn it."

Payne said, "Are these the guys?" But it seemed to Terry that he was the only one who'd heard the question. His stomach churned. Terry shook his head in response or he thought he did.

J. D. said, "Find something to tie them up with. I got it." He stepped over the legs of the blond man and tore the Confederate flag from the wall. "We'll cut this into strips."

Cap leaned into the face of Black Vest. "Where's your guns?"

The man said nothing.

The blow from Lee came so fast it was just a blur. It made a sickening smack and Black Vest fell to the floor with a groan.

The blond man growled.

Terry backed up without realizing it until he was again in the kitchen. "Um, Cap," he said quietly.

Cap and his friends were shouting at each other.

"I ain't gonna ask again where you keep your guns."

"No way. You gonna shoot, shoot us with your own gun."

"We want 'em for evidence."

"You boys shot a black boy last week, didn't ya? You thought we was gonna let that go? You think he didn't count for anything?"

"Hey, get back in here," Payne called to Terry.

Terry swallowed and returned to the room.

They were tying the white men's hands behind their backs with strips of the Confederate flag.

J. D. was saying, "What you boys doing with this flag anyway? You're Hoosiers, ain't you? Indiana weren't part of the Confederacy. Was it?"

"Hard to tell at times," Lee said.

"I ain't ever shot nobody in my life ever!" the blond man said.

Terry blurted out, "Cap, these ain't the guys."

"No names," Payne said. "God damn it."

"Sorry. These ain't the ones."

Cap and Payne looked to Terry.

Black Vest was staring at Terry.

Cap stepped in front of Terry, shielding him from the prisoners. He took him by both shoulders. He whispered, "You sure? How can you be sure? You couldn't give the cops no facial features."

Terry looked down. His mask was slipping. "Now that I've seen these guys, I know they aren't the ones. I'm sorry I used your name."

Cap pulled down his mask. His back was still toward the pot growers. "Don't worry about that. Ain't my real name. Nickname. Ain't in the phone book. Look at me. Are you saying these ain't the guys 'cause you're worried about what we going to do?"

Terry shook his head. "No."

"We found these guys cruising our part of town and followed them out here."

"It ain't them."

He whispered, "The truck is exactly like you said."

Terry just shook his head.

"Shit." Cap pulled his mask back in place. He turned to Payne, who hadn't moved a step since entering the house. "Go look in the truck. Look for the gun."

Payne left as if he couldn't wait to be out of there.

"I'll look in back again," J. D. said.

Cap crouched in front of Black Vest. "Did you shoot that boy on Gum Street?"

He looked at first like he wasn't going to answer. "Ain't shot nobody. I sell pot. Nothing harder or meaner. And I only do that 'cause I'm between jobs."

Cap stood and stepped quickly away from him.

"Fuck this. They gonna admit it." Cap turned to the one called Troy, brought his foot up, and stomped high on the blond man's back. "Admit it!"

The man cried out.

"Stop," Terry said.

Morris made to kick Black Vest, but Terry jumped between them and nearly fell over the man in the process. "Stop," Terry said holding a palm out.

Morris's eyes blazed behind his mask.

"Be cool," Cap said to Terry. "Be cool."

J. D. whooped and pounced back in the room. "Lookee what I found." He had a rifle in one hand and a gym bag hanging from his shoulder. "A Winchester 30-30 like Chuck Connors and . . ." He opened the gym bag showing dozens of dime bags in it. "Herb."

Cap said, "Put it back," but J. D. clutched it to his chest like it was a baby.

He said, "Screw that."

Payne returned, retying his mask as he entered the room. He looked at Cap and shook his head.

Cap looked stuck. He stood in the middle of the suddenly silent room. The white men looked toward Cap. He finally said, "Take the handset from the phone and throw it in the bushes. Let's go."

Terry backed out of the room. The man named Troy watched him the whole time. Once outside he pulled off the mask. Moments later, the others came bounding out. J. D. still clutched the gym bag.

They raced by Terry, who quickly sprinted after them.

The men squeezed into the car and pulled off their masks.

Lee got behind the wheel but had to get the keys from Cap.

Payne said, "Let's go. Let's go."

Lee turned the car about and peeled out, rocks and pebbles clanking against the fenders. They'd driven four blocks before he remembered to turn on the headlights.

Morris had his mask clutched in a fist. He still had his pistol out. "How come we so sure now they ain't the right boys?" he asked, but no one answered him.

Cap was up front with Lee and Morris, his face buried in his hands. He looked back at Terry before hiding his face again.

Lee drove too fast. Lights from the houses and streetlamps fell quickly in the distance.

Terry constantly looked left and right and behind. He expected pursuit or maybe the flashing lights of a cop car racing after them. He didn't know where they were until they pulled onto Franklin Avenue.

Lee slowed the car to a legal speed. He said, "What can they do about it? Tell the cops somebody smacked them around and stole their pot?"

Morris said, "Hell, should have killed them 'cause of the Confederate flag alone."

twelve

TERRY TWISTED THE handle of his father's razor, and the head parted like metal lips, revealing the Wilkinson crossed swords blade, which he removed and took to his bedroom closet. He already had his notebook and pen in there. He closed the door behind him and stood in the darkness. He tried to imagine what things would be like in just a few moments. His imagination tried to simulate nonexistence, but all he could come up with was a weightless feeling surrounded by total darkness. Briefly, he thought about hell. But he'd never understood how he would burn in eternal fires if he no longer had a body. Still, the thought of his skin blistering and cracking for the rest of time made him shiver.

First Lawrence and then Terrell, people would say and then shake their heads. They'd realize that they never really listened to him or let him do the things that would've made him happy. Mom, Dad, and Cap would all say, "Poor Terrell." When he thought of Cap, he wondered what his uncle might know. He had a strange look on his face when he looked back at Terrell from the front seat of the car. The lights from a store had briefly lit Cap's face and there it was turned on Terry, examining him.

After a minute he pulled the bead chain and the lightbulb glowed harshly. Terry sat on the closet floor and put the razor to the side and picked up his notebook and pen.

Dear Mom and Dad.

He read the four words. The pen grew slippery in his hand. The air in the closet became stuffy. His index finger and thumb tightened on the pen and he pressed the ballpoint to the page. He scratched a jagged line across and down the page, then threw the notebook from him. He began to cry from frustration because he knew that dying wouldn't help. He forgot to return the blade to his father's razor handle.

His stomach ached mildly, but he wasn't hungry. He had not eaten his lunch because sometimes after he ate, he'd throw it up in an hour or so later. So he only ate little bits at a time and not very often. He found he often just wasn't hungry.

Terry finished his math homework while in history class. He sat in the desk he'd always occupied in this class, second row back, next to the window. The sky was pale and empty. He could not pay attention to what Mr. Mrzek was saying. He wished he hadn't finished his math so quickly. He wondered how the sky could be white all over.

The last bell of the school day rang and immediately students started leaving the room. Terry still gazed out the window, isolated from the abrupt flurry of movement and scooting chairs around him.

If he had money, he would go away. He would go out to California or Alaska and he'd get a job and no one would know him, and the people here in Evansville who did know him would wonder about the entire thing and say to each other, wonder whatever happened to Terrell Matheus. He got shot. No not him, the younger one. Oh, yeah, he disappeared off the face of the earth, didn't he? Think he had anything to do with his brother's death? Guess we'll never know. If he had money, he could leave, he could fly away.

Denise Geary sat down in the desk in front of Terry and turned to face him. Her brightly striped sweater fit her tightly. Large African earrings of brown beads dangled on either side of her face. She had big, uneven teeth, but they were very white and her smile looked nice. She began talking about how the teachers had been treating the black students since the protest.

Terry had not noticed the resentment and the attitude, "the bad vibe," Denise described.

"Mr. Keller graded all of us harder on our essays," she said. She was leaning toward him, speaking in a loud, breathy whisper. "But we can't prove it." Her breath smelled of Juicy Fruit. She said something about more planned protests at the other high schools in town and even a sit-in.

It keeps growing, Terry thought. The image of Lee's punching that man came like a punch itself to Terry's mind, making him shake his head in an effort to cast it away.

"We'll clog up the hallways so that even the white kids won't be able to get to class. Can you dig it? Larry's already setting it up."

They want it this way. They're getting off on it. They won't let it all just go away.

"Mr. Keller will flunk me for sure, but I don't care."

I should have said black boys did it. I should have said I didn't know anything, that I came home and found him there on the porch. I should've gone to a friend's house and let someone else find him first.

". . . friends in St. Louis or Chicago." Denise had begun discussing her Christmas break plans. Terry liked the sound of her voice, though he paid little attention to what she was saying. He asked enough questions to keep her talking. There was a time when he would have been floating to have received even a glance from Denise Geary.

Maybe she sensed his preoccupation. Abruptly, she broke off the conversation.

"What?" he asked.

But she was already standing and waving good-bye with a brief flutter of fingers.

"Is everything okay, Mr. Matheus?"

Terry was surprised to see Mr. Mrzek still behind his desk. He'd been so quiet.

"Yes," Terry said, "I'm trying to figure things out."

Mr. Mrzek had been looking over the stack of papers in front of him even while asking Terry if he were okay, but now he looked up. "I suppose you would be," he said.

Terry had always liked Mr. Mrzek, who never seemed to take himself or his lesson plan so seriously that he couldn't have fun with his students.

Mr. Mrzek said, "There are two prevailing schools of thought and everything else is derivative of them. One, that God moves in mysterious ways—there is a plan, but it's beyond our ken to figure it out. The other, shit happens. Everything is random and it's a waste of time to try to figure why."

Terry smiled. He hadn't heard a teacher say "shit" before.

Mrzek picked up his briefcase and shoveled the papers into them. "I'll read these at home, maybe."

Cedric Thomas walked into the room. "Hi, Mr. Mrzek."

"Hello, Cedric," he said. "It's incumbent upon all of us to try to figure things out. Some come up with answers that work for them. But don't feel discouraged if you come up empty. Many of our best . . . it's a toughie."

"Are you in detention?" Cedric asked Terry.

Terry held up a hand. "Which 'prevailing school' do you belong to, Mr. Mrzek?"

"Hah. I'm a simple man, Terry. For me, the simplest way always seems closer to the truth." The history teacher smiled and shrugged. "Would you get the board for me?"

"Sure."

"What were y'all talkin' about?" Cedric asked, jerking a thumb over his shoulder at the departing teacher.

"He thought he knew what I was thinking about, but he didn't."

Cedric climbed on the desk beside Terry's. He put his feet in the chair's seat and his butt on the desktop. "First time I walked by, I seen you talkin' with Geary. Smooth, boy." He grinned. Cedric always wore a misshapen afro that made him look as if the top of his head angled off to one side.

Terry slid his books out from underneath his seat. The brown bag on top of them contained his uneaten lunch—a ham sandwich and an apple. He peeked into the bag. "You want this?"

"This is the third time this week you ain't ate your lunch." Cedric eyed Terry with suspicion.

Cedric had seven brothers and sisters. After the first time Terry had given Cedric his lunch, Terry suspected food was a precious commodity at the Thomas household.

"You don't want it, fine with me, Ced. I can toss it."

"Well, don't throw away perfectly good food." Cedric snatched the sack off the top of Terry's books. He started eating the sandwich immediately. "So, man, Denise is D-nice, huh?"

Cedric talked with his mouth full.

He continued talking, not noticing, apparently, that Terry didn't hear a word.

What Terry heard in that empty classroom after-hours was his mother's scream. Her mouth when she screamed had looked like a chasm. Denise Geary's smile had looked like a necklace, bright, white, uneven strings of pearls. Maybe she was attracted to his celebrity. Lawrence was still the focus of hallway discussion. The students were drawn to Terry, who was somehow the hero. The black kids saw him as a victim of white aggression. Other kids, white and black, saw him as a victim to authority, "to the man," who could not or would not resolve the case. Here was an excuse for activism and excitement. "Hang in there," someone had said to him from the mass moving in the hallway between classes today. Terry hated that. What did that mean? Why couldn't they leave it be? Hang in there. If, when a murderer was caught, the victim came back to life, he could understand the pursuit of and the demand for justice. But Lawrence was going to stay dead no matter what.

Dear Mom and Dad . . .

There was no fair exchange for Lawrence. There was no way out of this. None. The look on his mother's face, like she was broken way down deep inside, would never go away. Nothing could take that away, nor the intensity in his father's eyes when he said, "I hate now." There was no fair exchange.

"Hang in there." No one knew what Terry was going through, and each word of encouragement, each fist raised in solidarity or look of compassion, made him flinch, pushed him deeper into the quagmire of his lie.

He knew what he had to do, and he was suddenly more frightened than ever. Terry felt the tears come to his eyes and he jumped from his desk and went to the blackboard. He picked up an eraser and started clearing the board. He would have to tell everything. His heart raced at the thought. The moment of facing them. Maybe he could find Cap, who maybe had already guessed, and Cap could help him tell them. "I don't think I ever really hated anybody my whole life. But I hate now," his father had said.

Terry saw his hand holding the eraser against the dusty board tremble. "Oh, no," he whispered. His face fell against the board. They would hate him; Cap would hate him. Everyone would. Tears ran down the blackboard leaving thin, clean streaks.

"Terry?"

Terry sniffed. He blew chalk dust from his nostrils. "Leave me alone," he said.

"You okay, my man?"

"Yeah. Could you just go?" Terry didn't dare turn his face from the board.

"You want a ride home? Dingham is still around. He'd give us rides."

Cedric had gotten a free lunch; now he wanted a free ride off Terry's celebrity in Dingham's car.

"Just go. Don't say how sorry you are. Don't tell me how cool Lawrence was. Or how much you wish we could lynch those three crackers," Terry pleaded. "Just go." He kept his face toward the board, and he sensed Cedric finally leave rather than heard him.

Terry gathered up his books. He tasted bile. His stomach knotted.

Cap Porter would be hard to face. In fact, he might be just as hard to tell as his parents would be, now, after that night. He pictured Cap's angry eyes peering through the holes in a ragged strip of sheet.

The other students had deserted the school. It looked cavernous when empty. Only a teacher or two and the custodians were left. Terry heard a floor polisher somewhere and a locker door slam, and faintly heard squeals and shouting from the gym, which meant some after-school activity was going on. He wished he'd never come back to school. Everyone from Larry Dingham to the white girl who'd loaned him a pen the first day had made everything worse. Tamara Groves had made everything worse too.

The walk home took three times longer than usual. His dad wouldn't be home when he got there and he envisioned sitting at the kitchen table waiting. His mama used to come straight to the kitchen when she got home, but these days she remained hidden in her room. He would have to go up there then. And when they were both together, he would have to tell them, "I've got something I have to say."

In the middle of Bayard Park, children played on the swings. Their high pitched yelping joined the tumult of thoughts and visions that filled Terry's mind. He leaned against a tree. The maples and syca- mores reared up around him.

A woman with a small child at her side walked by. She gave him a quick glance and pulled her child close to her.

What courage he had, faltered. Tomorrow occurred to him. If he waited maybe some better way to say it would present itself. He began to walk. He passed the swings, the mother's suspicious eyes following him.

By the time he reached Evans Street, he knew he could not wait another day, especially another night. He swallowed back the acid rise in his throat. He wiped his eyes. He would go home and he would wait.

He turned the corner onto Gum Street and froze again. This time he stopped as if he had slammed into an invisible wall. Three police cars and an unmarked car were parked in front of his house. He saw a policeman crawl from under the porch and dust himself off.

There was a cop on the porch; another went through the front door. One went into the backyard. Two went down the side between the houses. They swarmed over the Matheuses' house like bees.

He must have kept walking. He must have covered the half block to his house but had no knowledge of it.

His father's car was in the driveway.

Two cops stopped to watch him walk up the steps. Terry opened the front door but did not step inside immediately. He held there, caught between two moments. There was the moment the gun had gone off that had separated his life in two: all that had gone before and all that would happen after. And now there would be this point and everything that followed. He leaned in with one foot still on the porch.

"Terrell," his father's voice said. "Terrell, get in here, boy."

Terry Matheus went into the living room and saw his parents sitting on the couch and Detective Bill Carson sitting in the big chair. Terry had run out of time.

His mother's eyebrows were wrinkled and she looked at him as if he were about to step off a cliff. He couldn't look at her.

Terry still held his books under his arm.

"Terry . . ." his father began.

"Mr. Matheus, as we agreed."

Terry said, "Daddy, I got something to say."

"Wait, Terry," Detective Carson said. "I was here first, so why don't we let me speak first?"

"I want to tell my parents something."

Terry heard the squeal of furniture being scooted and footsteps from overhead.

"I'm sure you do now."

"I have to talk to my mom and dad. I want to—"

"Terrell, shut up," his father said, glaring at him.

Terry tried to look back at him but couldn't. "Mama—"

"Terry, your parents and I have been talking about what happened to your brother and specifically how some of the things you've told us don't jive with what we've been able to determine from our investigation. Terry, do you know what some of those discrepancies might be?"

Carson paused. Terry glanced at the detective's face and thought he saw a little smile.

"Maybe you can clear these up for us. The shot that killed your brother was fired by someone standing from between one and three feet away from him. There were powder grains in his T-shirt. That's the big one. The angle of the shot is funny too." Carson jammed two fingers into his own chest. "With Lawrence standing on the porch, that shot would have had to be fired from someone either lying flat in the front yard or, standing close up to him."

Terry's mother was shaking her head in tiny, rapid movements that looked more like trembling.

Carson's eyes didn't sag in his face now. The detective studied Terry. He said, "You see the problems we have with your story? Just doesn't add up, does it?

"Add to that, we couldn't find a trace of that white pickup. Not even tread marks from where they took off after the shooting. You'd expect the driver to get excited and to stomp on the gas after his buddy fires the gun, you see, excited and adrenaline pumping, but not this guy. Like he didn't care if someone stepped out on their porch and saw him.

"I've got another one too. This is what we call circumstantial evidence but pretty telling, I think. I noticed it the day of the shooting but confirmed it in the photographs. The table your parents keep on the porch has a wet ring on it. You know, from condensation from a glass? Now you said you had your glass of punch with you until you dropped it. But there was no other glass out there, Terry. What do you think about all of that?"

Terry's mother rapidly shook her head. It looked like she was having a little fit. His father seethed.

The books fell from Terry's arms. He stooped to pick them up, but then left them at his feet. He couldn't think.

Carson continued, "Our initial suspicion was that Lawrence knew who'd shot him. We thought Lawrence was tangled up in something and that you weren't being straight with us because, maybe, you were going to take matters in your own hands. We found out that your brother purchased a gun just a few days ago; he showed it to some of his friends. So that, we figured, confirmed our line of thought that Lawrence was mixed up in something bad. But then, why would you lie about a glass? Why no tire tracks? Why continue to protect your brother's killers? We know about Bread. He and his friends have solid alibis." He paused. "All roads lead back to you, Terry.

"So I have one question for now. Where's the gun?"

His father rose slowly to his feet. "Boy, I can see it's all true. It's all on your stupid face. I can see it, God damn it." Preston shouted, "What have you done! What have you done!" He reached for Terry, though still steps away.

"Mr. Matheus," Carson said. He moved to be in between father and son.

Terry stepped back and bumped into an officer he hadn't realized was behind him.

His mother's hand was over her mouth. She looked terrified.

"If it's in this house, in the backyard, or in your school locker, we're going to find it. Where's the gun, Terry?"

Terry covered his face. He didn't want to see his parents. He didn't want to see or hear anything. He should have killed himself. He'd had the chance. He had the razor blade. He had just been too scared. He should have done it. Terry shook his head.

"What? You don't know where it is? Speak to me, Terry."

His mother screamed.

Terry uncovered his face in time to see his father lunging toward him.

Carson was shouting at his father.

His father was on him. Terry was struck in the side of his face and on his head.

"Get him off."

"Damn it, I shouldn't have done this here. Pull him free."

Terry saw spit spray from his father's snarling mouth. Terry was on the floor and his father was on top of him, straddling him.

More officers ran in.

His father had a fistful of Terry's shirt.

"Preston, please!" his mother screamed.

"God damn you, boy! What did you do? What did you do?" He kept repeating.

The coffee table was knocked over as his father was tackled.

"Damn it. Stop, sir."

"Calm down! Calm down, sir."

"Take the boy out of here. Arrest him."

Terry was pulled to his feet.

He saw two cops lying over his struggling father. His father's arms and legs flailed and his growl sharpened into a high-pitch whine.

"Terry Matheus, you are placed under arrest at this time. You have the right to remain silent. Should you elect to speak, anything you say may be held against you in court."

They pulled Terry's arms behind his back. The cuffs pinched his skin against his wrist bone.

"This isn't happening to my family." His mother seemed to be choking. She was on her knees near her husband.

Terry said, "Mama."

"If you can't afford an attorney, the court will appoint one for you at no charge to yourself. Do you understand these rights as I have told them to you?"

Terry was jerked around.

"Do you understand?"

Terry nodded.

"Do you understand?"

"He nodded. Good enough. Let's go, before the neighborhood gets home from work and this gets nasty."

A cop pulled Terry from the room by his upper arm. They led him outside. Attracted by the police cars, people were already gathered on the sidewalks. They made an audible gasp at seeing Terry appear on the porch, handcuffed and flanked by officers.

Terry kept his head down. He couldn't look at them. He saw the black, shiny shoes of the police officers on either side of him, and he saw the fresh porch boards his father had put in, but had yet to paint. He kept his eyes on the sidewalk and let the officers steer him. This wouldn't be happening if I had done it, Terry thought. I should have done it. Then he thought to look back and see if his mother was following him. Only Bill Carson stood at the doorway.

"What's happening, Terry," a woman said. "What do they want with you, boy?"

They bent him into the police car. Everyone was watching. The door was slammed and Terry waited. All eyes were on him. They were guessing at the truth by now. They were figuring out what really had happened at the Matheuses' house on Gum Street. Terry slid down on his side to hide from the stares. The police car had a partition of Plexiglas and steel grating above the back of the front seat. The back doors had no handles or locks. His shoulders began to hurt from having his arms pinned behind him. Why weren't they taking him away?

He heard his name called.

Someone knocked on the window.

Terry lifted his head to see who it was. A woman he vaguely recognized stood at the door with a microphone. A large camera aimed at him. "Terry, did you shoot your brother, Lawrence Matheus?"

"Get away from there," a cop shouted.

"The entire city has been in a state of racial turmoil for days over this incident. Did it begin by a hoax perpetrated by you?" The woman said, "Tell the city the truth, Terry. Did you kill your brother?"

A police officer blocked the camera and forced the woman away from the car.

Terry said, "Why don't we go? Let's go!"

After a few more minutes, two cops got in the car. One cop was black and young. He sat on the passenger side and turned to study Terry from behind the scratched-up Plexiglas. His lips and right cheek turned up in distaste. He shook his head, saying softly, "God damn, little brother."

thirteen

AS BREAD CAME through the doorway, Tamara saw his flat, poker-faced eyes and the hint of a smile at the corner of his mouth. She had been running water in the sink and had not heard the second set of footsteps behind him. Bread knew she hated it when he brought his boys to their apartment, but there was Carl in tow so early in the morning she hadn't had the chance to get dressed. She still wore what she'd slept in, a threadbare, translucent T-shirt and red terry-cloth shorts that covered her only slightly better than panties. Carl, whom she called the Rabbit—not to his face—because of his ears, was dressed in a leisure suit and his bubble-toed semi-platform shoes, which he kept very shiny. She had seen him on many occasions spitting on them and wiping them with a handkerchief. Recently, she had been able to get him to drive her a few places, including the errand that she had not wanted Lawrence Matheus to know about, the one she accomplished days before he died.

Carl the Rabbit knew he was cool because he was a part of the Bread Williams family. No one screwed with him. He talked about clothes and partying, and he looked at her as if she never wore a stitch of clothes. Of all of Bread's goons, though, Carl was the least objectionable. He mostly did the driving. Unlike Bread's enforcer, Angelo, who was ready to hit someone at the drop of a hat, Carl seemed to prefer the lifestyle more than the life.

Tamara felt desperate enough to put up with Carl's mushy, un-blinking eyes if it provided her some wheels. "I got a new album today, Ohio Players," he said that day when she came out of the clinic. "I don't feel well, Carl. Take me home." He helped her up the stairs and got her a bottle of RC that she didn't want. He never said a thing to Bread about their errand.

"Hold up right there, sugar," Bread said.

"I want to put something on . . ."

"Wait up."

Tamara crossed her arms over her breasts.

"I been wanting to get you two together for a while now, but what with the police doggin' me and all . . . Shame about your friend again. You hear about that, Carl?"

"What that, Bread?"

"Turns out that friend of Tamara's, the guy who was the symbol of the new civil rights movement in the tristate area, was really just a fool horsing around with a gun."

Carl laughed for as long as Bread wanted him to.

Bread chuckled, "Yeah, that's why we don't get you a gun, Carl. 'Fraid you might end up shooting your own corncob face off." Bread laughed.

Carl's face contracted.

"Yeah." Grinning widely, Bread shoved his face one inch from Carl's. He pivoted toward Tamara. "Yeah," he said again.

For whatever was coming next, she wished she had clothes on.

"Carl," Bread said, but he eyed Tam now, "what do you think of Tam? What do you think?"

"Think?"

"Yes, Carl. You've done that before, right?" Bread laughed.

"Bread, I need to get dressed, honey."

"Wait up. Wait up."

She recrossed her arms. "Bread."

"Do you think . . . think, Carl, do you think Tam is sexy? You find her attractive, Carl, what do you think?" Bread stepped quickly to Tam, grabbed a wrist, and pulled one of her arms away from her chest.

"Bread, stop it, God damn it."

"You seen these tits before, Carl?"

Tam pulled away. She used her crossed hands to cover herself.

"Carl, I ain't hearin' anything."

Carl was as confused as Tam. Little beads of sweat had broken out on his forehead. He held his hands out as if to show he was unarmed.

Tamara was about to speak, but Bread held up a warning finger. "You shut up. Carl is talkin' right now. Your turn comin'. Well, Carl?" He slapped him.

It had happened so quickly Tamara had only seen the follow-through and the shock in Carl's eyes as he held his cheek.

"I still don't hear anything." The next two slaps staggered Carl. His eyes welled up, but he made no move to defend himself.

"Stop it! Stop it! Bread, we don't know what you're talking about." She jumped between Bread and Carl.

Carl managed to say, "I ain't done nothin'."

"I've heard how Carl and you been going around. I got eyes that work for me. They see things. You been spotted looking chummy, all up under each other, coming right into my own crib. Right here. With your arms around my girl."

"Bread, I was sick and he helped me up the stairs. That's all."

Carl said, "I ain't done nothin'."

"You two been goin' around. Nothin' happens I don't hear about it."

"Hey," Tamara said softly. "He gave me a couple of rides when you were busy, baby. Wasn't nothing to it."

Carl was sniffing.

Bread looked from Carl to Tamara.

"You niggers keep thinkin' I'm dumb. But I'm smarter than both y'all. Carl, quit cryin'. Shit. Sound like a bitch. You might have thought it was nothin'," he said to Tamara, "but my buddy here didn't. Oh, any other time, Carl tells me everything. Don't you, boy? Yeah, nod your head. Fine. What Barney Miller said on TV last night. What damn flavor milkshake he had for lunch. But he don't tell me he gave Tamara any rides. Why were you sick?"

Tamara looked at the poor rabbit, who stared at the carpet in embarrassment.

"Why were you sick?"

"Women's problems," she said, betting he would not ask anything further.

Showing his teeth, Bread leveled a finger at Carl. "Don't keep secrets from me, knucklehead." Carl nodded. "Okay, wait for me outside. Go on."

Carl turned to leave, looking broken by those three slaps. He hesitated at the door, and that caused Tamara to meet his eyes. In them she still saw a secret, though she had not confided in him nor let him drop her off directly in front of the clinic, and still he knew, Carl the Rabbit knew and would not tell.

As soon as the door shut behind him, Bread said, "Maybe I'll buy him a watch or somethin'."

Tamara said, "Maybe next time, you don't hit nobody."

BREAD USED TO apologize to her when he shoved her around or shouted in her face. Three weeks had passed since he'd accused her of "going around" with Carl—usually, by now he would have bought her something cheap but cute like a stuffed bear or a bobble-head dog, and he'd say he was sorry he blew up. He did give Carl a watch. Sometimes, to assure him he was indeed forgiven, she would have to have sex with him right then or that evening. He had not apologized for his latest blow and Tamara was relieved actually.

She sucked in the smoke from a joint. She was going to take a bath and then she was getting out of that apartment. Its smallness was driving her crazy, its old creaking wood, old dust, the voices from downstairs that seeped through the warped floors, and the stained wallpaper.

Tamara held the smoke in her lungs and could feel it rise to swirl in her head. It was a funny, airy feeling. She released the smoke. She pushed the chained stopper in place and turned the hot-water spigot on full and the cold-water spigot a quarter turn. She poured in some Calgon powder from the shiny box and the suds grew like rapidly reproducing cells. Steam misted her face. The scent made her wrinkle her nose. She was hoping to hide in the smoke and water for a little while, to keep Bread and the Matheus family and everyone else outside the bathroom door for just a little while. But trying not to think of one family opened the door to another, her own. She had a family once, a mother and a father, and she was their only little girl. There was an aunt too, who lived somewhere in Virginia. She did not know the woman's last name, her married name. And there was Daddy, somewhere out there, who blamed her for everything he could no longer blame her mother for. She used to have daydreams of their reunion. Even when she had difficulty bringing the exact contours of his face to mind, she thought she could smell him. She could smell the hot sun he'd absorbed all day long on his clothes and black skin. And she could smell the cigars and the alcohol too, but back then these smells said nothing to her beyond this is my dad and he's home. And when she was a little girl, a little girl that belonged to a family, she would wait on that mostly vacant corner, where weeds had obscured the fencing and the grasshoppers were loud, and she would play with the vines and the ladybugs until she heard her father's truck bumping down the street, and she would wave her hand over her head and be rewarded by a hand sticking from the cab of the truck waving back at her, and then the race would be on. She would dash for home as she heard his Ford straining through its gears and the girl and the truck would manage to get to the driveway at the exact same time. "That's my girl," he would say as the door squeaked open and arms that seemed unbelievably long reached down to scoop her up. His girl, he had said, so she thought he knew that she remained his girl even as she chose to live with her mother when her parents divorced.

She sat the joint on the edge of the tub and slipped into the water. The suds and the perfumey smell surrounded her.

The divorce had made her feel stupid because she had not known it was coming. She had chosen to live with the woman who had done her father wrong, who had betrayed him with another man, a man he knew. For him, the last insult was his daughter had chosen to live with the woman who had broken him, and so they had broken him together.

And then her mother died.

She had chosen to go with her mother; she had not chosen to leave her father, an obvious distinction in her eyes. On some level, she had come to believe, she must have known even then, at ten years old, that her mother needed her more. And she would have assumed he would see that too because she was still at that stage where she thought her parents knew all there was to know, and the divorce had only begun shaking that type of naïve faith.

The phone rang. She submerged herself under the water and suds, holding only her left hand and the doobie up and dry. Enjoying the sensation, she remained under water until the dulled ringing stopped. That would be Mrs. Matheus; she just knew it. She took another long drag and tried to let the water and smoke combine to help her ease through the remainder of the day.

Mrs. Matheus had called her up the first time weeks ago. She had asked Tamara to go check on Terrell for her. "Just see that he's okay. He's out now and at his uncle's. I'm sorry to have to ask. He hasn't a friend in the city now." Stupidly, Tamara said she would, but that was weeks ago and she still hadn't taken a step in that direction.

The young woman shivered. There was nothing left of her joint except twisted paper. She looked at her hands. They had turned white; her fingers had pruned. She had soaked long enough. She absently washed herself and rose from the water.

"I want to hear from you again, dear. I mean it." The woman had looked so delicate, and though she had tried to smile, her eyes gave her away. Those eyes that Mommy had in those last days, Tamara thought.

She had left Judith Matheus with the impression that she had been Lawrence's girlfriend, but she had not lied. Tamara had been careful to tell the desperate woman only the truth and not all of that. Still, she could see that her words were being received differently than she was transmitting them, and she had done nothing to correct the impression. Tamara went over her own testimony to Mrs. Matheus, hoping she had not added to the woman's delusion.

The real liar had been outside, across the street, waiting on her.

"That little punk!" It was Bread who had brought her the news, and clearly he found it hilarious.

He was smiling as he handed her the newspaper, and she immediately brought up her defenses, immediately had decided that she would not give him the satisfaction of reacting to whatever article he wanted her to see.

But this news had blindsided her. She hardly heard Bread chuckling as she read the story: BROTHER ARRESTED IN LAWRENCE MATHEUS MURDER. *The case that had the entire city turned upside down for days has apparently been solved by the Evansville Police Department.*

"Girl, I heard about this dude works over to Whirlpool, white dude, he say he been pulled over four times by four different cops because he drive a white pickup. Hah. I guess they can call off the dogs now." Then he had flipped the newspaper into her lap. "Maybe they'll quit tagging around after me too."

She hated the fact she had to learn this from Bread. Of course, he liked that he was the one to tell her. He wanted everything she knew or owned to come through him first.

"They weren't following you."

"The hell they wasn't."

Tamara had taken the lie personally at first.

The last time she had seen Terry, his uncle and his uncle's friends had come tearing up in a car and practically kidnapped the boy in front of her. She wondered what the emergency had been and if it was in some way related to Terry's big lie.

He'd been standing in the shadows across the street when she left the Matheus place, waiting out there, perhaps, for her to leave.

Poor Mrs. Matheus. Tamara tried to imagine the woman in the twisted skirt and wrinkled blouse learning her son had lied to her and to her husband and to everyone else in the city and that the truth of it was one of her sons had killed the other. Now he claimed it was an accident, but who would be willing to believe him?

Tamara wrapped the towel around herself and padded into the bedroom. Still wet, she climbed on the unmade bed.

She did not know if it would have been Lawrence's or Bread's, but she knew it would be hers. There is a dream too tantalizing to dwell on: she is accepted into the Matheus family and she brings them their grandchild.

She cannot fathom how she did not hear Bread come up the stairs, except that the grass had addled her more than she realized. His arms encircled her and she slumped into them. "Bread."

"I got you. I got you. C'mon. Let's get you dry. Stop those tears now."

And she saw, while he held her, the roughed-up, torn skin and drying blood on the knuckles of his right hand. She was suddenly awake and sober enough.

"It's all good," he whispered. "It's all good."

fourteen

KNOWING SHE SHOULD get out of bed, and getting out of bed were two different things entirely. Getting out of bed was such an optimistic action. The only reason she could think of to push away the blankets was that it was too easy to stay under them. She knew she would get up eventually. She knew she would take a bath. She knew she would do something with her hair. She knew she would look in the mirror and put on her face. Put on a bra. Put on panty hose. Heels too. Because it was all she knew to do. She had no idea what else to do.

Judith felt the mattress sag with her husband's weight. He was waiting on her, though he hadn't said anything. It seemed everyone was waiting for her. They waited for her to smile, to feel better, to "get on with it."

It must feel doubly awkward for the girls at the bank, for the neighbors, for family to be around her. It's hard enough to approach someone who's lost a loved one. Anything you might say seems small or, at least, wholly inadequate. But what could they say to Judith whose first son was killed by her second son, a boy whose lie had set people against each other in virulent ways not easily dismissed or repaired? There is poor Judith, they will say, maybe for the rest of her life. But as difficult as it was for her, she knew it would be so much worse for Terrell. They will look at him and shake their heads, they will puzzle over him or pity him, never realizing they were looking at a boy as normal as any other.

The boys used to argue, but it was natural. Siblings argue. Except for the fights, it was no different than the tiffs Cap and she used to get in to. Lawrence and Terrell had been good brothers to each other. She thought so.

Terrell. Only a few chose to believe the whole thing was an accident, though police evidence supported his second story. If it were an accident, they reasoned, why would he lie? She thought she knew—and then wondered if she knew anything.

Preston had been talking, and she only caught the tail end of his voice inflection that told her he'd asked a question. She wanted to reply to him, her husband of twenty-one years. She wanted to reassure him, if that would make him go away. What she did not understand was why the entire situation had to be handled his way.

Terrell was not home because of Preston. He cannot face his son. This did not surprise Judith.

"Well?" he asked.

"Preston," she said.

"Eggs or cereal?" he asked.

"Preston." Pushing the sheet from her face, she breathed out. "Maybe some juice."

"You should eat something. We have those Brown 'N Serves."

Mothers have favorites. They do, though they would never admit it. Mom always preferred Cap; their personalities were so similar. Judith had tested her own feelings in this regard, however, and decided she did not have a favorite. The boys were endearing in different ways. Lawrence was more confident and adventurous and Terrell more eager to please and brighter, better at school. Terrell would be the first to sit with you and watch TV even though what was showing hardly interested him, whereas Lawrence would have to be on the move. Preston had a favorite, though; she could see it and wondered if Terrell ever did. Preston and she would sit in the bleachers during the track meets, and as Lawrence set his feet in the blocks Judith would glimpse her husband's face. Lawrence had kindled a glow in his father's eyes that no one else was capable of igniting. She wanted to confirm what she suspected, that Preston had a favorite.

She said, "Preston?" She sat up.

She had caught him just as he was rising from the bed, and he let his weight sink again. "Hmm?"

Was Lawrence your favorite son, she wanted to ask, or is he just your favorite son now? "Nothing," she said. "Your wrist is dirty. Is that oil?"

"I was working on Lawrence's car. I changed the air filter and the oil filter."

"Why?"

He opened his mouth, and for a moment it appeared he had an answer. His mouth opened but nothing came out. He shrugged. "Are you getting up?"

"I was thinking about nursing Lawrence, in the hospital bed. I remember more things with him because he was first and he and I had to figure them out together. Like nursing . . . I didn't know how to get him started. Or potty training. Or when to pull his first tooth. I went through everything with him first. I knew what to do with Terrell."

"Judith."

"So, if you think about it, the boys didn't get raised by the same exact mother. One got the unsure, hesitant mother, and the other got the got-it-worked-out mother. I think he got the more tired mother too, Terrell did, and much less time too. I stayed home with Lawrence, but we couldn't afford it with Terrell." Judith didn't need or want Preston to respond. She was just saying it, just working it out. But she heard him clear his throat.

"That's no excuse for anything," he said. "There's always advantages and disadvantages to being the first or the second."

"I know," she said, feeling impatient with him. "I'm just thinking. It's not Terrell's fault if . . ."

"If what?" His words sounded like a dare. A wall in him had risen astoundingly fast. He realized it and took a breath. He shook his head. "I, um . . . I'd been looking at every white pickup I come across," Preston said. His hands patted together silently. "Catch up with them in traffic so I could look in their window. Looking for them. White men in a white pickup."

"What did you expect to see?"

He shrugged. "Do you realize how many white pickup trucks there are in Indiana? Maybe I thought . . ." Preston swallowed. "I thought because of how I felt, I'd get led to the right one. I followed one for blocks one late afternoon, getting along toward suppertime. I don't recall what made me say, Oh, this one, this could be them. But I followed him on up Highway 41, past the Whirlpool plant to a truck stop. He parked but didn't get out for the longest time. I sat there wondering what to do. I could run to a phone. I wanted to call Cap. I thought it was suspicious that they were taking so long to climb out. I wrote down the license plate number on the back of an old bill. And that's when the door to the driver's side of the pickup opened. I pulled a tire iron from in back of my seat."

"Preston!"

"That pickup was an old Chevy just like Terrell had said. It was dented along the sides and rusted out along the bottom just like he'd said. And I said these might be the ones who killed my boy. Right here in front of me.

"This guy steps out with long blond hair coming from under a green John Deere cap. I walk toward him. He didn't see me at first and I wasn't really thinking. I told myself if I get close enough, I'll know. I'll see it in his eyes or something or he'll run. Give himself away."

"Maybe a black man coming at him with a tire iron might make an innocent person run."

"Hah. Yeah. I'm stupid. Somebody still in the truck hands the guy something. And that's when he sees me. When his hands are full with a kicking baby. His eyes get big. I stop. The passenger is a woman. She gets out on the other side, holding a balled-up diaper away from her. So they were in the truck so long because they were changing their kid's diaper. He's looking at me and he's a little scared. And I go to say something to him, but I couldn't think of what to say. And he says, 'What do you want?' real loud. And his wife tries to hush him."

"He could have called the police. What did you say to him?"

"Nothing. I backed up, holding up my hands. He was still shouting at me, 'What do you want?' as I drove away."

"I don't know what you could possibly have been thinking."

Preston turned toward her. He looked lost, Judith thought. He said, "I think I thought as long as I had that truck to look for, I could do something for Lawrence."

He sat at the foot of the bed, a boy himself, not understanding what had happened to him. Her tears flowed and she could taste them at the corners of her mouth. Almost she reached out for him, wanting to console him but not finding the strength to even say another word. Instead, she gripped the edge of the bedspread. She pulled it up to her neck, just under her chin. She had never seen Preston as he was now, and certainly could never picture him brandishing a tire iron at a stranger. She sniffed. She wanted to say something to him. She could see him floundering right there. She pushed her face into her drawn up knees, covered by the spread. She remained that way for a long time, well after her husband left the room.

fifteen

THE CELL TERRY was put in was narrow and long and felt as cold as a refrigerator. It had been a long day. He'd been fingerprinted. He'd been stripped. He'd stood in lines, wearing handcuffs until his shoulders ached and he began to feel faint. Finally, he was led to a cell and immediately all daylight seemed to cease to exist. The florescent light stuttered and winked and finally went out altogether, leaving him in a blue dark cold.

After what seemed an absurdly long time, he finally heard voices, distant, and echoey and impossible to understand. Footfalls accompanied the voices and they echoed also. He knew the voices and footsteps belonged to more than two or three people, and he knew they were coming his way. As they came closer, there seemed to him something familiar about the voices, but he wasn't sure. He at first welcomed the thought of any kind of human interaction and any distraction from the silence and the blue dark, but then he realized that maybe they were bringing him a cell mate. Maybe they were dragging in some drunk or worse, someone who would intimidate or abuse him if for no reason other than boredom. The footfalls grew closer and heavier, until the sound filled the cell, and Terry could feel the cot fairly vibrating. The talk continued too, though it was not like a conversation. The voices seem to talk over each other at times as if no one were paying attention to what the other was saying. Terry thought about going to his cell door and peeking down the corridor so he could see who was coming. But he was afraid to find out, afraid to unwrap himself, afraid even to put his feet on the floor.

Finally the footsteps reached his cell. He looked up. The figures were dark at first, but as they slowly paraded by, enough light played over their features that he could identify them. He saw his uncle Cap, and his dad and mom, and the girl, Tamara Groves, and Lee, J. D., Morris . . . and surprisingly the two white pot growers were with them, their faces still showing bruises and cuts. They were all talking, and they all looked straight ahead. Terry's lips trembled. He wanted to call to them, but something wasn't right so he kept silent. Slowly, they walked in single file straight by his cell, never looking his way. Only the last person in the line shot a quick glance at Terry—that was Lawrence. Terry jumped from his cot with a scream caught in his throat and awoke when he hit his head on the cot above.

He opened his eyes and the muted colors of the cell had returned with the morning. He felt the back of his head, felt the tender cut in his scalp, and took away bits of dried blood on his fingertips.

Terry believed he had not slept one minute straight through while in jail. The cell had been chilly and drafty and smelled of linoleum and cleaner and urine. He had lain in his cot and pulled his feet up and hugged himself and stayed like that, a wary ball, watching the comings and going of cops and the handcuffed people they ushered back and forth. The cops looked exasperated and bored at the same time. The prisoners looked either embarrassed or resigned. He thought it peculiar to see people restrained like that, to see them forced into the cages and to hear the metal gate bouncing shut. He was one of these caged people.

Ink still delineated the cracks around the edges of his fingernails and the whorls of his fingers. The police officer had taken control of each finger, one at a time. Even in this, the simple act of applying his finger to paper, they did not trust him.

HE DECIDED HE didn't care what happened to him anymore. They could put him in the electric chair or lay him on one of those medical gurneys with the paper sheets and inject him with poison—he wouldn't give a damn. Nothing mattered anymore. Everyone hated him.

Sometimes he'd try to console himself with the mantra "It was just an accident," forgetting, for a moment, his great lie.

The cell everywhere, the iron frame of the cot, the cement block wall, was cold to the touch. He drew into himself and waited for the next thing, because none of it was up to him. He told himself he didn't care.

When his mother came to visit him, he refused to leave the cell. In that moment, it became a cold womb that kept everybody away.

The first night he did not sleep at all, curled on the cot with a florescent light from down the hall as the only light, hearing voices that carried on all night, cursing and laughing and arguing and boasting until an officer went down the corridor and told them to shut up. The silence wouldn't last five minutes. "My God, don't they get tired?" Terry would whisper into his hands. "Don't they want to just shut up, just shut up." He tried not to cry, but he let himself down on that account and soon after heard loud laughter and believed it was aimed at him and he willed himself then to stop.

He wanted his father to come by and charge at him again. He wanted that detective with the bags under his eyes to come to his cell and interrogate him again. Almost.

He tightened up every time a new prisoner was brought in, praying that he would not be put in the same cell with him. And each time the prisoners were pushed on by. He breathed in the stale odor of himself and waited to start at the next jangling sound.

He had dreams. Each time sleep finally came, the dreams came, and each time they woke him up, sometimes three or four times a night. Some he remembered, but most would leave only an uneasy feeling behind, the residue of the emotions they had stirred up.

There wasn't a trial. Terry had pleaded guilty on the advice of his lawyer, who hardly looked at him. He filled out paper work and asked Terry only questions whose answers fit into blocks on a form. "As far as your plea," he said, "not a lot to think about. They have you for obstruction of justice and involuntary manslaughter. You did it, right?" He didn't wait for Terry to answer. "They are going to drop the involuntary manslaughter. They don't have a weapon and if we fight them on it, well . . . EPD already is a bit embarrassed by how long it took to solve the case. The judge may want you to tell the court everything that happened. Do that. Don't embellish. Don't mention anything that they don't already know. You hear me? Right."

The judge was the only person who looked at him with anything close to sympathy. Terry kept his eyes on the judge's robes, though he was tempted to turn around and see how Dad, Mom, and Cap were reacting to what they heard. He told himself he was past caring about what people thought or what they did to him. He had not seen his parents and Cap Porter come in the court room, but by the time the judge was seated, there they were in the back, Mom between Cap and Dad. Other than seeing that they were there, he could not look their way again.

The judge seemed to try to look at everyone. He went from the DA to Detective Bill Carson to Terry to Terry's lawyer. "The police and

DA are embarrassed by how they rushed off on tangents on this one, trying to prove gang connections and drug connections and all this will come out. The victim could not have been just an innocent high school track star. No, he had to be into something, and that made them blind, and if we make a big deal of this EPD is going to look a lot worse than they already do. My opinion. Son, you watch the news? Didn't President Nixon teach us anything? The cover-up just makes it worse. So let's make sure you know that. They weren't the only ones to rush to judgment either. Out entire community was taken in. You're either a good liar or the lie had an appeal it should never have had." He held up some papers that had been in front of him. "Do we have the truth here now?" he asked Terry.

Terry could not see what the papers were, but he nodded.

The judge was silent for a long while. Everyone waited on him. Everyone was quiet.

Detective Carson eyed Terry.

The judge scratched the side of his face and took a long look at Terry, a look that forced Terry's eyes down. "Hmm, neither you or your brother had been in trouble before. But when you do . . . it's a doozy. Playing with a firearm and old enough to know better. But still a minor in your case." He waited a bit longer. "I did some homework. Lawrence Matheus, by all accounts . . . teachers . . . friends say he was a good kid. A good kid. I'm betting not a bad brother either?"

Terry rubbed his eyes furiously. He wiped his wet hands on his pants.

"We've also lost everything that good boy was going to become. Do you understand that?

"Okay. Prosecution wants three months in jail. Eh, time served, two weeks, is good enough. Community service, yes, lots and lots. You put this community through a lot, so maybe you can make it up to us, eh?"

Terry was led away. His parents were already gone. Only Cap sat there and he did not look Terry's way.

They sat him at a desk. He signed papers. And then they left him there for a long time. Maybe he was free to go, but they had forgot to tell him. Four hundred hours of community service.

Finally, Detective Carson entered the room and beckoned Terry with a finger. He led him into a small alcove off the main corridor. Carson slammed him against the concrete block wall. Terry felt a burning in his chest as his air rushed out. The detective pinned him there with a hand spread on Terry's chest. The detective looked left and right quickly to make certain they were alone.

"You think you got away with something, don't you?" Carson talked rapidly and spit flew from his mouth. "You think you finally have them snowed. Tell lie number one, you figure, and if they stop swallowing that one, go directly to lie number two, which will be a lot more believable 'cause it shifts a piece of the blame back to you. But there are two people in this town who know exactly what happened aren't there, Terrell? Everything you did after the shooting were the calculated acts of a murderer trying to hide his crime. You've benefited from all the publicity. All the whites want this all to go away so they can look superior to the black community that was condemning them just days ago. But I know how deceitful you are, don't I? We both do. I think you think you just got away with something." Carson's sad eyes were livid. His face was just an inch from Terry's. "You watched while people grew angry. Your uncle and father shaking with it . . . Your mother collapsing . . . And you just worried about covering your own ass. You think you got away with something. It's going to catch up with you. I promise.

"Were you jealous of him? Was he the handsome, popular brother and you the chubby, little brother who could never keep up? What pissed you off, Terrell? Doesn't matter now does it?"

"Get off me."

"I mean, doesn't matter what the reason was. It's looking like a bad idea now. Sure. It's not how you pictured it. You didn't account for all that blood, and the look on his face, did you?"

"Let go." Terry tried to move, but Carson was too strong.

"When the blood spurts out and it's gotten over everything, and the body is lying as still as stone, it all looks different doesn't it? Different than you imagined it would look. Everything's messier . . . more fucked up than you thought possible. And now everybody's looking at you. People in your neighborhood, your friends, and family. Hell, they think you did it. Whether they say or not, they think you killed your brother on purpose, and they'll never be the same around you again. Not really. See, and that's how it starts catching up with you. That's how it all begins to turn sour. You'll see the turned-away glances, you'll hear whispers when you walk by and know they're talking about you. It'll catch up with you, punk. It always does."

An officer came toward them. Terry hoped he would help him. Not looking up from the opened file in his hands, the officer chuckled as he passed. "Carson, why're you wasting time with that punk?" he asked.

"Oh, I'm done," Carson said. He took his hand away from Terry's chest and looked at it. He wiped the hand on the side of his pants as if he'd touched something rotten and then he walked away.

Outside seemed bright, and Terry shielded his eyes, though it was a cloudy, grayish day. Cap was in the parking lot, leaning against his car. He said, "Your mom told me to come get you . . . You're going to stay with me for a while."

"My mom told you?"

"But don't say nothing to me. Dig? Nothing. Don't you dare say shit to me."

When they were young, Lawrence and he used to hang on the big man's arms, and Cap would hold his arms out at his sides and lift both of them into the air at the same time. Watching his dangling brother, Terry would hang on for dear life. They would all laugh, the two brothers and their uncle, the mighty giant.

WHEN THEY ARRIVED at Cap's house, Lynn had a meal ready, ham and mashed potatoes and brussels sprouts. She had a colorful scarf wrapped about her forehead, And her red hair leaped from the top of it like a fountain spray.

Cap looked at the table then looked at her.

"I thought jail food might be . . ." She turned to Terry. "Was it bad? Jail food. I can't imagine it being anything to write home about. Though I did hear about a homeless man who got himself arrested just so he could eat . . . so he could get warm. It was wintertime, get warm and eat."

Cap crossed the kitchen to the refrigerator and took out two beers. He carried them both with him when he walked out.

"Porter? What? Porter?" Lynn sat down and motioned Terry to sit too.

She adjusted the flatware. She put a big serving spoon in the mashed potatoes. She took a napkin and put it in her lap.

Terry wasn't hungry. The food looked like more than he could manage. He tried to remember the food in the jail, little sack lunches.

Lynn was not looking up.

Terry sat down. "Jail food is horrible," he said.

"I figured," she said with a small smile. She passed him the ham, asking if he would please slice it.

• • •

Tuesdays he reported to the Parks and Recreation Commission and climbed with six or seven others into a van without air-conditioning for a quick drive to the outskirts of town. They were all issued orange safety vests. If you wanted gloves you brought your own. Terry brought a pair of Lynn's Playtex gloves the second Tuesday he went, but his hands couldn't breathe in them and the gloves filled with his sweat. They combed the shoulders of highways, bagging trash. It was hot work, but Terry endured it while listening to the others complain about the heat, the gross garbage they would find, or how some cars seem to swerve closer to the shoulder when they saw the orange vests. When they returned, the supervisor would call in their hours worked to be put against their outstanding balances.

He found tires, which were common, and used condoms and Styrofoam Big Mac boxes and dirty diapers. And of course there were beer cans and soda cans, beer bottles and soda bottles. The returnable bottles went into a bin. They collected the refund and bought themselves sodas with the money. He went into prickly bushes and weeds and vines made of wire to fetch these items and bag and tag them along the side of the road. Some people slowed when they came upon the workers in their orange vests, some moved a lane over, most zoomed right by as if they weren't there at all.

Sometimes people shouted at them as they grazed for trash on the side of the highways. Terry was called nigger a couple of times, once by white kids and the second time by black kids.

On the second Tuesday, they walked the levee, which was harder work, but much more pleasant because of the view and the danger of being hit by a car was removed. One guy found a bra. Terry believed he pocketed it.

He tried to ignore his fellow inmates and parolees, but they all knew who he was, which made the job of ignoring them nearly impossible.

Four days a week he reported to the Evansville Rescue Mission. They fed people who came into the premises, no questions asked as far as Terry could tell. He rode his bicycle, which he picked up from home without seeing his parents, downtown to the old building between Seventh and Eighth avenues. He locked it to a downspout in the back. He put on one of the stained aprons that hung from a row of coat hooks in the kitchen. He opened giant cans of green beans until his hand hurt. He washed dishes and trays and pots encrusted with spaghetti sauce that had been simmering all day. He washed the warming trays. He swept up everything that everybody else dropped in the course of preparing and eating these meals. Carol, a slightly plump white woman, who wore Earth shoes and wore an ornate leather necklace, supervised him.

He watched the people who came in, and the people who volunteered. If the volunteers knew he was working off a court sentence, they didn't say anything. Maybe they thought at first he was a volunteer like them. What gave him away was that he was there too often and for too many hours in the day.

The people they served were familiar strangers, no one he knew, but faces he could have known. Sometimes he imagined he could see their problems in their eyes and fantasized that he had something in common with these struggling people. They had all seen trouble.

"Some are homeless. Some just need help making ends meet," Carol told him. "We don't want them to become homeless because they had to decide between food and heating oil or the rent. So you don't look down on anyone who comes through these doors. Financial hardship is just that. It doesn't mean you are intellectually or spiritually bankrupt. Don't depersonalize anyone."

His second week at the mission, he spotted a little girl eating a biscuit from a batch he had helped make. She had a cute round nose, big dark eyes, and an absolute riot of long, crinkly hair. She was alone at her table, though the nearly emptied dishes next to her indicated she was with someone. She was savoring the biscuit when her mother returned with a page from the newspaper in her hands. She sat down and proceeded to read and circle want ads. The mother did not seem older than maybe Lawrence's age; it was hard to tell. She was not bad looking either. Her top was tight and she wore no bra. Terry smiled, thinking, maybe she lost the bra at the levee.

sixteen

No one spoke to him. No deacons came up to him to voice their support. No schoolkids stopped by, not that they knew where he currently lived, to raise their fists in solidarity. His mother had not called. He did not expect his dad to call. The look on his father's face when Bill Carson told Terry's parents who really had pulled the trigger would stay with Terry forever. No one spoke to him.

It all seemed unfair, though not because he did not deserve it. He felt he deserved this treatment and worse. He thought the situation unfair because there was no way to make it up. He could not make it up to any of them except to let them be.

He had the jail dream again, where the voices echo down the corridor and everyone including the bloodied pot dealers and Lawrence parades by his cell. This time he woke up before Lawrence could shoot him that look. He woke on a small mattress in a small room. He kept his eyes closed until he was able to convince himself that he was no longer in jail, that he wasn't lying on an iron-frame cot, a toilet two feet away. "We've also lost everything that good boy was going to become. Do you understand that?" He opened his eyes finally and saw wallpaper, green vines with leaves of various green colors on an off-white background. This was not his bedroom. After the jail dream, seeing the unfamiliar wallpaper threw him off and he did not know where he was. He wanted to make sure he was not in the middle of another dream, so he lay there until he was fully awake, until he remembered that he lived at Cap Porter's now. "Don't say nothing to me. Don't you say shit to me."

He heard water running through the pipes in the wall next to his head. That might be Lynn, he thought. He had gotten up early yesterday and seen Lynn—seen more of Lynn than he was supposed to—coming out of the bathroom. She covered herself and said, "Oh, crap! Sorry!" and raced to the bedroom she shared with Cap. Once safely behind the door she peeked around it and asked, "Did you see anything?"

"Plenty," Terry said.

"You're not supposed to say that. A gentleman would say he saw nothing, in order to make the lady feel better."

"I saw a whole lot."

"Terry!"

"Gonna remember it always."

"You . . ."

"Fantasy stuff, really."

"Hah! Now I know you didn't see anything." She shut the door, and he heard her laugh.

So Lynn spoke to him. Once or twice she tried to engage both Cap and Terry in the same conversation. Terry wished she would not try. Each time, Cap just walked away.

Terry slid halfway out of bed, his feet on the floor but most of him still on the mattress, hoping today wasn't Tuesday. He hated Tuesdays. Working on the side of the road made him nervous, and the other boys in the work gang made him nervous too. But it was not Tuesday. If he stayed home no hours would come off his sentence.

There was a soft rap at his door, and Lynn with her red porcupine hair stuck her head in. "You're running late. You want a ride downtown? I'm going that way."

"No," he said a bit too abruptly. "Thanks," he added.

"Okay. I know it's a hassle, but it must feel good doing good. You know, helping people and all."

"Feels fantastic."

"You're being funny. Why? Cap talks like that. When he's not slurring his words. Did you see him last night?"

He turned his face into the pillow. "No." The only person who talked to him and he wanted her to leave.

"Well, I think it would at least be satisfying to be down there helping, you know?"

"I think for it to feel good, Lynn, it has to be your idea. Not your punishment."

"Oh, I didn't know that," she said. He thought she was still there, hovering, waiting for him to say more. But then he heard her footsteps going down the stairs.

Dust swirled about him. Sneezing with every other breath, Terry worked his way to the very back of the garage. He knocked something over and it broke, and he cursed.

"Hello?"

He thought it was Lynn at first. He backed out of the tight jumble and stepped half out of the garage. "Yeah?" He shielded his eyes from the morning sun. It was Tamara Groves. He had not seen her since that night Cap and his friends had dragged him off.

She was wearing worn bell-bottoms with a yellow, lacy shirt that was almost but not quite see-through and her hair was brushed back and tied off. She did not have on much makeup. He could not imagine what she could possibly be doing there or what she wanted, and because he could figure no way to ask, he said nothing at all.

Her fists were on her hips.

He decided quickly that he did not need to take any crap from her, especially from her. Everyone he ever knew had that look for him now. They looked to see if he was a liar or a killer or what. If they were sure they already knew, they did not want to hear from him at all, and looked away.

"What do you want?" he said, leaning back against the garage.

"You're kidding, right?" she asked. "You think you get to have that attitude with me? You get to be angry with me?"

His defensiveness crumbled immediately. "Well, I . . ."

" 'Well, I . . . '?"

He looked away for a moment, then back. She was still looking hard at him so he looked away again. "I got something for Bread Williams," Lawrence had told him. Lawrence had gotten that gun to defend himself from Tamara's boyfriend, so in Terrell's mind that gun was her fault. And why had she visited his mother?

"What are you up to in the garage?" she asked.

He nodded toward the garage's dusty darkness. "I think my uncle's old motorcycle is in there."

"You ride motorcycles?"

"Maybe soon," he said. He stepped back into the garage and to his surprise, she was behind him. "There's a bunch of junk in here all pushed back. Cap puts his Harley in here in the winter."

"Can't the door open wider?" she asked.

"I've been trying." Terry put his hands on the door's edge and pushed again. Tamara placed hers under his and tried to lean into the door. It moved an inch or two, but no more.

She said, "You're going to have to get it back on the track first."

"This is enough to see by."

"I thought you eventually wanted to take the bike out of the garage."

"Oh, well, yeah, there's that."

Terry found a crowbar to leverage the door back onto the rusty metal track, with Tamara helping, pressing against the door in case it decided to fall. Finally, it dropped onto the track and opened grudgingly.

Terry began dragging away cardboard boxes and what looked like shelving. He had to find a place to put aside an old door. Instantly, he was hot and sweaty. The dust mixed with his sweat.

That shiny curve of chrome, belonging to the bike's front fender, shone dully against the back garage wall. Terry stepped over a stack of warped boards. "Watch it back here." he cautioned. "There's nails on the floor."

"I am not going back in that dust bowl," Tamara said.

Terry pulled off a plastic tarp, and dust flew everywhere. Under the tarp was a blanket. Terry carefully pulled this away.

This was the very motorcycle on which Cap used to give them rides. Terry would get to go first, mostly because he was younger and didn't have the patience to wait until Cap and Lawrence had returned. Their mother would be there to warn and worry. "Cap, don't lean around the turns," she would say. "And there's no need to go fast. And for God's sake, don't do any of those front wheelie things." He remembered Cap tightening his helmet and how he could feel his heart beating faster just getting near the engine. It was the first time Terry realized you could be afraid of something and attracted to it at the same time.

Cap was a giant then. Cap was the biggest man Terry knew, an adult who played like a kid, who did what you would do if the adults let you. "Hold on tight. Cause if you come off . . . well, I get a ticket, like a ten-dollar ticket, plus the police would make me clean up the street myself."

He remembered the noise it made, a fierce noise, as Cap worked the throttle, and you couldn't hear anything else. Their mother only got on it once. They could hear her screams clear down the block and around the corner. Lawrence and Terry laughed the entire time from the moment she threw her leg over the motorcycle until they came up the driveway and she scrambled off.

Terry looked around for Cap's old helmet but couldn't find it. "He had a white helmet . . ." The one he wore nowadays was a metallic aqua that matched his Harley.

Terry held the motorcycle by the handlebars and wrenched it free of all the junk around it.

"Both tires are flat," Tamara said. "There goes my ride home."

Terry looked at her and wondered if that was why she was here, because she needed a ride.

He rolled the Honda CB450 outside in the sunlight and walked around it several times.

The key was still in it. Terry straddled the bike and held on to the handlebars.

"It's cute," Tamara said.

"Cute?" It was smaller than he remembered.

He flipped the kickstand down and swung his leg off. He was wishing Tamara would go away so that he could be alone to think about the bike. He sat down on the concrete next to the bike, ignoring her or trying to until she sat down next to him.

"It's gonna take some work to get it running, isn't it?" she said. "Did your uncle give it to you?"

"He's not talking to me."

"But you're living with him."

"We have something in common; we blame me for everything."

She seemed to study him for a moment, then turned back to the motorcycle and asked, "What's this do?" She grabbed a part that looked like a tiny lever and pulled down on it.

"Don't touch that. That's very important."

"You have no idea."

"Looks important."

"What about this?"

"That's the seat."

"No. This thing under it, silly."

"That's . . . looks like . . . well, clearly there's a learning curve."

"Clearly."

"Do you want some juice or Kool-Aid or something?" Terry gained his feet.

"Sure. Yes." She put her hand out to be helped up. Terry hesitated, noting quickly its slimness and the manicured, shiny nails, before grabbing it and briefly feeling the soft padding of her palm.

"Cap's not here. He's in and out these days."

"His girlfriend lives here too?"

"Lynn. Yeah."

They went in the side door, which took them right into the kitchen. Terry poured orange juice. He found it hard to look at her, but curiosity and her attractiveness kept him glimpsing her way. He found he wanted to ask her what was the last thing Lawrence had said to her? What had they done? How did she feel about his big brother? Did his death hurt? And why was she here, right now, helping him take a motorcycle out of the garage? He wanted to see what Lawrence had seen. Why was his big brother so crazy for this girl so crazy that he would go get a gun?

"So you're over here with a man who won't talk to you. Must be crap at home?" Before Terry could even consider the question she said, "Forget I said that. Stupid question. Sorry. Better question. What happened last time I saw you? Your uncle, right? Jumps out of the car and practically drags you in."

"Yeah."

"And then goes tearin' down the street. What was all of that?"

"Yeah, that." Terry exhaled loudly, not meaning to. He opened his mouth and nothing came out.

"Hey, if that's stupid, awkward question number two, that's fine. We can go on to number three. I've got at least a dozen . . ."

Terry smiled. "No. It's just that . . . well, that night is like one of the reasons he ain't talking to me anymore. And, I'm betting, the only way I could make it worse would be to go tell people about it."

"Oh."

"Screwed-up night."

"Well, now I'm not curious. So, he's pissed. What makes you think he's going to give you his motorcycle."

"Give me his motorcycle . . . guess I think he's too busy ignoring me to care. He's changed; that's my fault too."

"How?"

"Let's go look at the bike again. God, I'm tired of pedaling everywhere."

"You're psyched about that thing." She got up, leaving half her juice behind.

He followed her out. He sat on the same spot on the cracked concrete, but she mounted the Honda and cast about until she found the foot pegs.

He said, "I have a plan to get out of here to go and go and go. Find someplace else. I have to."

"Me too. Maybe."

"No maybe for me. No one is going to know me where I'm going. I mean no one. Do you know how freeing that will be? That is true bird-in-the-sky freedom there. No one will look at me and know, there's the guy fucked up his family beyond all recognition and almost brought down the city too." His hands fluttered. "No one will know. I might write a suicide note, then disappear so they'll all think I'm dead."

"You'd like that?"

He looked up into her face, meeting her gaze for the first time. "I'm the reminder of all I've done. I'm the reminder of how bad it can get."

seventeen

HE WAITED UNTIL her mother was down the hallway, then brought the little girl an extra piece of toast with grape jam spread on it. She accepted it greedily, almost snatching it from him. But then, before she bit into it, she gave Terry a gap-toothed smile that was more than polite.

He went back into the kitchen where a stack of metal and plastic trays waited to be washed in scalding hot water.

Yesterday, while the little girl's mother was talking to friends across the room or checking out the job board in the front hall, he had sat with her briefly. He held a broom in both hands, locked between his legs and asked her what her favorite cereal was.

"Cocoa Puffs."

"Oh, koo-koo for Cocoa Puffs, huh?"

She had looked at him shyly.

The clap slap of her mother's heelless flats came up behind him.

"You okay, Christy?" she asked her daughter.

"Christy, is that your name?"

The mother was beautiful. She had wide-set, light brown eyes, and long dark brown hair and big cheekbones and her shirts always fit her tightly. She had a nice smile, even with a gold tooth, and an even nicer laugh. "You're here every day, ain't you?" she asked.

Terry tried not to stare, but she was pretty and he had found himself rooting that her and Christy might overcome whatever had brought them to mission house each day for meals. He answered, "Just about."

"Lots of hard work needs doing around here." She had a rich voice with an accent that Terry's limited scope could not identify.

"Yeah, guess so."

She was beautiful and she was smiling at him, but edged around her eyes was something vicious, which he did not notice until she sprang at him. "I know who you are," she said still smiling. "You're the little shit who shot his own brother and made up make-believe stories to cover your sorry self, yes?"

"Wha . . ." Startled, Terry jumped from his seat, sending it falling backward. His feet tangled in the legs of the chair or with the broom he forgot he was holding. It clattered to the linoleum floor too.

Little Christy's big eyes turned up to him saying she didn't understood what her mother had said.

"Stay away from us, okay? Do your work."

Terry staggered backward, not stopping to pick up the chair or the broom. He retreated to the kitchen where he stayed the rest of the day.

He had hoped to cloak himself with anonymity at the mission. He had gone about his duties smiling at people, not knowing they knew. He wanted to ask his supervisor, Carol, if everyone knew who he was, but he didn't ask.

He did not think he could face returning to the mission the next day. He told Tamara Groves what had happened between him and the mother and daughter. She convinced him he could return.

She said, "You're working. Most people are gonna respect that and let you be. Did you expect to make friends?"

So he hauled himself back the next day. He had not found Cocoa Puffs for Christy, but when the mom left her alone for a while, as she did every day, it seemed, he hurried out to her with an extra slice of toast.

When he peeked out later, hoping the mother and child had left so he could go in there and start sweeping, a man was sitting down at Christy's table. The man, dark, in his midthirties, thin, and tall, did a lot of smiling, but the girl did not smile back at him.

One of the volunteer ladies called Terry back into the kitchen for help. A minute later, he was walking by the dining hall entrance and saw the man leading Christy out the side door. He looked about for the mom, but the room was empty. He ran to the job board. No one was there either. "Hey . . ." He dashed back to the kitchen. "That guy just left with . . ." Two old ladies were discussing rice pudding; they were not going to be able to move fast enough. "Stay away from us. Do your work." Even as he raced to the door, he wanted to shrug the whole thing off.

Outside, he saw no one except an older couple on the sidewalk, making their way toward the mission building. There were several cars in the parking lot. That man must be up to something to disappear so fast, Terry decided. The next moment he heard a car door slam and saw the man making his way around the car to the driver's side. Terry looked back inside the mission; he saw no help coming his way.

"Um, excuse me. Excuse me. Hey."

The man opened the driver's side door before turning around. "Yeah?"

Terry jogged to him, but stayed about ten feet away. "Um, hey, yeah. I work at the rescue mission." He didn't know what to say. "I know Christy. Um, is that your daughter?" Terry thought maybe he should have just made note of the license plate and gone back inside.

The man's eye narrowed. "Who wants to know?"

"Like I said"—Terry pointed a thumb over his shoulder at the building—"I work here. I'm a member of the staff."

"So?"

"Hey, I just want to know who . . ."

"Nigger, you better get away from me." The man pointed a finger at Terry as he put one foot in the open car.

Terry stepped forward. He placed a hand on the door and tried to place himself in a way to stop it from closing.

"Get the fuck away from here, fool." The elbow connected with Terry just under his left eye on his cheekbone.

"Wait a second," Terry hollered.

He was hit again, a glancing blow off his left temple.

"What's goin' on over there?"

"Y'all stop that fuss, you hear? Leave that boy alone." It was the old couple.

The old lady had a walking stick that she shook in the general direction of the parking lot.

The old man was hustling inside the mission. "We need some help out here," he called out.

Terry was hit again as he tried to hold on to the door. "Christy, is this your daddy?"

On the verge of tears, the little girl looked wide eyed at the two men.

The man said, "You better goddamn well say yes!"

Christy managed something that might have been a nod before busting out in a loud wail.

"There, satisfied?"

Brandishing her tripod walking stick over her head the old lady asked again, "What's goin' on over there?"

Now several people ran from the building toward them, including Carol and Christy's mother.

"Someone tell this fool to get away from me before I kill him," the man said.

"What's goin' on? Jackie, what are you doin'?" Christy's mother went around to the passenger side and Christy nearly leaped into her arms when she opened door. "What in the world, honey?"

Carol looked to Terry.

"He took the girl. I didn't know who he was."

"I said I was her daddy."

"No, you didn't."

Carol turned to the mother, who was bouncing the crying girl and whispering baby-talk to her. "Jeanetta?"

The mother didn't say anything at first. She looked up and met Terry's eyes. The meanness of yesterday was not there, and that told Terry a lot. She then looked to Christy's dad and a lot of unsaid words passed between them too. "We got our days mixed up," she said. "I didn't know Jackie was taking her today."

"Today's my day. I tol' you," he said effecting a tolerant smile. He repeated this two or three times. "I tol' you."

Terry did not want to hear anything else and maneuvered himself away. The old couple was on the periphery of the circle of people. Terry put out his hand to the old man, who took it tentatively. He met the old lady's eyes. "Thank you," he said. He felt her pat his back as he went by her.

Later, in the kitchen, Carol came up to him, arms crossed. "I convinced the boyfriend not to call the police. I think that's the last thing you need."

Terry rolled his eyes. "What was I supposed to do?"

"You did all right. But next time try to find me."

"I did."

"Okay. Does it hurt?" She briefly touched his forehead and cheek, testing the tender skin. Her touch made the skin sting, but the hand felt good too, motherly. "Jeanetta says you tried to hit on her yesterday."

"I was not trying to hit on that woman. I was just . . ."

"You're not surprised if anyone has a hard time believing you, are you?" She shook her head. "Terry, it doesn't matter. We're here to help these people, not argue with them." She turned and walked away. Over a shoulder she added, "Just leave them be."

THE SECOND TIME Tamara Groves showed up at Cap's house, Terry was as surprised to see her as he was the first time. She did not stay long. She had said a few words to Cap and Lynn, apparently, and then came up to his room. She did not enter the room but leaned against the doorjamb and asked Terry how he was doing. Terry did not for a moment think the girl had a thing for him so he was at a loss to explain her presence or concern. She had looked preoccupied and not in the same humor she had been during first visit. This second time, she had left quickly, and Terry had not asked her how she was doing.

Two days later, after Terry had been dressed down by Christy's mother and then gotten a fat lip trying to foil a kidnapping, he rode his bike over Tamara's place.

He rode by it looking for signs that Bread and his gang were about. He did not see any of the cars that he suspected were theirs, the pimpmobile-looking cars with the portawall tires and padded vinyl roofs. Still, he suspected that just climbing that flight of stairs and knocking on her door might not be good for either him or Tamara. The third time he coasted his bike by he saw a girl sitting on the first-floor porch. He stopped but continued to straddle the bike. "Hey," he called.

The girl got to her feet and moved closer to the door. "Will you do me a quick favor, for a quarter?" He pulled a quarter from his pocket and showed it to her. "Do you know Tamara?"

The girl nodded and seemed to be a bit less wary at the mention of the name.

"Go up and tell her I'm in the alley. Just her. Just ask for her. Don't give nobody else the message, okay?" Terry flipped the quarter, expecting it to land on the porch in front of the girl, but to his surprise, she snatched it out of the air. They both smiled at her catch. She leaped toward the stairs and Terry turned his bicycle around and walked it quickly into the alley. He hid behind the tall, untrimmed bushes and a leaning toolshed. Houses on the newer east side of town did not have alleys; people there put their garbage in front of their houses for collection. He thought he knew every alley in the city. Then he wondered how he could have gotten rid of the gun if not for the alley.

He got off the bike and sat with his back to the old shed. He waited ten minutes before telling himself to leave, but still he did not move. It was late afternoon, and hot, and he was tired, but had really wanted to talk to Tamara.

He closed his eyes for a moment but was sure he had not napped. Still when he opened his eyes Tamara was there, arms crossed and looking irritated.

"Bread is home. He's pissed at me these days as it is, because word is getting spread around that I was Lawrence's girlfriend."

Terry shrugged. He hoped she would sit down next to him. "Just tell him it's not true."

She let this comment go. "It would have been nice if you told Shevette to whisper your message."

"Shit. Did he hear?"

"No. I don't think so. And heaven help us if that girl's mother knew you sent her up those stairs to the den of iniquity. She can't stand the fact that we live up there, sin and corruption above her head, but she's not the landlord and Bread pays his bills. Always late, but not too late to get kicked out . . . How'd you get the fat lip?"

Terry waved his hand in the air as if to say, it's nothing. "I had a hard day," he said. He told her about the little girl and the tussle by the car and how the woman had said to him he could not expect people to believe his story.

During the telling, Tamara had sat down next to him. Honeysuckle grew along a dilapidated fence that leaned into the bushes. She pulled the flowers to her face and inhaled their fragrance. "So the mom, this Jeanette whatever, didn't say anything to you later? Did she go off with the boyfriend?"

"Nope. Everyone came back in the mission. Everybody except the boyfriend, but nobody said boo to me."

"It's okay, Terry. What did your uncle Cap say? About your lip?"

"Cap and Lynn—they didn't notice. Thing is, I think Cap lost his job and didn't tell Lynn about it till like yesterday or something. She's pissed. The vibe in that house is . . ."

"I can imagine."

"Everything is worse. Cap . . . They all hate me. I don't blame them." He wanted to say more, but he was afraid of what would happen if he did, how he would feel, what she would think. Tears came to his eyes. He was surprised by them and quickly wiped them away.

"Hey," she said. "Give it time. The woman at the rescue mission, your uncle, me. No one can just get over . . . Look, why don't you call your mom? I'm sure she'd want to hear from you."

"I can't."

"I think she could use hearing from you."

"What did you two talk about anyway? Y'all talk about me?"

"Some."

"You talk about Lawrence." Terry was sure that was all they talked about; of course it was.

"She just wants to know what she can about him."

"What do you know?"

"I think I knew just a bit, but it's . . . it's different than what a mom would know." Tamara picked a honeysuckle. "She just wants to hear things she didn't know, something new."

"You have a boyfriend," Terry said, and he felt an anger toward her that had always been waiting just under his skin. "You just needed rides home, right?"

"Terry . . ."

"And you didn't mind leading him on, right?" Terry felt the heat in his face. He wanted to tell her if she hadn't been playing her games, Lawrence would not have gone out and gotten a gun. He saw the look on her face, briefly the hurt was there, but she looked away, and he could not bring himself to say more.

They sat quietly. Cars drove by the mouth of the alley. In the other direction, they heard someone rattling a garbage can. The closest part of her to him was her shoe, her white Keds. He reached out slowly, let his hand slide over the dusty ground until the tip of his longest finger touched the rubbery side of her tennis shoe.

She watched his hand.

Shevette came around the shed. "Bread was out on the steps looking for you," she said.

Tamara thanked the girl, who grinned as she retreated backward.

"I better get back in." She stood, dusted off her backside. "I'll tell Bread I went for a walk. He might . . ."

"See. I don't get that. Why go with someone you got to worry about how he takes every little thing?"

"I've got to go. And that is none of your business." But then she said, "Most boyfriends probably don't want to hear about their girl sitting in an alley with another boy, right? Even if he's like way too young for anything to be going on."

"Thanks."

"And, Terry? Don't come visit me here again, okay?"

eighteen

WHEN WHITE TEENAGERS drove by and gunned down his oldest son for no reason, Preston Matheus didn't choke on his hurt because he was so angry, so filled with rage, he could practically spit the venom from him. Some days his fists were kept so tightly balled his hands hurt at the end of the day, and the muscles on the back of his hands afterward would twitch of their own accord. His jaws ached from the viselike set of his teeth. The hatred was insulation. He didn't have to confront the great void in his family because that space was plugged with anger.

There was no failure as a father with Terry's cover-up story either. His son had not been shot at a nightclub over some girl or in a drunken stupor on a street corner on Lincoln Avenue. His son had been home, where he belonged, on his own porch, minding his own business. Preston had not lost control of him.

And when the white boys had murdered his child, Preston had wrung enough pain from the rag of rage to ignore the collapse of his fragile wife and the rapid withdrawal of his other son.

Preston had set himself to repairing the porch. He had taken out a clawhammer and crowbar and ripped up the bloodstained boards. He returned from the lumberyard—the second lumberyard—with clean, straight boards, which he measured carefully, cut exactly, and fit into place. He had attempted to hammer the orderliness back into his house.

He held his wife that first day and felt her sobs shake through him and remind him of his helplessness. He recalled something of talking to Terrell but nothing clearly. He thought back at it constantly now in a search for clues.

But out-of-town white rednecks had not driven by his home. His home had not sustained an unprovoked attack from outside. There were no pale phantoms in a pale truck to blame. The knife had plunged even deeper than that. One son had killed the other. The gun had been brought into his house by his older son. The family had turned on itself, had exploded from within with startling suddenness, leaving him shocked. His wife had collapsed. His living son had been banished from his house.

His house had unpainted boards leading to its doorway.

Inside, the ordinary machinations of a day, such as taking a shower or cooking dinner, seemed to make no noise against the quiet. The tomblike hush could only be broken by the nightly whimpering of a mother whom he could not comfort.

He did not know what to do for Judith. She no longer sought comfort from him. He had tried to give it, but she used the distance to blame and convict him. Her tears were weapons. The robe she never took off was a weapon. The days spent in a ball on the edge of the bed were meant to condemn him for his failure as a father, his failure, for allowing it all to happen. The loss of both Lawrence and Terrell was placed on his shoulders. So when he reached to hold her, because he needed to do that, to be a husband if he could no longer be a father, she would not allow it and would slip from his arms and pad away on bare feet.

Judith pulled herself together only for that girl, Tamara Groves, who claimed to have been Lawrence's girlfriend, but Preston had heard from one of Lawrence's track teammates that she had a live-in boyfriend. The detectives had confirmed this even if Judith chose to forget it. The girl had visited twice now and they had talked in the kitchen, the only time Preston could look at Judith and think it was possible to at least survive this hell. But he was wary with the girl and waited to see what she was up to, fearing the day would come when she would be asking for money in exchange for another tidbit about Lawrence.

He had been working on Lawrence's Dodge each day and now had it in fairly good shape. Maybe a new fuel filter would help. He should have done these things with the boy. He could have taught him a few basic automotive skills, because the boy had none. He recalled telling him once that if the tires weren't properly inflated, his performance and mileage would suffer. Lawrence had run right by him saying, "Okay, Pops, got it."

The decision to visit Terrell took him by surprise. Preston was under the hood swapping out a hose in the car, but twilight had snuck up on him and he couldn't see his way around very well. Then the idea to drop by Cap's occurred to him. He would talk to Terrell. They would talk calmly and lay things out.

He had lunged at the boy and struck him again and again until the police had dragged him off. He couldn't recall anything the police had shouted to him or anything Terrell may have said or even what he himself had said. He only had his wife's screams in his ears and he only saw Terrell on the floor, trying to protect himself from his father.

He cleaned his hands at the kitchen sink, then dialed Cap Porter. Lynn answered the phone and he hung up. The phone would not do. You had to see a person's face for any important conversation. Words could mean anything and Preston was determined not only to hear the words but to see between them this time.

He went down the driveway to his car and started it up. He let his car roll down Gum Street, barely going twenty-five miles an hour.

He turned on the radio. Ronald Reagan had beat President Ford in the Texas primary and Governor Carter beat Senator Bentsen in the senator's own state. In Boston, antibusing whites rallied at Bunker Hill to show the mayor they were not going away or giving up their neighborhood schools. In sports, Muhammad Ali had won against Jimmy Young, but, the announcer said, the champ looked sluggish and overweight. Over twelve thousand fans booed the decision, according to the newsman.

Preston did not like to hear that Ali was out of shape. Retire or be ready to fight, one or the other, he thought. C'mon champ.

He turned the radio off partly from anger and partly because he wanted to be alone with all the thoughts he had to sort out. When he got near Cap's house, he turned away. He went up to a gas station and filled up, which earned him a free *Flintstones* glass from the attendant.

He went by the boys' school, pulled into the parking lot, but when a cop car circled twice he started his car and pulled back onto the street.

He should have told Judith where he was going. Judith was never what one would call tough, but she had been strong. She had guided her boys through life in the projects, pushed them in school, and they would never have been able to afford the house on Gum if she hadn't worked. She deserved better than this. She did.

He asked himself what he should do about Judith. Maybe he should take her somewhere, he thought, to visit family in the country or maybe she should go to a psychiatrist. But then, he had no money for that and besides, she wasn't crazy. Would bringing Terrell back home do any good and be good for her, he wondered.

He tried to put himself in Terrell's place, and that only made him angry. He gave the steering wheel three hard blows then had to jerk it straight quickly to avoid sideswiping a parked car. What could the boy have been thinking? Was it on purpose? Did he kill his brother on purpose? Only that could explain the lie and the cover-up. Despite the findings of the police, Preston had his own ideas—ideas that he did not allow full form. They made his jaw ache. Now he thought he would confront the boy and wring the truth from him. Exactly, what did you do? Exactly, why did you do it? And why did you lie?

Yet, as he thought about it, Preston realized it would do no good to confront the boy. Certainly, the shooting was an accident. They were horsing around. They were always horsing around. He had warned them about that.

He had tried to make them into more serious boys on countless occasions. The mistake had been that Preston's generation had worked hard to make it easy for these kids nowadays. Any time they came up against a wall, they protested. They fought the authorities at every turn, in the house and out. Nothing about the way things were was good enough for them. Instead of working through the bigots and the corrupt system, they punched black power fists at it. They grew afros like shrubbery and dared anyone to tell them no. If they shouted black power, wouldn't that make the whites shout white power? In the end, who did they think had the numbers to shout loudest? But you couldn't tell them nothing. They had the answers. In their minds, the adults were just stupid.

"Cap, ask him why Lawrence had a gun."

His brother-in-law had waved him off. "You ask him," Cap said. "Can't you ask him, Preston?"

He finally pulled up in front of Cap's house and let the engine run for a while, the car was still in drive. After a couple of minutes, he killed the engine but left the keys dangling from the ignition.

He peeked at Cap's house; lights were on. Based on when he'd left home, he guessed it was only eight thirty or so. Cap had not come by to see Judith at all since the truth of the whole thing had come out. Preston would have to talk to him about that. It wasn't right. What was his girlfriend's name. He had just heard her voice on the phone earlier this evening and had known it then. What was the matter with him? Millie. No, that was the other girl. Lynn—that was it. Being a man meant being in control of your house, your family, and yourself. Preston felt totally out of control now and had to reclaim it.

His eyes felt dry.

Maybe bringing Terrell back would snap Judith out of her downward spiral. She seemed to be shrinking daily. Eventually, that dark pink terry-cloth robe she wore constantly was going to swallow her whole. She was shrinking before his eyes. He'd made her come down for breakfast yesterday—eggs, toast, orange juice, and coffee. She pinched a corner off the toast and took little kitten sips at the orange juice. The coffee she stayed away from.

Maybe he should talk to that girl too, Tamara. He should know what the girl with the live-in boyfriend was saying to his distraught wife. This was just another example of Preston having lost control of everything in his own home.

He heard raised voices coming from the side of Cap's house and strained to hear them without getting out of the car. He recognized Cap's voice and that of a girl's he supposed was Lynn's.

". . . you worry about you. I'll worry about me," he heard Cap say. That was followed by the gruff start of Cap's big Harley. The bike, ablaze with lights and reflectors, shot from the driveway and made sparks on the street as it turned. Cap was gone in an instant.

Judith had always worried about her little brother, but then, to know Cap was to worry about him. The boys liked him though. Preston let his mind slip into an unexpected recollection of the boys coming home on their bicycles just as he pulled into the driveway at the end of the day. He had asked if they wanted to help him mow and edge the yard and, to his surprise, they had agreed with near enthusiasm. They were new in the house then; yardwork was a novelty. But then Cap came rolling up on his motorcycle, not the big one he has now, but a smaller more agile one—and the boys were off, the yardwork forgotten.

HE WOKE UP with a start. He had nodded off. The clock on the dashboard didn't work so Preston had no idea how late it was. His hands were damp. Muscles in the back of his neck twitched. He climbed from the car feeling worse for the nap. He stood for a minute, trying to figure out what to do.

His thoughts were mushy and had a dreamy quality. He would save his family. He would bring his surviving boy home. With Terrell around the house, Judith would have to come to her senses. She'd have to wake up. And Judith was still just young enough; they could have another baby, a girl this time. He could see what must be done but not how it could be done. He had no solutions on how Terrell could regain his life. Preston only saw things in terms of salvaging his family. Yes, he would bring Terrell home. He had to teach him what a man does as far as owning up to his responsibilities and owning up to his mistakes too. He thought he'd taught them both that lesson. He'd been stern with them. But Terrell was so hardheaded—and Lawrence was even worse. He'd had a way of showing you that he wasn't listening even while he looked you in the eye. When they were young, if you gave Lawrence a cookie, he would give a piece of it to Terrell. But when they got older it seemed they couldn't share anything.

KNOWING THAT CAP was not home, Preston knocked on the front door instead of going around to the side. The porch light came on. He heard locks flip. "Hey, Preston," Lynn said. "What's wrong, is it Cap?"

"No."

"I thought," she said, holding the door open so that he could come in to the dark room, "you were here to tell me some bad news."

"Naw."

She smiled. Her hair was in a sleeping cap, and she was wearing men's pajamas. "He flew out of here more than two hours ago." She clicked on a floor lamp that dangled its shade over one end of the couch.

Preston saw Terry's sneakers were on the floor. The heels were run down.

"Two hours . . . I had no idea what time it is, Lynn."

"It's after eleven. Cap has no consideration. Do you think I'm going to get a call just to let me know he's okay?"

"Is Terrell here?"

"Yeah, he's here. Hardly ever stays out late. Sometimes does, but even then I think he's just in the backyard or something."

She sat down on the couch. "Preston, how's Judith?"

"She's coming along, I'd say. We're progressing one step at a time." He did not want a conversation right now, least of all with a woman who apparently felt more comfortable with him than he did with her.

"Oh, that's good. That's good, isn't it? Good. Preston, your brother-in-law lost his job."

"What? I didn't know that. What . . ."

"Exactly, he doesn't tell anybody anything. Just let's the checking account get overrun and then, oh, by the way, there's no money. No damn money. What am I supposed to do?"

"I . . ."

"Look, Preston, since you're here. Teen boys eat. He ain't a great eater, but . . ."

"We've been sending Cap money."

"You have?"

"Gave him the checks myself, one for fifty last week."

She looked away for a moment and then whispered, "The shit."

"Lynn, I came to see Terry. Maybe later, some other time, we could talk about . . ."

"Sure. Sure, Preston. Come on. I'm glad you came. Terry needs to see you."

"Is he asleep?"

"Don't think so. Go on up. Take a left up there, then straight."

Preston slowly climbed each of the steps.

Behind him, he heard Lynn whisper, "That shit."

As was his habit, Preston did not knock at the door. Dim light shone from under it, so he turned the knob slowly and put his head through. The bedside light was on, its glow muted by an old shade.

Preston gasped. "Terrell?" For a moment, he thought it was Lawrence in the bed, and a sudden queer sensation froze him there.

Terrell lay there with his clothes still on, on top of the sheets. Only he was so thin. The boys had never resembled each other much, but for a moment his mind couldn't tell them apart. Terrell had lost even more weight since Preston last saw him, and there was fuzz on his chin that had not been there before. Preston tiptoed into the room and stood over his son. The light threw Preston's shadow on the wall. He put his hand out. He could see the hand and the shadow of the hand trembling. He thought to cradle Terrell's head as he had done when he was a little boy until he woke. Hold him up and say, It's going to be all right; it's time to come home now. He heard Terrell's uneven breathing. The hand hovered and then retracted. The police had to pull him off the boy or else he would have killed him, and Preston was certain he would have. The thought made his guts tremble. Maybe I should just apologize, he thought. Apologize for what he almost wanted to do, apologize for wanting to do it. His fists clenched. Lawrence! Gone. And here lay a boy who lied about the death of his brother. Lied to his mother. Lied to him. Lied to the police, the town, the world. Let people grow angry, let people protest. Where had that come from? Watching his mother agonize with only a care for his own skin. What was in this boy?

"Preston, do y'all want coffee? I made . . ."

He rushed past Lynn without saying a word. He was outside so quickly it had not registered that he had left the room or run down the stairs. He whipped his car into the middle of the street and gunned it down the block. After several blocks, he slowed down, looking around to get his bearings. He knew he'd better get home quickly; he hadn't told Judith he would be out.

nineteen

TAMARA GROVES PUT the Kotex box on the sink where Bread would see it and hopefully leave her alone. She called it her "scarecrow," and it had worked before.

She peeked from the bedroom. Though it was well past midnight, Bread was not alone. Three members of his goon squad followed him through the door. Tamara closed the bedroom door and leaned against it, pressing an ear to the wood. Bread said, "Sit him" or maybe "Sit them there." She heard voices but could not make out the words, which she found ironic because usually she could hear everything that went on downstairs in the Dorsey's apartment, and they could hear every bounce and bump in Tamara and Bread's bed. The first week after they moved in, Mrs. Dorsey had used a broom handle or something to knock on her ceiling while Tamara and Bread were making love. Bread had become enraged. He jumped from the bed and pulled on his pajama bottoms, then stomped down the stairs. Tamara tried calling him back. From the bedroom, she heard and felt the thumping as Bread tried to pound his way into the ground-floor apartment. Even after the police left, Bread would fall to his knees and shout to the floor at the top of his lungs, "Call the pigs again and see. Just call and see," and he would hold a finger warningly to Tamara if she tried to say anything.

Tonight Bread and his goons must have been whispering for her not to hear them, which, of course, meant they were up to no good, because these were not considerate boys, concerned with not waking her or the neighbors.

Deciding she really did not want to know any more of Bread's secrets, she turned away from the door and let herself drop to the bed. Only the bathroom light was on so that the bedroom was half dark. It had been hot all day, and it was still. Tamara had showered, but already she lay above the scrambled sheets feeling sticky.

She heard Mrs. Dorsey's television, which sometimes stayed on all night. And she heard boards creaking under the feet of Bread and his boys in the outer room. She heard a rush of incomprehensible words from Bread, followed by grunted replies. Suddenly, the bedroom door flew open and bounced against the wall.

Tamara sat up.

"Sorry, Tam," Carl said. He had Angelo's arm around his neck and they were bulling their way to the bathroom, but only Carl's legs seemed to be working.

"Is he smashed?"

"Yeah."

"Don't worry about him. He's fine," Bread said from the front room.

Tamara buttoned two more buttons on her light pajama top that she wore with a pair of boxers.

They closed the bathroom door. Tamara heard water running in the sink. Angelo groaned, and Carl said, "Man, you stink."

A police car running its siren raced up Garvin Avenue. Tamara heard movement in the front room and, as the car sped by, nervous laughter.

Carl came out of the bathroom and glanced at Tamara but did

not meet her eyes. He never looked her in the eyes anymore, she realized.

Tamara lay in bed, listening. Bread and his boys were waiting for something. After a while, Tamara fell asleep.

She awoke to find Angelo standing over her. She did not know if Bread was still in the front room because it was quiet in there. Angelo was half lit by the light from the bathroom, and he was looking at her legs. He appeared wobbly.

"Tamara," he said. He pronounced her name differently than everyone else, "Tuh-MAR-uh."

Instinctively, she wanted to try to cover herself with her arms but did not. She did not want him to know he made her that uncomfortable. "You don't look good, Angelo," she said.

That fact did not seem to register with him. His eyes appeared red and small. He still used them, however, to look Tam up and down. He leaned a bit forward and almost lost his balance. Momentarily, his hands flailed in the dark space. He whispered, "Things almost got fucked up, Tamara." At first she wasn't sure if he wasn't talking about having just nearly fallen or something that happened with Bread earlier, but he sounded scared, so something must have gone wrong earlier. "Almost fucked bad . . ."

"Is that you, Angelo? Come on out here, jackass."

Angelo whispered again, "Oh, now I'm the jackass because he done decided to blame me. That makes me the jackass." He put a finger to his lips as if swearing Tamara to secrecy and then he limped out of the room.

The apartment began to smell of smoke, so Tamara opened the bedroom window, but there was no breeze. She began to dream of the other Tamara Groves, the one whose mother had successfully resisted temptation and did not cheat on Tamara's daddy. In that world, the family stayed together and no one got cancer. In that world, Tam raced her father's pickup to the driveway of the house, and he leaped from the cab of the truck, arms wide, and scooped her up.

But people cheat. She knew Bread cheated. And she had cheated on Bread, twice, with Lawrence Matheus, the first time, a totally out-of-the-blue compulsion while stuck in the middle of a cornfield, and the second, over his uncle's in the middle of the day, when no one else was there. So she had cheated even after she saw what it had done to her father. But she was not in love with Bread. And Bread was not in love with her, at least, not in that romantic Peaches & Herb way.

Judith Matheus had apologized before saying, "I just have to ask, were you two in love?"

Tamara knew that was all the woman really wanted to know and all the other discussions had led up to being comfortable enough to ask. Tamara had promised herself not to lie—there'd been enough lying about Lawrence already. But her mind flashed back to that after-noon at Cap's house, when Lawrence pulled the sheet over both their heads and they snuggled in the diffused afternoon light. Thinking about that moment, Tamara met Judith's desperate eyes and surprised herself when she said, "Yes, we were."

Yesterday and today, she had gone job hunting and had two solid maybes. She gave the potential employers Cap Porter's phone number so that no calls would come to the apartment. She counted on Terry or Lynn to somehow get the word to her if she got one of the jobs or if someone wanted a follow-up interview. She wanted to know for sure she had a job before she told Bread. Either job was a bus ride away, which meant getting up early. The first thing she would do with her money would be to buy a car.

She heard the front door open. They were talking on the front landing. Bread was whispering and then he said in a normal voice,

". . . everybody get some sleep. 'Cept Angelo, maybe you should stay awake." They laughed. Heavy footfalls descended the stairs. Tamara jumped to the bed, placed her legs beneath the sheet, and feigned sleep.

Bread came in heavily. "Long night," he said. He stood over the bed for what seemed like a long while.

Tamara made a few sleeping sounds, even turned a bit, but did not open her eyes.

He went into the bathroom. She peeked in his direction but then resumed her possum sleeping.

"Tam? Tam?" She heard him breathe loudly. He let his weight drop onto the bed. "It's late, but I'm keyed up. I'm real keyed up."

She knew it was stupid to try to pretend sleep through all of that. "Hmm?" she said, and yawned.

"I'm keyed up," he whispered. She felt a tickling at her ear and felt his warm breath on the side of her face.

"Bread, I'm trying to sleep," she said.

A wet tongue outlined her earlobe while a hand was pulling down her boxers. She jerked away from the tongue and grabbed the hand. "Stop it."

"What's wrong with a midnight raid?"

"Let go," she said. But he would not relinquish his hold on her boxers. "It will be better in the morning. Let me get some sleep."

"Naw, I need it now."

She was surprised to see he was already naked. "Listen to you, 'I need it now.' What went on out there anyway? Why were the guys over? What happened to Angelo?"

"What you want to know what it was all about now for? The whole time we was out there you never peeked in to say shit or to see if we needed anything or nothin'. Now what? You'd like a report? Woman, please. You been hanging around too many high school boys." He tugged at the boxers. He could fend off both her hands with just one of his. She was lifted and the boxers were gone.

She slapped him hard across the face, letting her nails rake him.

He looked momentarily stunned. "Damn," he said as he touched his left cheek.

She tried to scramble out of the bed, but he had her by an arm and an ankle and pulled her back in and under him. He hit her with open hands and would not let her turn away from the blows. She pleaded for him to stop, but he was laughing. "I'll take it rough," he said.

It was almost an accident. Her wildly kicking legs were trying to dislodge him when the ball of her foot connected with his swinging package, and the midnight raid was abruptly over.

Bread grabbed himself and crawled away. Tamara jumped to the floor. She dived partly under the bed and fished frantically around the bed slats until her fingers found Bread's backup gun. She squirmed out just as he was about to make a grab at her, and his nose was suddenly inches from the gun's barrel. "Yeah, I've always known where you kept it. So get back."

He sat back on the edge of the bed and began inspecting his groin as if she were not in the room.

Tamara was breathing so quickly that she was afraid she would pass out.

"You almost maimed me."

"You almost raped me."

"I didn't almost rape you. You ain't a stranger."

"What!" Bread's twisted reasoning infuriated Tamara, and she thought she should shoot him for that alone. Instead, she said, "Get dressed and get out of here. Go spend the rest of the night with one of your jackasses. Especially the one that looked me up and down."

"Angelo looked you up and down?"

"Get out . . ."

"Ah! Ah! You crushed it," he said still holding himself.

"Get your clothes on and get out of here."

"I ain't gettin' thrown out my own place." He drew his legs up and lay down in a fetal position, facing her.

Tamara switched the gun to her left hand. Her right elbow had been locked and so tense that it began to throb with pain. She stayed on the floor with just the pajama top on.

"Oh, man. Tam, you did a number on me."

Bread was trying to be disarming through humor, a new tack for him and one he wasn't particularly good at. She knew if she did not stay wary he would be off that bed and on her in a second.

"I can't believe you," he was saying.

"Don't you believe I'll shoot you if you don't go?"

"No, I don't believe that." He gasped, apparently in some pain. "That gun don't do you as much good as it would me or Angelo. The hand is as important as the gun. My hands take less provocation than yours. My hands are more part of the gun; they don't know better. Angelo's, hell, they ready to squeeze off at a moments notice, just like tonight. But you. That gun is a foreigner. Different texture. Alien. You actually have to think before you could squeeze one off. If I try to jump you, you might, just might, shoot. But any other reason? Naw, you won't shoot for no other reason. I'm safe."

"I hate you for what you tried to do tonight."

He waved a hand.

"What's that mean?"

"Means you're full of shit, Miss Groves. I've done the same thing before, a bunch of times, and we had fun and laughed about it. The difference now is your attitude."

"Bullshit," Tamara said, growing hot again. She put the gun back in her right hand. "The difference is when I said no before, you respected it. This time you kept going. The difference is your attitude, Mr. Williams."

He did not reply and in the darkness she could not make out the expression on his face. She didn't know if he would continue to try to hurt her. She just did not know. And that meant everything. Tears rolled down her cheeks.

She brought the gun into her lap. There had been a few other times, not many, when she had been tempted to grab the gun, but she was glad she had waited for this time. A gun much like this had killed Lawrence when no hand had intended for Lawrence to be dead. The stupidest thing she had ever heard a person say was that guns did not kill people, people killed people. That was like saying jetliners don't fly people to Europe, people fly people to Europe. Okay, but the planes make a tough job real easy. A gun had killed Lawrence.

She did not want to think of that boy at this moment. It would be dangerous to think of anything other than the large, dark shape sleeping—or not sleeping—at the end of the bed. She wanted morning to come. She was afraid to move before there was daylight.

"I used to feel so safe with you," she said. "You were larger than life. You were independent. You didn't have any knuckleheads working for you then. You were Bread. Why were you called Bread, I asked you. The first day over—"

"Selma's house. You and some other girl were sleeping on the floors at Selma's."

"Yeah. You said, 'Because Bread is the word that puts money in perspective. It's sustenance.'"

"It's sustenance."

"I said, 'Man don't live by bread alone . . .'"

"And I said, 'But he sure ain't goin' far without it.'"

"You were braver back then . . ."

"People weren't kickin' my nuts up my . . . back then."

"No. I mean it. Now you got these jerks watching every which way for you."

The shape at the end of the bed said, "That's not fear. That's complications. I have more enemies now. I'm making money; people want that money. You can't watch your own back. It's a physical impossibility. Unless you're a fly or something."

She repeated more for herself than for Bread, "You were braver then."

"Maybe so," he said.

"I thought you and I were going to make it. The world had abandoned both of us, you know. My dad . . . both our moms had passed . . . you put the past where it belonged for me. Or so I thought. We had a plan for the future. We were going to be somebodies."

"Be somebody? What does that mean? You forget where you came from." He sat up momentarily, then perhaps didn't have the energy and fell back on the bed. "You were a hungry girl from the hills of Kentucky. Nothing more. Just hungry itself, walking like a person. To be somebody means to be somebody who eats every day." Tamara could tell he liked that turn of phrase. "How's that? You're somebody who eats every day and who knows where she is going to sleep every night."

The floor was hard, and her butt was getting sore, but it reminded her of sleeping on Selma's floor with the rest of the strays that woman used to take in. Tamara once asked her if she were afraid one of the girls would rob her. She had said she makes it a point never to own so much that the idea of being robbed could hold her hostage. Bread used to come over, never empty handed, with groceries or cake or chicken for frying. "Bread is sustenance." The other girls liked him too, of course. How was Tamara to know at the time that his dream was this small?

She recalled the conversation she had with Bread back then that had brought them together. She had told him she had run away from a foster home.

"Do you think they still look for me?"

"No. They ain't."

"How can you be sure? They lose a kid . . ."

"And they save money. Naw, you ain't gotta worry about them lookin'. I'll tell you who might be lookin'. Your daddy."

Tamara had scowled at Bread.

"No, I'm not kidding. When you went missing, they probably made an effort to get a hold of him. He's lookin', I'd bet."

Tam just shook her head. After Mom died, Dad did not take her from the foster home. She had thought she would be there temporarily, but he had left her there.

"You could contact the authorities in Kentucky. Tell them where you are and they will point him in the right direction." Bread put an arm around her. That had surprised her because it was such a sweet gesture.

She never made that call. The notion that her father may be looking for her was like a sliver of sunshine, a small, warm notion Bread had placed in her mind that she could play with forever. She did not want to call and find out it was not true.

Bread turned her face toward his. "We'll get a place," he said. He kissed her. "He'll find you there."

Tamara awoke with a start, thinking Bread was kissing her. She looked around. He was gone. The gun was still in her lap. The first feeble light of morning was coming in the window. Water ran in the bathtub. She did not think she had dozed long or he would have taken the gun from her. He was, no doubt, in the bathroom now, taking inventory of his parts for the thousandth time. Well, she had proven one thing to herself—she could still sleep on the floor.

twenty

THE BIKE'S KICK-START snapped back and spanked Terry's calf. Terry jumped off the motorcycle and eyed it. "Who's in charge here?" he asked the machine. Tamara and Lynn were watching. The motorcycle gleamed in the morning sun. Even the black vinyl seat glistened.

He had discovered the bike's owner's manual in a compartment under the seat and had followed the instructions carefully, charging the battery, cleaning out the cylinders, and tightening the chain. When that was done, he had cleaned everything on the bike with meticulous care.

A few days prior, Cap had caught Terry with the motorcycle. It was in the early evening; Terry was losing his light anyway and should have already rolled the bike back into the garage.

He worked on it around the back of the house, where his uncle never went, but there Cap stood looking down at Terry, who had the rear brake drum open and was dusting it out. Cap said, "I almost forgot about my old buddy." Immediately, Terry could tell Cap had been drinking.

Terry had a proposal for his uncle: in exchange for getting the bike back in shape, Terry would be allowed to ride it while he lived with

Cap. Also, he would remind his uncle, he needed the bike to get to his community service jobs.

Before Terry could get his proposal out, Cap said, "Don't know what you think you're doing. Glad you reminded me about my old bike, though. I'm gonna sell it. Yeah, that's what I'm going to do. Could use the bread right about now, yeah." Then he left. Terrell heard the side door open and shut.

His first reaction was to fling the disassembled parts all over the backyard. Let Cap have an Easter egg hunt if he wanted to sell the motorcycle, he thought. But instead of throwing the part in his hand, Terry took a cloth and worked the accumulated dust from it.

Today, Tamara and Lynn were watching as he tried to get the bike started.

"Who wants to go on the first ride with me?" he asked, anxious to put up a brave front, especially in front of Tamara.

She looked beautiful in a white linen dress. Only the bruises around her lips and nose marred her looks. He had not asked her about them yet.

Neither woman responded to his question, so he asked again.

Tamara took one step forward, but Lynn pulled her back. "We'll let him take a shake-out cruise or two before we join him on that thing," she said.

He mounted the bike again and checked the switches. The neutral light shone; the kill switch was on "run." His right foot went to the kick-start and he kicked it around for what seemed like the one-thousandth time. The bike would bark and chuff at him and then fall silent.

"C'mon. Gas, oil, lubed chain, charged battery. What do you want now?" Terry was embarrassed that the bike wouldn't start. He hoped he had not done all that work for nothing. But he still had confidence.

The bike looked good, like it wanted to go, grateful for being rescued from the garage and the dust.

Terry heard Lynn whisper to Tamara, "I'm kind of relieved."

Just then, Cap stumbled from the house, and Lynn's smile vanished. Cap shielded his eyes even though there was little sun.

He said, "Terry, you gonna have to drop the clutch."

"Huh?"

"Get started by letting it roll down a hill and popping the clutch."

"Huh?"

"Squeeze in the clutch. Roll down the driveway in first gear, and when you get a bit of speed just let that clutch out and the engine will take."

"Thanks, Cappy," Lynn said with a brave smile.

Now Terry wished he didn't have an audience. He sat not moving for a while.

"Need a push?" Tamara asked.

The driveway suddenly looked steeper than it had before, and he realized he would have to make a ninety-degree turn immediately in order to avoid running into the cars parked across the street. "Um, no, the driveway seems steep enough, I suppose."

He squeezed in the clutch and immediately the bike began to roll. As it picked up momentum, the street rushed up to him. "Oh, hell," he said to himself, as he let the clutch out. The bike roared into life. Terry executed a wobbly turn before being carried away down the street. It occurred to him as he was being swept away that he should have asked Cap about braking while he had the chance.

HE RAN EVERY stop sign he came to, afraid the engine might stall and he'd be unable to get it started again.

After an hour of driving, almost running into parked cars and nearly colliding with cross traffic, he began to get the hang of the motorcycle. He braked too hard once and nearly went over the front of the bike. It was then he remembered to always apply the rear brake before the front brake. "Okay, you can do this," he said, a grin affixing itself to his face.

He had enough false confidence after one hour to go back to the house to offer Tamara a ride in earnest, although he figured there was no chance she was still there. So he was surprised to see her sitting on the front stairs, talking to Lynn.

"We were sure you crashed into a tree somewhere!" Lynn shouted.

Cap's big Harley was gone from the driveway.

Terry felt an unexpected weariness in his arms. "Want to go for a ride now?" he asked Tamara.

"Lynn, do pilots fly passengers after their first—and only, I might add—solo flight?"

"I'd bet they don't," Lynn said. "We could call TWA, but I'm betting . . ."

"So, I'm with Lynn," Tamara said, They laughed. "Go practice!"
And he did.

He couldn't identify all the scents, but he detected pine and cow pasture, and wet earth, and something oily under the light wind. And he thought he could smell the river itself, though sometimes the road led away from it. There was a wild, verdant backdrop that grew or diminished with the curves of the road.

He found he no longer needed to keep a death grip on the handlebars and could move through the gears with little thought.

He dropped to fourth gear and the little motorcycle in its effortlessness seemed to vanish, leaving him gliding just above the live pavement, following wind currents. No experience he'd had was anything like this. He was as much a part of the air as a bird or a cloud. He did not think about the curves in the road; maybe there was something called tire memory. He leaned one way, pressing down on the handlebar in the direction he wanted to go, and the bike behaved as if it knew the road, or read Terry's mind. Leaning to one side and then the other, he and the bike flowed through the curves as liquid as water through a river's bend.

Back off throttle, squeeze clutch, pop up to fifth, release clutch, more throttle. Gone. Now he was a part of the transparent, sharp wind.

THE BIG SURPRISE had been seeing her asleep on Cap's couch the morning after his first ride on the bike. She was curled up facing the back of the sofa, her shoulders and legs shining. Terry didn't hear Lynn come up from behind him.

"Quit staring," she whispered. "My word."

"I'm not staring," Terry said, not taking his eyes off of her.

Later, Tamara explained: "Bread knows every place I would go to spend the night. Everybody I know. I have to stay with people he doesn't know."

It was Cap's place, but lately Lynn paid the bills, and it was more up to her than Cap if Tamara could stay there. Lynn had no problem with it. Cap had only shrugged when asked if it was okay with him. He gave Tamara a look that Lynn noticed and frowned over. Terry did not think there was anything to the look except that of a man who no longer gave a damn what happened around him.

Terry offered Tamara his room, but she declined. That night she sat on the couch with her two grocery bags of clothes. Lynn and Cap were upstairs. It was very late. Tamara told Terry about her long night. "I should be sleepy," she said. "But . . ."

"Does it hurt?" Terry asked, indicating the bruises.

She waved a dismissive hand. "No," she said. "He can't hurt me."

"You have the gun?"

"No, that's not what I mean. I left the gun in the apartment. When I asked Lynn if I could stay, she said, 'Fine, but no drugs or guns.' I said, 'That will be nice.'"

Terry was going to say something like he knew Lawrence would be glad she was out of there, but it sounded lame in his head and the truth was he did not have any idea if that would have made Lawrence happy.

She said, "Most of my clothes and shoes are still over there, damn it." Tears rolled down her cheeks. "Well, just don't sit there. Help me make up this couch."

Terry went upstairs, thinking about the motorcycle, Tamara Groves, what Lawrence would think if he knew she had finally left Bread, and most of his sleepless night he spent thinking of his parents and of Cap. Everyone's life seemed to be in a jumble, and it was all his fault. He wondered if he should go by the house the next day and see how his mother was doing. Just say hi, he thought; he wondered if that would be okay. He wondered if he could do it, just say hi.

He had logged mile after mile in the days that followed, taking Tam to her new job, going to the rescue mission, and just riding every free chance he got. If Cap was going to sell the bike, Terry was determined to get as much use out of it as he could until then. And, because Cap was going to sell the bike, Terry never worried about the annoying fact that he was in no way legal. The bike had an expired license plate, no state inspection sticker; he had no insurance, nor did he have a motorcycle operator's endorsement on his driver's license; and, of course, the bike wasn't his, and technically, he had never gotten permission to ride it.

Tamara bought his gas and he took her to her new job.

One day while she was at her job, Terry scooped up her few belongings and took them up to the room he slept in. He stuffed his clothes back in his suitcase and placed her clothes in the chest of drawers. He remembered to switch the sheets too.

When she came home and saw what he had done, she told him she was perfectly happy on the couch but then thanked him with a hug.

AFTER FINISHING HIS work at the rescue mission, he still had a couple of hours before he had to pick up Tamara, so he went to several restaurants and filled out job applications. He wished he could put down a fake name just in case they might recognize him from the papers. He was all but certain that one woman did recognize him, it was the way she looked at him longer than people usually did. He would have bet she balled up his application and tossed it away as soon as he left.

He did not want to find a job that was so far away that he could not get there by bicycle once Cap sold the motorcycle, which severely limited his choices. Still he put in the applications and did not meet the gaze of the people he spoke with. He told them he was in school and would not be available in the mornings or on Tuesdays.

When he got back to Cap's he told Lynn he had been job hunting and she said, "Well, at least someone has." Then she broke down suddenly, crying. "I don't know what he thinks these days," she said in a high shriek. "You see it right? I don't know what I did to deserve any of this."

Terry could not get out of her exactly what had happened. Cap, he was able to gather, had called her a bad name, which she would not repeat, cussed her, and stormed out. Lynn cried and Terry patted her on the back. He had grown to really like her and felt her current troubles with Cap were his fault. The fact that he was here, the fact that Cap lost his job, the fact that Cap was ashamed and embarrassed about that vigilante night—all that stemmed from what Terry had done.

Lynn was the breadwinner in this dysfunctional household and it would not stay together without her. "This is my fault, Lynn," he said, but he said it so softly she did not hear over her own sniffling. He sat with her on the couch for a while, neither speaking.

She stood up suddenly. "Well . . ." she began, but let the rest of her thought go unspoken. She went upstairs to her room without looking back at Terry. It was almost as if she had forgotten he was there.

He left shortly after to pick up Tamara, bringing with him Cap Porter's tightly folded old army duffel bag, which he sat on. Tamara was waiting for him with Lynn's motorcycle helmet, in front of the print shop where she clerked and cleaned. "Sometimes the place smells liked baked bread. Other times it stinks," she had said.

He pulled up right in front of her. She rapped her fist on his helmet in greeting and then tugged on her own. After a moment, she tapped him on the shoulder and indicated the chin strap, which he had to cinch for her each time.

"When are you going to learn to do this for yourself?" he asked over the bike's engine.

She said, "Why should I?"

Only when he was this close to her could he see that her nostrils and upper lip had not completely healed from her fight with Bread.

"Did you bring it?" she asked.

They were on a mission today. He nodded and heard her say, "Good boy."

Even though she wore a skirt, Tamara managed to throw a leg over the bike and wrap her arms around his waist, giving Terry a guilty thrill.

They rode to the apartment she and Bread had shared, circling the block twice before pulling to the curb a block away, near the corner where they had a good view the house.

"Two cars," she said.

"I'm getting tired of sitting on this bag. It's going to make me slide off," Terry said. He pulled the folded duffel from beneath him and handed it back to her. "Do you think he changed the locks?"

"Heck, no." Their helmets clacked; she rested her chin on his shoulder.

Her easy familiarity thrilled him and, at the same time, weighed him with guilt.

"That's Bread's car and Angelo's car. They won't hang around long. He can't make any money sitting around."

Terry killed the engine.

"You know what he's like," she said as if he had asked a question. She spoke into his left ear. "You ever been around a kid in school who plays that game where they try to make you flinch by pretending they're going to hit you. You know." she reached around Terry and made a motion with her fist. "They jab at you to make you jump?"

"Yeah," Terry said. "And then they yell psych or gotcha."

"Yeah. That's what living with him for the past six months or so has been like. He makes you flinch."

Terry thought of a few things to say in reply, but none of them felt very smart, so he just nodded. Her chin was still on his shoulder. He kept thinking, this is what Lawrence wanted so badly, for Tamara Groves to leave Bread Williams and to be with him, Lawrence. He wondered if she had asked Lawrence for help and that was why he had gotten the gun. Was it his brother's idea, or had she told him to get the gun? He wanted to ask, but he did not want to hear the answers.

"Will this carry a lot?" she asked, and he knew she referred to the duffel bag.

"Yeah. Just stuff it. It has shoulder straps and . . ."

"I see them."

They waited. It started to feel like a long while.

He felt her hands on his back. "He probably wouldn't try anything. I should just go up there and get my clothes. I need to wear something besides the same three things to work. Damn."

"Maybe he won't try anything, if I go up there with you."

"I should have packed everything and then hid it in the shed or in the bushes out back. He wouldn't have thought to look 'cause he would've thought I'd taken everything. God, all I had to do was call a goddamn cab!" She slapped him on the back of his helmet. "As if I had money for cabs."

"You had to move fast. You said you were afraid he might return and catch you leaving."

"I panicked."

"Unlike you, I think very clear headed where guns are involved." Surprised it had come out of his mouth, Terry twisted to see how his poor joke was received.

There was no hint of a smile on her face. She slapped at his helmet again, but suddenly her face brightened. "There they go."

A block away, Bread Williams and three other men came walking down the steep outside staircase. Terry had seen Bread once before in the high school parking lot picking up Tamara. He remembered a fierceness in his face and imagined he could see it even now from this distance. Bread had a cool car and clothes and reputation. And Tamara Groves had been a part of Bread's persona, just like the sunglasses and the goatee or the black-tinted glass of his Cadillac. So

Terry knew that when Lawrence began his attempt to catch the attention of Miss Groves, it must have seemed like an impossible task.

They watched now as one guy got in the first car and three got in Bread's Cadillac, with Bread climbing in the back. Terry started the motorcycle.

As soon as the cars turned a corner two blocks down, Terry brought the motorcycle up to the curb at the side of the apartment house.

"Stay here," Tamara said getting off the bike. "If they come back, which they won't, honk or something. Get this helmet off me. No, never mind. It'll be quicker if I just wear the damn thing." She ran up the stairs shaking out the duffel as she went.

He hoped she would not be long. He used the cuff of a shirtsleeve to wipe the tachometer and speedometer clean. He was fogging up a rearview mirror with his breath when he saw Bread's Cadillac charging right at him in the reflection. The other car followed and pulled in front of Terry at an angle, blocking him in.

"Oh, we should have got a cab," he said to himself and then remembered to honk the motorcycle's feeble horn. He expected to see the apartment door erupt open and Tamara to come racing down the stairs, but the apartment door did not open. He pressed the button again and again as the men climbed coolly from their cars.

"Don't let this punk go anywhere," Bread said, and he looked up at the apartment. The others were grinning. "This is my place," he said to Terry. "Did you come to see me?"

Three of the men surrounded the bike. One of them, tall with a narrow face and small mouth, put his hand on the handlebar.

Terry twisted the handlebars back and forth, but the man held on. "Hey," he said.

"I'll be back," Bread said, and started up the stairs.

Terry leaned on the bike's horn, and finally the door opened, and Tamara leaned out.

Bread was halfway up the staircase by then.

Tamara and Terry's eyes met.

The narrow-faced guy twisted Terry's hand away from the horn.

Tamara said to Bread, "Don't start nothin'."

Bread continued climbing the stairs, a grin on his face that Terry could see from his spot at the curb.

Tam pulled a half-filled duffel bag from behind her. "I just came back for my things," she said.

One of the guys behind Terry said in a low voice, "Can I take a ride on your motorcycle? I want to check it out. Carl, you ever ride one of these here?"

The man on Terry's left shook his head. His attention was more on what was happening on the staircase.

"Hop off and let me have a ride," the big guy at Terry's side said, stepping so close that his legs pressed against Terry's right leg. "Brother, I'm asking you for a ride. What do you say?"

"Leave us alone," Terry said, and immediately felt stupid saying it as the men around him laughed.

Tamara cinched the duffel and dropped it from the top landing. It fell with a thud and everyone looked up then.

Bread was only six steps from her. "Good thing you have a crash helmet on. Get inside," he ordered. "Go on."

Though she did not say it loudly, Terry heard Tamara's firm "No."

Bread did not advance farther.

The guy with the narrow face said, "I know who this punk is." And then louder to Bread, "Bread, I know who this punk is."

Bread continued to stare at Tamara.

"This is the brother of that guy. This punk is the brother of the other punk. He shot him."

Now Bread looked in their direction. "What the . . ." He pointed at Tamara as if to say, stay right there and he came down the stairs.

"You sure, Angelo?"

"Yeah, he capped his own brother," narrow-faced Angelo said.

"Why ain't he in Joliet or someplace? Alcatraz?" asked the one who wanted to ride the motorcycle. He was the biggest of the men and very dark complexioned.

Bread picked up Tamara's duffel and dragged it behind him. Above them, Tamara seemed frozen in the doorway, and Terry wondered why she didn't come down. He wanted her to come down from there and make a run for it. Maybe she could run to a neighbor and borrow a phone. But she just stood up there.

"Lawrence Matheus's brother," Bread said.

Tamara ran into the apartment.

"It ain't up there," Bread called up to her. "I'm not stupid." He looked at Terry as if examining him. "She's looking for my gun again. So here's the killer. Here he is. Here he is."

"What you messin' around with Tamara for? That's a bit too much woman for you, ain't she?" Angelo said.

"Shut up, Angelo," Bread said, still looking at Terry.

Terry grinned and regretted it instantly. Angelo slapped Terry on his lips so quickly Terry had hardly seen the hand.

The other two laughed.

"Carl, go up . . . no, not you, Carl," Bread said. "Angelo, go up there and make sure she stays up there. Don't hurt her."

Angelo pointed a finger in Terry's face. "You and me, when I come back," he said, and raced up the stairs.

Terry hoped Tamara had locked the door and barricaded herself in, but Angelo easily opened the door and disappeared inside, closing it behind him.

"Carl, have I ever messed in this boy's shit? Have I, to your recollection, messed with this dude?"

Carl shook his head. "Naw, man. Nothing."

Terry began, "I ain't—"

"Shut it," Bread said. "Yeah, you messin' in my shit. You here, ain't you? I live here."

"I'm just helping a friend."

The dark guy who wanted to ride the motorcycle said, "He's just being helpful," and laughed again. He straddled the front wheel of the motorcycle so that the headlight was at his midsection.

"Where she been all this time?" Bread asked. "With you?"

Terry said, "No."

"'Course can't believe anything you say, can we?"

Terry heard shouts from upstairs. He tried to think of what to do, but his mind just fluttered, unable to focus. Bread kept talking, but Terry listened only for Tamara's voice. The apartment door opened six inches, then slammed shut again.

"I'd better get up there before somebody is beat to hell. And you know we won't get no work out of Angelo if he's all bruised up." Bread and his friends laughed. Bread leaned toward Terry and said low, "Why did you do it?"

"It was an accident," Terry said, hearing his voice shake.

"Accident! Accident!" Bread laughed and the others laughed too, but they didn't look so sure as to what was funny. "Wasn't no goddamn accident, butt punk. 'Three white boys shot him.' Does that sound like an accident to you?

"You know what I hate about you, punk? Tamara's gotta watch who she hangs with. It's niggers like you that ain't done squat that makes it hard on black people. Oh, not on hustlers like us here. But on the rest of us. You've made it harder for next time. For anybody who's looking for some real justice. You put that doubt in people. They'll think for a second, Is this just another sham? Those lying niggers; you can't trust them. Remember the one who shot his own brother and blamed it on white men? Yeah, that's what they do, you know, just make up shit. You've given the police an excuse to drag their asses next time, to doubt, to be suspicious, to just ignore us. That's your contribution to the cause of equal treatment for your people, weasel."

He turned to the others. "Let him go." He waved a dismissive hand at Terry. "You get," he said. "Start your bike. Start it."

Terry pushed the starter button; the bike roared to life.

Dark guy jumped to the side as if the bike gave off an electric shock.

Bread said, "Now get your sorry ass down the road, and I do not want to see you with Tamara ever again. Do I? Do I?"

Terry shook his head.

Bread and his background singers turned their backs on him and headed toward the stairs. Bread had forgotten about the duffel bag. It lay on the sidewalk.

Terry watched as the three men climbed the stairs. He felt the bike vibrating through him and realized he was squeezing the throttle. He stepped on the gear shifter. Maybe he should go, and come back with Cap, he thought. And maybe his dad as well. He knew his mother would want to see that Tamara was all right. Or maybe he should just call the police, he decided. But then the face of Bill Carson loomed in his mind, and he told himself he'd better hurry and get whatever help he could find. Assuming, of course, Tamara really needed help. Bread was, after all, her boyfriend. She had chosen him over Lawrence. Let her have what she chose, Terry thought. He felt his chest tighten with his decision. He turned the key, killing the engine, but left it in the ignition. He dismounted quickly and ran after the three men, sprinting up the staircase to just a few steps below them.

"What the f—"

"I have to talk to Tamara first," Terry said.

"Carl," Bread said.

Carl's arm shot out, but Terry ducked and fell against the right side railing. He took two steps up, trying to slip under Carl's reach on all fours.

Bread kicked at Terry, connecting with his upper arm.

The other guy pushed Terry down and his helmet bounced on a step, making him glad he hadn't taken it off. Carl had grabbed Terry and was trying to push him down the stairs, but Terry had the rail by one hand and dark guy's pants cuff in the other. One of them hit Terry hard on the back. Then Terry grabbed Carl's belt. They shoved and pushed him. The steps and railing creaked.

Bread looked as if he were going to join in, then thought better of it and dashed up the remaining steps.

Dark guy managed to pull Terry's hand loose from the railing and shoved him backward. Terry teetered, nearly a story above the ground. He reached out with nothing but the air in front of him yet managed to grasp Carl's arm. Carl yelled as they both went tumbling over each other down the stairs. The sky and the stairs rolled over each other until there was a jarring and abrupt end.

Carl groaned and held his left ankle with both hands.

Terry lay on the ground only a moment, trying to get his bearings. Then he heard Tamara yelling for him.

"Let's go, Terry," she said, bursting from the back door of the downstairs apartment. A woman and a little girl followed her out.

Terry clambered to his feet almost tripping over Carl.

Tamara thanked Mrs. Dorsey and her daughter as Terry jumped on the motorcycle.

Scooping up Cap's duffel bag, Tamara said to the woman, "I bet you'll be glad to see me go."

"Glad for you, honey," Mrs. Dorsey said.

Terry started the engine just as Bread exploded from his upstairs door. "Tam!" he called. "Tam!"

Terry felt Tamara's weight on the back of the bike. An arm encircled his waist.

"Go," she said to Terry. "Go."

twenty-one

"WHO IS HE and what is he to you?" Terry heard the low music in the upstairs hallway, the accusing voice of Bill Withers. He suddenly felt hesitant and tapped softly on the door instead of knocking. He waited, hearing only the music, then pushed the door enough to poke his head in Tamara's room.

"What do you want?" she asked, not looking his way.

Wearing a worn, thin T-shirt that gave little cover, she sat in an old upholstered chair she had turned toward the window. Morning sun reflected golden in her eyes and painted her face, neck, and arms. The sun etched highlights in her hair. She drew her knees up, putting her heels on the very edge of the seat. The bottom of her long T-shirt fell back showing her thighs. She made no move to cover herself.

Terry eased into the room.

She faced the window, but there was nothing to see outside except the gables and roofs of nearby houses and the limbs of trees. She touched a finger to her lips. She wore no lipstick, but her lips looked like they had been colored in copper. In that light, the tiny strands of delicate body hair caused her to glisten. He watched her chest rise with her slow, casual breaths.

"It's too early for Bill Withers," Terry said. "Maybe Earth, Wind & Fire?"

Abruptly, the light streamed in strongly, growing harsh. The sun must have cleared the tops of the trees. She blinked, then continued to stare out the window.

He knew she wanted to be alone, but Terry needed her. He had woken that morning with a choking feeling, as if his mind were awake but his body was not, and he could not draw breath until he could again master his own limbs and lungs. It was a scary feeling. He was in a silent fight, screaming and flailing about on the inside, while his body lay like stone. Finally, he found his way out and woke with a start, gasping.

He wondered if that was what paralyzed people felt like, trapped in unresponsive bodies while their minds were like rats on metal wheels, working furiously yet going nowhere.

Terry had lain there on the bumpy, uneven sofa whose cushions had separated like a fault line threatening to swallow him. He pulled in great gulps of air as he looked around in the darkness, taking inventory of Lynn's cheap ceramic statues that populated the shelves and tabletops. There was even a Chinese boy and tiger on the TV near the rabbit ears. In the semidarkness, he could see all the frozen gray figures stripped of their garish colors. He was not supposed to be here.

Nothing was as it was supposed to be, and he knew where the fault lay. This parallel dimension he had struggled to wake up in was of his own making and everything was off kilter. His parents living alone. Lawrence gone from the earth. Gone. Cap changing before his eyes. Lynn distressed and unable to do anything about it. Tamara Groves was not where she was supposed to be either. His hands shook. It was too early to do anything, so he waited and waited for the light to reach the Chinese boy and his tiger so that he could go upstairs to talk to Tamara Groves.

"Hey," he said softly. She wasn't looking his way. He wanted to tell her how hard it had been to awaken this morning. He wanted to tell her that the world she was looking at out that window was different than it was supposed to be. "You want to go for a ride?"

He heard her breathe out.

"Men," she said. "Men offer you a ride, then take you for a ride."

She looked at him then for his reaction, but Terry did not quite understand what she meant. She looked different in the full light, not as ethereal but still beautiful.

She said, "Sure, but later, okay?" and turned back to the window.

Terry thought maybe he could sit on the floor and wait. Maybe she would start to talk. "Do you want to go down and get something to eat? I'll scramble the eggs, you cook 'em?"

"Terry," she said.

And he slipped out of the room.

HE WAS MAKING up the couch, folding the sheets and blanket, when Lynn came down the stairs.

She looked at him and hovered nearby and he tried to ignore her, mostly because he was embarrassed to be in her house and sleeping on her couch.

"Terry, I want to ask you a question. Now a good time? Everyone else is still asleep." She sat down on the couch, moving the sheets out of her way and indicated with a pat on the cushion for Terry to sit too.

Terry's first thought was that she was going to ask him to leave or ask that Tamara leave. He didn't know why, but he was sure that was coming.

"Money is short for all of us, I know. If your uncle would just . . . just snap out of it . . . just . . . Everybody needs some cash and . . ."

Her face twisted and her lips tightened. Her froth of hair bobbed when she shook her head. "I had fifty dollars in my purse," she said quickly. "Please, did you see it? Did you need some money?"

"God! No, Lynn. I didn't take your money."

She put a palm up to stop him. She looked more hurt than Terry and that calmed him. "Okay, I believe you."

"No, you don't," he said. "No one believes me."

HE GOT DRESSED and splashed his face with water and went outside. He sat on his motorcycle, wondering where he might go and fantasizing of places he'd like to go, epic one-way trips across plains, under vast skies. He went back inside, found a little something to eat, and turned on the television. The *Phil Donohue Show* was on.

Cap came down. He had on a pair of jeans and his pajama top. He sat in the big chair without ever looking Terry's way. They both watched TV, not speaking. Terry's attention was on his uncle, who would nod off from time to time but would awaken and look determinedly at the tube. Terry thought this might be a good time to say something to him. Other then threatening to sell the motorcycle, and a tip on how to start it, Cap had said nothing to Terry during his entire stay. But now, Terry could not think of anything to say, not about the weather or sports or motorcycling, or even about the fact that yesterday was Terry's mother's birthday, and no one had done a damn thing about it. He thought he might tell Cap it wasn't supposed to be this way and that he was sorry. Sorry was the only word he could think to actually say. And it seemed much too large a word for a first conversation.

Terry finally jumped up from the couch and went back outside.

He had walked to the corner of the block but saw people coming out of their houses, and so he pivoted about and headed back.

Tamara sat on the front stairs in a yellow dress printed with small flowers, wearing sandals, and holding Lynn's motorcycle helmet.

He felt a flush of awkwardness, as if he didn't already know her. She looked pretty, but he wondered why she wore a dress and sandals if she knew they were going motorcycling.

"I believe I was promised a ride," she said.

Terry felt a wash of relief. "You're wearing a dress," he said.

"It'll be okay."

She smelled good too. They went up the driveway past Cap's Harley to the little Honda.

"I can sit on it like this," she said, pulling the skirt between her legs. More of her legs, well above the knees, was exposed. "I told Lynn we should put some flower decals on her helmet."

"Flower decals?"

"Sure. Flower power. Dig?"

"That is such a bad idea. Let's go."

Terry got on first and kick-started the engine. He gave more twist to the throttle than was necessary and Tamara seemed appropriately impressed with the motorcycle's growl.

Tamara put her helmet on and stepped up to him. She tilted her chin up so he could cinch the chin strap. Their faces hovered close together for a moment. He was aware of her breath on his face and couldn't help notice that she gazed directly at him.

She pulled the front of her skirt between her legs and straddled the bike. She was pressed against his back and her bare brown legs were right alongside him.

He brought the bike onto the road.

"Did you ever get a valid plate on this bike and insurance?" Tamara Groves asked.

Terry tapped his helmet. "Can't hear you," he said.

They rode to the old side of the town near the river where some of the streets were still cobblestone, which made for a bumpy ride.

Tamara would point at things and Terry would nod.

They rode out of town headed south on Highway 41, and crossed the huge bridge over the Ohio River, which poured wide and brown below them. "Whee hoo!" Terry heard at the back of his head.

In Kentucky, they stayed away from traffic, riding the black-topped, tree-shadowed back roads that led them between barns, flat stretches of crops, around and over hills, and through intersections that claimed to be towns.

In no time, Terry was lost, but he didn't let on to Tamara, and eventually he found his way to Highway 41.

After that, Terry headed back across the bridge and to town because he wanted to be on familiar pavement. They stopped at a little diner downtown called the Rocky Top.

"My hair is molded to the shape of a helmet," Tamara said, attempting to fluff her hair back to life.

They sat at the counter. The waitress took overly long to acknowledge them and take their order. After that, nothing happened. Others came in and were served and their orders were brought to them promptly. Terry and Tam looked at each other and got up at the same time.

"You should put up a sign so we'd know," Tam said to the girl behind the counter as she walked out.

They went to a McDonald's where they talked about returning to the Rocky Top one day with a reporter or maybe TV cameras.

"Do you want to go home?" Terry asked.

"I want to go back to the river," Tamara said.

They rode out to the west side of town around the looping curve of the Ohio that the city perched on, past Mead Johnson, where Cap used to work, and turned on Old Henderson Road, a thin spaghetti strip of a road that followed the river for miles. Terry zoomed along, passing cars on the two-way road and eliciting shrieks from Tamara, which just encouraged him. He leaned into turns and felt Tamara tighten her hold on his waist. Terry stole looks at the brown legs clamping him.

Tamara tapped him on the shoulder and pointed at the brief glimpses of river seen between the black trunks of trees. "Let's go down there!" she shouted over the wind.

Terry found a flat piece of bare shoulder along the river side of the road and rolled the bike onto it.

They left their helmets behind a tree and picked their way down a steep, rocky embankment through trees and overgrowth to a thin stretch of sand at the river's edge.

They wandered over the bank for a bit, enjoying the wide open, unencumbered view of the great brown river. No one else was anywhere about.

Tamara sat down in the crusty sand and used her heels to dig into it. She gazed over the wide, moving water while using her fingers to comb out her hair.

The river made a constant sound as it coursed by, carrying deadfall along with its sudsy white caps. Over the sound of the river, Terry could hear a barge-pushing river tug in the distance.

Suddenly, Tamara flung her arms out wide as if trying to embrace the entire river. "This river was here long before men ever saw it," she said. "It's been running like this, well maybe a little less soapy, for centuries and centuries."

"Yeah, and?" Terry eased himself down close to her, though not too close.

"Well, doesn't it feel good to know that there are older and bigger things than us out here, that they go on forever?"

Terry shrugged.

"It's called perspective, Terry. Our problems are fleeting really. We make them bigger and deeper by the perspective we look at them with. We just have to tune into the larger picture." She held her arms wide again but let them drop. Right then she seemed to lose enthusiasm for what she had just said.

Terry had never ridden the bike for so long at one stretch, and he could still feel the vibration of it in his hands. He began to think his dreams of leaving were really possible.

The friends sat without speaking for a while, content to listen to the sounds around them.

Terry's eyes went from the river to the smooth skin on Tam's outstretched legs. He wanted to touch her, but instead he rested a hand on his own leg, just a twitch away from hers.

Tamara, in her dress of yellow and flowers, looked as if she were formed from sunshine.

He wanted to ask her questions. There were so many. But he worried she wouldn't like them, and he feared angering his only friend. Then the moment of their victory, their escape, came back to him, and he asked her how she had managed it. "I know you must have gone down the stairs, the inside stairs," he began as if they'd already been discussing it awhile, "but how did you get away from Angelo?"

"Angelo's an idiot," she said. "I tried leaving, but he blocked the front door. So finally I told him I was going to finish packing and leave when Bread came up. I'm going to pack my closet, I told him, but instead I unlocked the door to the staircase and ran down to Mrs.

Dorsey's door and tapped until they answered. Mrs. Dorsey asked me very loudly what I wanted and I whispered back that I needed a little help." She looked Terry in the face. "I was glad you were still out there, buddy."

"Bread is a smart guy?"

"Hmm. I guess. Why you ask?"

"Something he said to me." The beach was littered with driftwood. The bones of old trees, Terry thought. He picked up a small stick near him and began to draw in the sand between his knees. "He said I'd given white people an excuse not to believe the next black person that makes a claim . . ."

"Bread has gotten mean. He wasn't always that way. I could see him turning bad, like an apple, you can see the bruised part just growing. I don't want to stick around to see what he becomes. I think with me gone it is going to happen even faster. I sometimes talked him out of things."

"How did he get bruised?"

"How did we all get bruised?" She shrugged. "We make mistakes, or things don't go our way."

"Yeah."

Loud enough to make both of them turn their heads, a small flat-bed truck rattled to a stop on the shoulder of the road above them. It was an antique truck, a rusted, dry red color, and it shook from palsy. The truck sat for a minute or so, idling and trembling, skittish before the engine was cut.

The door opened with a squeal, and the oldest woman Terry had ever seen stepped out, holding on to the person that followed her. The old woman had high cheekbones and pure white spun hair. Though she looked shrunken, there was something dignified and noble about her. She was wearing a blue dress that showed her lumpy shape, and she had spindly, fragile legs, or so it seemed from the distance. She never relinquished her hold on the door, but she stepped to the side to let a young woman out.

Tamara whispered, "Look at her hair."

The young woman, maybe Tamara's age, scooted out of the truck. She had jet black hair that ran well below her waist. She wore a brown skirt and an embroidered leather vest that had tassels. The third person out was the driver, a man whose face was mostly obscured by a straw cowboy hat. He came around the truck and put an arm out for the ancient woman. The young woman was taller than both of them, and she had a bouquet of white flowers in her arms.

The women spoke. These were Mexicans, Terry thought, or maybe Indians. The young woman's hair reflected light as her head moved. She seemed quite attentive to the old woman, to whom she nodded as the woman talked. The ancient woman patted the young one on her upper arm then pulled herself back into the truck.

The girl climbed down the embankment, picking her way over the broken rocks and dead fall to the shore. It appeared to Terry that she did not know she was being watched, though Tamara and Terry sat in the open. In her hands the bouquet of white flowers bobbed as she went.

She stepped to the edge of the river, maybe even getting her feet wet. What she had come to do must have been some obligation, for she began it without ceremony and without words, no praying to the waters, no beseeching the sky. The only thing that marked it as ritual was that she tossed the flowers into the water one by one, letting each soft cup float away on the current before tossing in the next. When she finished, she turned around and did not look back. Some weight is off her, Terry thought, as she bounced back up the rocky bank moving lightly now, unburdened.

The truck started before she completed her climb up the embankment, and the truck door opened and she jumped in. Terry watched the truck disappear behind the line of trees before turning to Tamara.

"What was that?" he asked.

"You got me," Tamara said. "I think it was a girl thing. The flowers were from someone important to her, and maybe they weren't going to make it to the next vase of water and she couldn't bear to just toss them out the truck window."

There was more to it than that, Terry figured. He remembered how the Indian woman had turned her back on the river and sprang up the embankment. She had looked freed. No, he thought, it was a funeral or something near to it. It was the final part. The last of the good-bye. He thought about the funeral Tamara had wanted to have in Lawrence's room.

After a silence, Tamara said, "We ought to come back here with one of those little hibachi grills and some steaks. Bring Cap and Lynn . . ."

"Cap and Lynn."

"I know. Did you hear them the other night? Not as bad as Bread and me mind you, but . . . He's a bully."

"No. He wasn't always that way." Terry thought of the man who had sat like a lump watching TV that morning. "He used to be a lot of fun. He used to be this character. He was a boy like us, except he could have grown-up fun too. Lawrence and I loved him. 'Let's go to St. Louis and see the Cardinals,' he would say, or some such, just out of the blue. I changed all that."

"You?"

"Yeah, me. My story. No, my lie. I was just trying to make the whole thing easier." He stood, dusting sand from his jeans. "I didn't know what to do. Wish I could say I panicked, but I didn't. I just

didn't want people looking at me like I knew they would, you know?"
He looked down at Tamara. "I thought I could make it easier. I lied
to people who knew . . . knew I would never lie to them. Did you
know that changes people? It does. People who trusted me that much.
I didn't know how much people trusted me until I betrayed them."
Terry crossed his arms. Tears ran down his cheeks. He walked to the
edge of the narrow strip of sand. "I'm just trying to explain about Cap."
His breath came fast. "He wasn't always this way. Tam, I broke . . .
Cap . . . and my mom and dad . . . I broke their hearts."

He laced his fingers together on the top of his head.

"Hey, hey," she said. She was standing next to him and he felt an
arm about his shoulders.

His face was wet, and he wiped it with his hand then wiped the
hand on his pants. "God, I miss Lawrence," he said. "He's the only
one who could help me out of this."

"I miss him too."

Terry looked up. Her face was near.

"More than I thought I would," she said. "I think of what might
have been, you know. We were really just getting to know . . ."

"I thought you just led him on to get rides home. I told him to
leave you alone."

Tamara stepped away. "Yeah? I wish he had . . . listened to you."

"You should have left Bread Williams," Terry said, and he felt a
swell of old anger.

"You know what? I always thought you had something you wanted
to accuse me of. I did."

"He got the gun, that gun, because of you. He was scared of
Bread."

"Oh." Her eyes glistened.

"Yeah, 'oh.'"

"You're being mean. I never told him to go get a gun. I never asked him to . . . Screw you."

She turned to walk away, but Terry held her wrist. "Let go," she said, but did not fight his grasp. After a while she said, "I'm an orphan, Terry. It's not so easy to just pick up and leave when you have no home to return to. No uncle to take you in."

"I'm sorry, okay?" Terry said.

She freed her wrist. "You think we weren't close, but we were, Lawrence and I. We just needed some time. I just needed more time. Or maybe you aren't forgiving of people who make mistakes?"

"I said I'm sorry. I mean it."

"Did Lawrence ever tell you that he and I . . ." She smiled even though her eyes were watery. "Never mind, I can see that he must not have told you. Well, track star got me pregnant. Maybe. He borrowed Cap's key one afternoon. Maybe I got pregnant in the very room I sleep in now. Maybe." Now her tears flowed. "Do you get the significance of the word *maybe*? Yeah, it's trashy."

Terry tried putting his arm around her, but she pushed it away, grabbing the bottom of his T-shirt to wipe her face.

"Unless you have a handkerchief? I didn't think so." She moved to a dry spot and blotted her eyes.

"Did he know about it?"

The tugboat Terry had heard earlier was coming abreast of them. River water slapped at the shore like small ocean waves. The tug pushed four barges each carrying a hill of black coal. Terry could see crewmen moving about the boat.

Tamara had paused a moment to watch them.

He watched her profile. She beamed a smile at the boat crew and waved.

Two crewman waved back.

One could believe she was using Lawrence in order to get away from Bread. That she told him he would need a gun. That maybe she supplied the gun or told him where to get it. Terry chose to believe none of this.

She said, "You're the only one who knows or ever knew."

The boat headed around the river's bend, showing its stern and the frothy water behind it.

"Your 'story' affected me too, you know. When I read what you said happened in the newspaper, my first reaction was Bread had something to do with it. Really. I thought, Oh my God. Bread found out about me and Lawrence. Then I started having second thoughts, but still I realized I couldn't be with someone who I thought was capable of such a thing. I began to free myself right then. And finally did with your help."

Terry thought, No, Bread didn't shoot anyone. That was me.

"We'd better head back," Tamara said.

SHE PUSHED HER helmet down on her head and stepped up to Terry, lifting her chin.

"You're not ever going to learn how to do this for yourself, are you?"

"Why should I when I have you," she said.

On the motorcycle, before starting it, Terry turned and asked, "You loved him?"

Tamara Groves said, "Your mom asked me the same thing. Yeah, I did."

On the return trip, Terry nimbly swerved to avoid what he first thought in the growing twilight was a large stone in the road, but as he zipped past he saw that it was a turtle crossing the road. In his rearview mirror he saw a car behind him straddle the turtle, nearly crushing it. He eased the bike to the road's shoulder and flipped the kickstand down.

"What?" Tamara asked.

One second, he signaled with a finger, ran down the road to the turtle, and picked it up from behind. It made a soft cry, which surprised Terry because he hadn't known turtles made noises. Then it peed on him. "Damn," Terry said, holding the animal farther away. He heard Tamara's laughter. He carried the creature to the side of the road it was heading toward and set it within the tree line.

"That was gallant of you," Tamara said.

"You use me for Kleenex; he used me for Charmin," Terry said.

twenty-two

LYNN SAT NEXT to a stack of suitcases in the middle of the kitchen floor. She and the suitcases looked posed: black woman and mid-twentieth-century luggage. Her usual froth of hair was tamed under a colorful scarf.

When Tamara and Terry stepped through the side kitchen door, Lynn's shoulders visibly slumped.

Her eyes were red. "Oh, it's you two," she said. "Is Cap with you? Did you ride around with him? He left just about the same time you did. I thought maybe he caught up with you."

"No, Lynn, we haven't seen him."

Lynn stood and kicked at her suitcases.

Terry asked, "What's going on?"

"I'm leaving him. But you can't leave someone unless they're here to leave."

Tamara said, "In my experience, brief but intense, it's much better to leave while the man is away. But, Lynn, don't go. I don't think you want to."

Lynn look confused. "I'd pour myself a drink, but there's never anything in the house anymore."

"Don't look at me," Terry said. "I don't drink."

"Cap took my money," she said to Terry.

Terry knew this was all his fault; now his lie was hurting Lynn too. "I'm getting a job soon, maybe," he said. "There'll be more money coming in."

"Is it me, Lynn?" Tamara asked. "I'm in the way. Maybe you guys could work things out if the guest would move on."

Lynn waved Tamara's suggestion away. "It's been coming way before you, sweetie. And," she added to Terry, "you don't get the credit either so don't try."

She was being nice, Terry thought. They both knew it had everything to do with him.

Terry took some ice water from the fridge and poured himself a glass.

Tamara took it from him and began drinking. "Yes, please. Thanks for asking. You're such a gentleman."

"It's late—where have you two been?"

Terry went for another glass.

He was reaching in the cabinet but still managed out of the corner of his eye to see Lynn point to him and then to Tam and mouth, "Are you two . . . ?"

Tamara shook her head so vigorously, it hurt Terry, not that he had thought there would be anything there. But she did not have to be so adamant.

"Hey, you guys are wet!"

"Rain stings," Tamara said. "Doesn't it, Terry? We almost beat it." She sounded momentarily giddy. "But it got us right at the end. It felt like needles. And I could hear it smacking the helmet. Oh, the helmet . . . Did you want to ride with Cap, but I had your helmet?"

"He hasn't asked me to ride in ages. Where could he be?" Lynn asked, kicking her suitcases again.

"We don't want you to leave anyway. Can I bring those up to your room for you?"

"No! Sorry, no . . . I want him to see them."

"So that he knows you mean business."

"Perfectly put."

"Hey, aren't a couple of those cases mine?" Sure enough the two bottom suitcases were actually his mother's, packed for his exile while he was in jail.

"Cap won't notice."

"But they're mine."

Tamara said, "He's missing the point."

"Well, if he does notice two are mine, he's going to think you're leaving and taking me with you." Terry pulled one case from the stack. "I need a dry T-shirt. And one without slobber on it," he said, smiling at Tamara.

He was still smarting from her forceful denial of anything going on between them. "I swear," Lawrence had once said to him, "you want everything that's mine."

He left the women talking in the kitchen and went into the living room to change his shirt. Then he looked out the window to see how hard it was raining. Across the street, a Cadillac with portawalls pulled away from the curb and zoomed down the street.

"Is that him?" Lynn called from the kitchen.

"No, Lynn. That was a car."

Tamara walked by Terry on her way upstairs. He whispered what he had seen. Pulling the blinds aside herself, she asked, "Did you see a face?"

"No. But how would he know you're here?"

Tamara shouted into the kitchen, "Lynn, he's probably at a friend's house waiting for the rain to blow over."

Lynn shouted back, "He could call."

"He's a man, Lynn."

"I know. Just picked a bad night to leave him."

Another couple of hours went by with Tamara and Terry and Lynn taking turns looking out the window at every engine sound they heard. Later, Lynn retreated upstairs and began calling friends.

Terry asked, "You don't think Bread has anything to do with Cap?"

"Bread is always my first suspect with anything."

Lynn came running down the stairs minutes later. "He was at his friend Morris's place up until eleven o'clock. He got tired sitting out the rain. It looked like it had slacked off a bit so he went for it. I asked Morris if he'd been drinking. He said, 'Lynn, that's all he do these days.'"

"So he let him go at night in the rain on a motorcycle?" Tamara said.

"How far away does Morris live? Should he be here by now?"

"Not that far." Lynn's brow wrinkled and her lips trembled.

"Well, let's go," Terry said. "Lynn drives. Tamara on one side. Me looking on the other. We drive the whole route."

Lynn grabbed her car keys and they were quickly on their way.

Terry sat in back on the driver's side.

"Gah! Did you see that?" Lynn started.

"What?"

"When I hit the headlights, for a split second, I thought I saw someone in the backyard."

Tamara looked to Terry.

Lynn said, "I must be jumpy. I'm glad you two are going to do the searching."

"We'll probably see him ride by us in the opposite direction," Tamara said.

Lynn drove excruciatingly slowly. Other cars raced by. One annoyed driver laid on his horn as he sped by.

"It's raining and black as the grave, and they want to play Indianapolis 500," Lynn said.

They headed north on Garvin Street until it turned to Stringtown Road.

Terry was wondering if Bread had found Tamara and he knew Tam must have been wondering that too. He guessed if someone like Bread had asked around town where does that kid, Terrell Matheus, live, he would eventually find out. Who knew how many people Cap had told.

There was hardly anything to see out the windows, but Terry could not bring himself to tell Lynn his idea was a bust. His concentration slipped. The rain and the dark obscured everything except the lights from houses and other cars. He started thinking about Tamara's having been pregnant and that Lawrence had never known. The big brother he knew, who spent hours in the bathroom and long minutes in front of mirrors would have freaked out to be a father. Terry had no idea how Lawrence would have handled it, but he knew his brother would have rather gone to college and had fun than raise a baby. Maybe Tam realized this too. Maybe it never really mattered which guy was the father.

They came to a bend in the road of almost ninety degrees, which Lynn took slowly. Her headlights played across a dot of red reflector, and Terry sat up.

"Pull over," he said.

"Do you see something?"

"Just pull over," he was opening the door. The rain burst in. "Just let me check."

He jumped out into the downpour, which soaked him immediately. He could no longer see the red reflector or much of anything else for that matter. There was no sidewalk here. He walked on the shoulder of the road to the bend where there was a hurricane fence set back about ten feet. It was shaggy with dark vines and nearly impossible to see. But he did see where the fence had been pulled down. In the tangle he saw the bit of red, the rear trunk reflector of a Harley-Davidson Electra Glide.

"Cap! Cap! Cap Porter!"

The motorcycle lay on its side on the downed portion of the fence. There was a bit of a drop off Terry had not noticed before and he fell while scrambling to the bike.

He heard his name called by one of the women in the car.

"Cap!" Terry shouted. Now Terry was both dirty and soaked. He touched the bike; it was still warm, and the rain sizzled when it hit the engine. There seemed to be nothing beyond the fence but darkness and trees. He continued to call his uncle's name. Behind him, Lynn was backing up the car.

She rolled down her window. "Terry, what . . . God! That's his bike! That's his bike!" The door swung open, and she jumped from the car. The car began to roll backward.

"Lynn!" Tamara shouted grabbing the gear shift and shoving it into park. The car lurched to a wobbly stop and skidded on the gravel on the shoulder of the road.

"Watch your step," Terry warned.

Tamara crawled from the car on the driver's side. Lynn stopped at the motorcycle momentarily before plunging into the blackness beyond the fence.

The rain increased right then, which had not seemed possible. It all but drowned out their voices. Terry and Tamara followed after Lynn.

"He's here! He's here!" they heard her call out.

They found Lynn kneeling over Cap, who was curled under a tree.

"He's bleeding. I can't see from where."

Terry bent over his uncle, who still wore his helmet.

"He's bleeding from . . ."

Terry saw no blood. "Cap," he said.

Cap grabbed Lynn's wrist. "Hey, Muffin," he said. "Did you bring a ride?"

"What?" she said, then, "We need to find a telephone. Find the nearest gas station and call for an ambulance."

"No," Cap said. "No ambulance." He gasped. "Oh, shit. Just help me up. Shit. Crawled over here to get out of the rain until I could catch my breath."

"There ain't no out of this rain."

"Help me up, nephew."

It took all three of them to pull him to his feet and get him moving toward the car. He screamed when someone held him by his ribs. They took their time, step by torturous step. Terry bore most of the burden, but he couldn't have done it without the women. Still he had to rest every few steps.

They nearly tripped over the fence because Cap couldn't lift his legs, and Tamara had to help him. At the car, they tried to ease him down into the backseat, but it was a rough landing and he cried out. "Is Morris here? Who's all here?" he asked.

Lynn answered him.

"Get my motorcycle, would you?"

Terry, Tamara, and Lynn looked at each other.

"One of his friends can get it early tomorrow morning," Lynn said. "I'll call them."

"Get my bike, God damn it."

"Cap, we'll get it tomorrow."

"Shut up. Just . . . get the bike, nephew. He'll get it for me."

"Okay. okay," Terry said. He looked at the fallen bike. He slogged over to it and tried pulling it up, clambered over to the other side and tried pushing it up. Then Tamara was beside him. She helped without saying a word. They grunted together and brought the big bike upright. Terry straddled it. He found the key and the ignition and got it started after a few tries.

"This is stupid," Tamara said. "This has foolish written all over it."

"I can do him a favor," Terry said.

"I'll get his helmet."

He put the kickstand down and let the bike idle. The fairing was cracked. The right rearview mirror was gone. The turn signals on the right side hung limply by their cables. If there was other damage, he could not see it.

He figured working the bike backward to the road would be tough. But he saw if he went forward, he would be free of the fence. He discovered he only had to ride over a stretch of grass and between some trees to gain a driveway that would lead him back to the road.

Tamara handed him the helmet. "Do you want me to hook that up for you?" she asked, smiling.

"We'd be here all night."

Terry took a deep breath. He was afraid of the hulking size of the motorcycle, he was afraid of the wet grass, and he was afraid of what he couldn't see in the darkness.

"Lynn says we're going to follow you."

"Through here?" Terry said.

"Foolish written all over it." Tamara stepped back. Terry flipped up the kickstand and let the big machine roll over the rest of the fence. He could see little more than rain in the headlight. He kept working the brakes and eased it over the wet uneven ground. He kept it in first gear when he went among the trees. He kept his feet down, dragging them along as guides. He bumped over what must have been roots. He had to give it gas to get it up a little rise to the driveway. Up on the pavement, his confidence returned. He rode to the mouth of the driveway and saw Lynn and Tamara waiting on him. He wasn't sure of the way home so he signaled for them to lead, and they finally understood.

The windshield, which he noticed was cracked, afforded him some protection from the stinging rain. Again Lynn drove slowly, thinking perhaps it was safer for him, but it seemed to only prolong the miserable ride.

Once in the house, they didn't try to get Cap upstairs. He managed to hold himself up with help and gasped at every step. They took him through the kitchen. He saw the stack of waiting suitcases, but they did not seem to register. Lynn laid out Terry's sheets, and they deposited Cap on the sofa. His face was bruised, his shirt torn, and he had scrapes over various parts of the right side of his body.

Everyone was soaked. Tamara began pulling off her clothes as she trudged up the stairs.

While Lynn fussed over his uncle, Terry noticed for the first time the deep parallel grooves that had been cut into one side of the helmet, probably by the wire of the fencing. There were matching scrapes on Cap's cheek. His uncle had narrowly missed a bad one. "Jesus," Terry said, showing the helmet to Lynn.

The temporary arrangement was for Lynn and Tamara to sleep together, and for Terry to take his room back. But Lynn never came up the stairs.

twenty-three

TAMARA HAD SLEPT fitfully at the foot of Cap and Lynn's big bed. Still sleepy, she scooted from the bed to look out the window.

She did not like Cap Porter, did not like having spent the night in his bed. There was no excuse for the way he treated Lynn and Terry. And it was sad to see Terry's face when Cap would enter the room, just like a puppy thirsting for a word of recognition. Cap Porter was a man who cared more for his own pain than anyone else's, and Tamara hated that.

He had his woman and his nephew tramping around in mud and bushes in a thunderstorm in the middle of the night, just to get his drunk ass home. And he'd thought nothing of risking Terry's life just to get his bike back and avoid the police and their questions.

As she stood at the window, relieved not to see what she feared she might, it came rolling into view. A Cadillac, the same rose color as Bread's, drove slowly by the house.

She saw the car's brake lights flare just as it disappeared from view. Still in her nightgown, Tamara ran downstairs and out the side door, running by Lynn asleep in the easy chair, and Cap, out on the couch. She ran around the back of the house so she would not be seen and peeked down the street from behind a column of the neighbor's porch. The Cadillac was parked near the end of the block, and she was certain it was Bread's.

She found herself wondering for the nth time what Bread was and was not capable of. Why not just park in front of the house, get out of the car, knock on the door like anybody else would do, and ask, "Excuse me, is Tamara Groves here?" No, he'd rather do a stakeout. He would be angry; he would be stewing in it. He would feel she was being unfair to him and will have conveniently forgotten that he assaulted her and nearly raped her. He had become just another man who saw only his side of the story.

She felt bad for Lynn and Terry. They did not deserve to be entangled in her messy dramas.

A man across the street came out of his house. He would have seen Tamara had he looked up, so she retreated around the house, tiptoeing in the wet grass. As she opened the side door, Terry came out.

"I wanted to check out Cap's cycle in the daylight. Let's see how bad off it is. Did you see his helmet? It saved him."

"Bread's out there."

"What?"

"Down the street in his car. He can't see us on this side of the house. Come to think of it. He has a bad spot for a stakeout."

Terry squeezed by her to go to the front of the house.

"No, Terry. Don't let him know we know he's there." She stepped inside but leaned out.

Terry stopped and pivoted. "Okay. Well, what do you want to do? We could call the cops. I know a few of them. They hate me, but they might come out to say hi."

"Yeah, look, I have somewhere I have to be. So let's . . ."

"I'll take you."

"No, rather walk this time, believe it or not." Not for the first time it flashed though her head how much of this would never have happened if she had not minded walking. Terry said something else, probably asking where she was going, but she was already scurrying through the house, using her arms for added cover in front of her nightgown.

Lynn still slept in the chair, but Cap was not on the couch.

She went to her room and picked out some clothes, feeling lucky to find a blouse that wasn't too wrinkled.

"I almost killed myself slipping on this mess left on the floor," Cap shouted, exiting the bathroom. He had a limp.

Tamara had left a puddle of clothes on the bathroom floor.

She stepped into the hallway and said, "Sorry, Mr. Porter."

He looked her way; she was glad she had a bundle of clothes and a makeup bag to hold in front of her.

"What, honey?" They heard Lynn from downstairs.

Tamara almost winced when she saw Cap. She had a smart-ass retort about why the clothes were wet in the first place, but looking at his face, she let it go. He looked like he had lost a fight, and it had not been close.

He seemed to sense what she was thinking and hobbled back down the stairs. He turned around just as she got the bathroom door. "Are you leaving?" he asked. "I saw suitcases in the kitchen."

"Um, I'm not sure," she said.

"You're still welcome here." He steadied himself on the stair rail. "Any friend of Lawrence's is a friend of ours."

Tamara nodded closed the bathroom door behind her.

She took a quick bath, then dressed even quicker. She told Lynn where she was going, but no one else, and even managed to slip out without encountering Terry. She beat the temptation to check on the Cadillac down the block and cut through the backyard to the alley.

She was on her way to the Matheus house and was happy for the time she had alone during the walk.

She sensed that to remain involved with the family, especially with Terry, was a mistake. She was not sure if the feeling stemmed from what had already happened or because of Bread and what might happen next. "He got the gun, that gun, because of you," Terry had said. "He was scared of Bread."

This will be my last visit, she told herself. I think Judith is getting better, and I am getting worse. She skirted standing puddles of last night's rain. After two blocks, she left the alley and walked down the sidewalk of a quiet side street. It wasn't the most direct route, but she was being wary, and the other ways meant too much traffic.

"Can I kiss you?" he had once asked, making him seem even younger to her than he was.

"If you have to ask," she had said, "then no, you can't."

She wished she had worn something else, just some jeans instead of the skirt. She just did not want to be pretending with these people but always seemed to be accusing herself of doing just that.

He pulled the sheet over both of their heads. It billowed above them and then settled lightly down. There was still afternoon sun filtering through it, and she could see that smile glued to his face. She was aware that she was smiling too. He put a finger on her nose and traced around her nose and mouth. The way he looked at her was embarrassing, but she liked it, in retrospect she liked it. He was memorizing her, absorbing her, taking in all of her. Her pretty track star. That boy. And why hadn't she realized it at the time, her boy.

Damn it, she thought, crossing another intersection. It looked as if the rain might return today. If they offer me a ride back this time, I'd better take it.

Not wanting to walk directly on them, she stepped over the unpainted boards that led to the Matheuses' front door. The door opened before she knocked.

"Saw you coming up the walk," Preston Matheus said. He always looked at her as if he were judging her. Obviously, he could not decide what he thought about her, and Tamara did not blame him. He'd been burned on the trust thing already.

She said hello and crossed her arms under his gaze.

"Judith will be down in a minute. Or she will if I tell her you're here. Judith! Judith, honey, Tamara is here. Tam!" he shouted up the stairs, then asked her, "You graduated this year, right?"

"Yes, sir, and I got a job in the print shop of Keller Crescent."

"Oh, yeah. That's good. You like it?"

Tamara nodded and then shrugged.

"Well, hello, Tamara."

Mrs. Matheus looked better than the last time Tamara had seen her. Her hair was brushed and neat and she wore a pair of slacks. Most of all, her smile did not look as miserable and fleeting as before.

The women greeted each other with a hug and immediately went into the kitchen.

"So have you seen Terrell?" Judith asked before sitting down. She caught herself. "I'm sorry. I'm being rude. How are you doing?"

"I'm fine. Like I told your husband, I have a job."

"Wonderful. Do you like it? I don't have any tea made up. Coffee? It's instant . . ."

"Ice water would be good. And Terry is . . ." She was going to say fine, but then she truly did not think so. And, of course, there was Bread to worry about; he would be pissed at Terry too. And then it occurred to her: Maybe he doesn't know that she is living there at all.

Maybe he only knows that Terry Matheus, the dude who lied about shooting his brother, lives there. And maybe Bread is blaming him for her leaving and wants revenge.

Judith was twisting the blue plastic ice trays. "Preston overfills them," she said. The ice cracked and she dropped the cubes in tea glasses and filled them with tap water. "Look, I know you must think I'm pitiful. Needing you to tell me how my son is. It's just that I think he needs the time. His father does too. If I go over to Cap's, it will be like going around him. I'm trying to let the men be men here. It takes a while."

"Yes ma'am. That can be a long wait."

Judith chuckled and held up her glass. They clicked glasses.

"He blames himself for everything," Tamara said. "Everything. His uncle's drinking. Oh, did you know your brother had an accident?"

"No," Judith said, her alarm showing.

"He's okay," Tamara added quickly. "He ran into a fence last night on his motorcycle. In the rain. He's okay. Lynn is nursing him. He has bruises mostly. She's worried about him."

"He's drinking?"

Tam nodded.

"No luck on the job front?"

"Ma'am, I don't even think he looks."

"Lord."

"Terry blames himself for all of this. He blames himself for you not going back to work either."

Judith clasped her hands in front of her as if she were about to pray. She brought them up under her nose. She said from behind her hands, "There's this parable in the Bible about human nature. It's about how a shepherd, if he's missing one of his sheep, will leave the entire flock, maybe in harm's way, to go looking for the missing one. It's human nature."

Tamara wasn't sure if she knew what the woman meant. "Terry's not missing. He's eight blocks east of here."

"No, Terry's not missing," Judith said.

The woman closed her eyes.

"Ma'am?" Tamara asked loudly. "The parents are the ones that are supposed to hold on. I chose to live with my mom. I thought she needed me more. That was all. She wasn't my favorite. I didn't think she was right to take up with that man like she did. It was an unselfish decision on my part. I didn't think she was easier, or that I'd be able to get my own way more, or even that girls should be with moms. I just thought she would need me more than Dad. But by choosing her, I made my daddy mad at me, and he never forgave me."

"Oh, honey."

"The parents should be better than all that. They should be above it."

Judith took one of Tamara's hands. A silence followed that at first felt awkward, eventually comfortable. She held Tamara's hand the whole time.

"Another business transaction to make, dear." She let go of Tamara and held up her index finger. She called, "Preston! We're ready here!"

"All right," came his voice from the front. "See you outside."

"Honey, did you walk here?"

"Yeah."

"Do you need a ride home?"

"Yes . . ."

"Well, let's see about that." Judith jumped up and went to the back door. She held it open for Tamara, who was a bit confused.

Preston Matheus was outside in the driveway. He stood beside a car covered with a tarp. His chest was puffed out and he looked directly at Tam, who couldn't read the look.

"What's going . . ."

"Okay, Preston," Judith said.

He snatched the tarp off the car.

"Happy graduation!" Judith and Preston shouted in unison.

There was Lawrence's old Dodge but cleaner and shinier and healthier looking than he'd ever managed to get it.

Judith said, "You kept the first part of your promise to your mom, and you still have to get yourself in college. So this is a reward for the first and a help to attain the second. Preston has worked on it, so assuming he knows what he's doing . . ."

"It'll run good, don't you worry."

"I couldn't," Tamara said, stunned. "I shouldn't, oh, but I will." She hugged first Judith, then Preston. "Thank you," she said to each.

Preston said, "We didn't want to keep it around. And I couldn't see just selling it . . ."

"Oh my God," Tamara said.

He handed her the keys and opened the door, which did not squeak. The interior was spotless.

"Is this the same car?"

"Papers are in the glove box," Preston was saying. "And you have a few days to get some insurance."

Tamara slid behind the wheel. Instantly, she saw Lawrence.

"What's wrong?" Judith asked.

"Lawrence and I got together because of this car," she said, laying a hand on the steering wheel. "He was proud of it. I'll take good care of it, Mr. Matheus. I promise."

"Just do better than he did," Preston said.

They all laughed, maybe a little more than the joke deserved.

"Tam, enjoy it," Judith said.

"It's gassed up," Preston added.

Judith leaned in the window. "I'm going back to work tomorrow. So you can tell Terry that."

"Okay."

"I want you to take him somewhere for me." Judith whispered even though Preston had stepped back toward the house. "I want you to bring Terry to our church Sunday."

Tamara wanted to get out of humoring that request, but the woman had just given her a car.

"I'll call you later."

"Start it up," Preston said, making a hand gesture like turning a key.

Tam started the car and gave Preston a thumbs-up. She remembered the weightless sensation of flying off the road in this car and into a cornfield. She remembered lying on the roof of this car and watching stars pop into view. And she remembered being with Lawrence in the backseat. She remembered this car waiting on her under the shade of a huge oak tree. She remembered following after a little boy to make sure he got home safely. Mr. Matheus must have done a lot of work on the engine, she thought; it rumbled low, without effort. She almost wished it had rattled and burped like it used to.

twenty-four

THE SMELL OF the gunfire refused to leave his nostrils. It was a detail he had forgotten from before. The gun smell.

Tamara was in the police cruiser at the end of the driveway. The back door was open, and he could see her by the car's dome light. Though it was dark, the police car's revolving beacons created quick scenes that kept repeating. There was Cap sitting in his front yard, his arms behind his back. At the back of her car, Lynn, in her robe, spoke to two cops. On the sidewalk there were neighbors and more police. One of the neighbors pointed at Terry.

They would not let him talk to Tamara. They kept them all apart in order to keep the stories separate.

This is the story Terry told the police:

"I had just finished watching *Baretta,* so I know it was nine o'clock. Lynn had asked me to take the trash out. That's why I was outside.

"No, the light over the door wasn't on then. I know where the trashcans are. I didn't need it. No, I didn't see anybody.

"No. She's just staying with us. She's my brother's girlfriend.

"Lynn turned on the light and came outside.

"I was over there. Next to the garage, at the garbage can and they kept blocking my path.

"They were just talking sh . . . stuff. They were hassling me.

"I shouted for them to leave her alone. Lynn told them they weren't welcome, that they were trespassing.

"Like I said, they kept pushing me and getting in the way.

"Four, maybe more.

"Then Tam came out. Bread started pulling on her. He was screaming. He said it was time she came back home. He said he wasn't going to put up with her shit anymore.

"I got to him. I don't know. He was pulling on her. I grabbed him. Yeah, I hit him or tried to.

"That's when my uncle came out. He saw that Bread had a gun. No, I didn't exactly see the gun, but . . . Yeah, that's when Cap fired."

A FEW MINUTES before Cap appeared at the kitchen door and fired his gun, Terry stepped out into the thick humidity. It was bad in the house because Cap's downstairs air conditioner was just too small for the job, but out here was awful. It felt as if it took effort to breathe. He lugged a bulky bag of garbage through the door with him. He took a step toward the cans beside the garage, but was drawn to the car, dimly lit by kitchen-window light. Lawrence's Dodge Dart, with the broad white rally stripe on the hood, sat behind Lynn's car. Letting the bag slide to the ground, he walked up to the car and placed a hand on the hood. Three days ago, Tamara pulled into the driveway in Lawrence's car, and she had been acting differently ever since. He did not begrudge her the car. But it was Lawrence's and had been a big part of Lawrence's life, and it felt strange to him, seeing it come and go, a teasing apparition. It was queer to be standing in the driveway and see the car pull up.

Tamara was clearly thrilled to have the car. "Your dad fixed it up for me. They said it was a graduation present." She also said to Terry, "You won't have to get up early anymore." By which she meant he would not have to take her to work or bring her home each day. These two chores, however, had become the highlights of his day.

"Finally," he had replied, pretending to be relieved.

He felt, though, that since getting the car Tamara was more distant. She spent less time with him, driving here and there, maybe visiting the friends she'd always denied having.

He retrieved the garbage bag and walked into the darkness next to the garage. He removed the lid and dropped in the bag.

"Liar, liar."

Terry jumped.

Angelo, in a dark shirt and pants, stood behind him.

"Pants on fire."

At the same time he heard rapid thumps. "Tam, I know you're in there." Bread Williams was pounding on the kitchen door.

Terry heard Lynn's voice. "Terry, it's not locked."

Terry shouted, "Don't open the door."

But he'd found his voice too late. The door opened and light from the kitchen illuminated Bread and part of the driveway.

Terry made a quick step, but someone pushed him from behind, and he staggered.

Angelo stepped in front of him. Terry felt the trashcan lid in his hands and like a gladiator with a shield he brought it up, catching Angelo under his chin. The lid was yanked from his hand and tossed across the driveway. Terry tried to run around Angelo, but now Carl blocked him too, shoving him against the garage door.

"I'm going to get you for that," Angelo said.

Terry had been shoved and hit a lot recently, first by his father, then Bill Carson, then some deadbeat father at the mission . . . The threat did not scare him.

Lynn was shrieking, and he heard Tamara shouting for Bread to leave. The women were trying to keep him out of the house.

Terry lowered his head and bowled right into Angelo's midsection; they both crashed to the ground. Terry swung and connected, and Angelo's hands went up defensively. Carl grabbed Terry by the ankles and pulled him off Angelo.

"Leave him alone!" Lynn cried.

"Call off your dogs, God damn it."

"Tam, you're coming home now."

They were all shouting at once.

Terry scrambled to his feet and swung at Carl, but got only air. He spun about, leaped over Angelo, and ran to the kitchen door.

Bread had Tamara by her wrists, holding her with both his hands. "You're not being fair!" he shouted.

Lynn held on to Tamara by the waist.

"I don't want no trouble. Tam, talk to me now, come on." Bread's voice had broken. The threat sounded more like a plea.

Terry pulled on the collar of Bread's shirt. "Let her go, you . . ."

Lynn was pushed out of the doorway and a blast deafened Terry.

Everyone froze.

"Get the fuck away from my house," Cap said. The gun was held over his head. He fired again. Bits of orange briefly glittered around the barrel.

"Now, God damn it. So help me . . ."

Tamara pulled her wrists free of Bread's grasp.

Angelo and Carl grabbed Bread, and they ran down the driveway. At their car, Bread shouted, but the ringing in his ears muted his voice and Terry couldn't make out what he'd said.

"It is over!" Tamara shouted back to Bread.

Lynn said, "Oh my God. Oh my God." She grasped Cap's arm. "Cappy," she said.

The four of them hurried back inside. Terry ran to the living room window to see if Bread and crew had truly left. Lights came on at two of the houses across the street. There was no sign of Bread's car.

Back in the kitchen, Lynn was saying, "Will Cap get in trouble? They were on his property."

"The cops won't care," Terry said.

The gun lay on the kitchen table.

Cap's left hand thumbed the palm of his right. His eyes were narrow and red.

Terry said, "The police will be here in a minute."

"Bread had a gun," Tamara said. "He did. He always carries one. Cap. Cap!" She clapped her hands to get his attention. "You saw Bread's gun. You wanted to protect me."

"I did," Cap said defensively.

Tamara squeezed his hand. "But you saw a gun too."

Lynn picked up on what Tamara was saying. "I saw him reaching for it," she said.

"Well."

"I did." She looked from face to face, trembling. "I did."

Terry said, "I didn't see anything. Sorry. But, you know, I was off to the side. I wouldn't have seen it anyway . . . at that angle . . . I couldn't see it."

"Okay," Tamara said. "I keep getting you beat up." She was rubbing her wrists. Already, they looked bruised.

"No," Terry said, "I was winning that one."

. . .

ILLEGAL DISCHARGE OF a firearm within the municipal boundaries—that was the charge against Cap. They took him downtown to book him. Tamara drove Terry and Lynn to pick him up. He was surprisingly sober looking, having sat so long handcuffed in his front lawn. It looked as though he would only get a fine. Fortunately, he had fired the one licensed weapon he owned.

The rest was handled as a domestic dispute. Tamara had helped frame it that way. The police said they would talk with Clay Williams and his friends, and they suggested that Tamara and her boyfriend work out their differences in a peaceful forum—maybe with their pastor? She thanked the officers.

At just after one in the morning, the four of them were again home. Lynn ran to her room crying. They heard her door slam. Cap, who had said little to nothing, dropped on the living room couch and was quickly asleep.

Terry and Tamara stood watching him. He began to snore immediately.

"Great," Terry said, "where do I sleep?"

"In my room," she said. "You can have any patch of floor that suits you."

She made out a place for him with a folded blanket as a mattress. She gave him a sheet and a pillow. In no time, she was in bed and the lights were out.

A stretch of silence passed. He could hear her move in the bed.

"Tam, you asleep?" he whispered.

"No. Still a bit worked up."

"Yeah. Your wrists hurt?"

"Yes."

"Will he come back?"

"Yes."

"I think Cap would have shot them if they hadn't skipped. Mom used to say he would sleep with pocketknives under his pillow."

"Terry, I'm leaving."

Another hit. People kept hitting him. He couldn't talk.

"He won't come back if I'm not here. And I want to go. I want to see someplace new."

Terry pushed his face into the pillow.

"And Terry," she added, "I want you to do me a favor."

twenty-five

THE NOTE HE placed on the coffee table told Lynn to tell his parents that he was leaving, but would call soon. The note told Cap that he intended to pay for the motorcycle: "I promise I'll get you the price you think is fair." And the note thanked Lynn for everything. "Thanks for being wonderful," he had written. He wasn't satisfied with the note. He wanted to say he knew what he had done, that he knew what damage he had done, and that with him gone, things could get back to normal. He didn't know how to put it, though, and in frustration he finally folded the paper into a square and left it on the coffee table.

The truth was—a part of the truth was—with Tamara gone it had begun to feel worse than ever being with Cap and Lynn. Lynn deserved to get her life back if she could, Terry thought.

He tiptoed down from the bedroom that was his, then Tamara's, then his again. He had traded his suitcases to Tamara for Cap's duffel bag. He slipped out the side door, leaving his key on the kitchen table. Using bungee cords, he strapped the duffel to the back of the bike's seat.

Tamara had said, "When I told Lynn I was leaving, the relief on her face was like a slap. There's bad vibes in that house."

"I thought y'all got along."

"Me too. You think she might not like thugs trying to bust into her house in the middle of the night? Anyway this feels right. I got a recommendation from my boss and . . ."

"Where you going?"

"Hmm." She smiled. "I'll call you when I get there. That's when we'll both know."

He didn't believe her. She had some place in mind. Back to Kentucky maybe? A search for her father or the family she remembered from her childhood?

He leaned into the car and kissed her on the mouth.

The day before she left, he had to perform the favor she had asked of him. His mother wanted to meet him at church. He had groaned. "Why not at home? Everyone there will all be looking at me," he had said.

He slipped outside. The morning was cooler than he'd expected after so many humid days, and he knew it would feel even cooler once he was on the motorcycle. As he turned his motorcycle toward the street he kept looking back to the house and its dark windows.

He mounted the bike and let it roll down the driveway. A half block from Cap's he pulled out the choke and started the engine; the bike awoke eagerly and the journey began.

The ride through the dark invigorated him. He had not ridden much at night, just the few times he'd taken Tamara home when she worked late and, of course, the time when he rode Cap's Harley. He took Kentucky Avenue to Highway 41 then headed south. He liked running through the shadows and seeing the black landscape beyond the road. Crossing the Ohio River at night truly felt like flying. He could look down and see the coffee dark waters below. He followed the highway's dashed lines picked up by the bike's headlight. Crossing the river into Kentucky made him feel the journey was truly under

way. To his left and behind him the sky lightened slowly. Farmhouses
and billboard signs began to emerge from the shadows.

He was being chilled to the bone, something he had thought would
be impossible in summer. Finally, he pulled off the road. The big rigs
blasted by him as he went into the duffel and pulled out two T-shirts.
He put them both on, over the T-shirt and long-sleeved camper's
shirt he already wore. With four layers on, he zipped back onto the
highway and the cold felt less severe.

More miles slid away. He stopped for gas and bought a sandwich
that had been neatly cut in half and wrapped in clear plastic. The sun
was climbing. The field in front of him chimed with the life of insects
wakening to the day.

Motorcycling felt like flying and falling. It made him feel giddy.
He didn't think he was leaving his problems behind, but the quick
transit through the wind and sun had him believing nothing could
stick to him for long. And it had been even better when Tamara's
arms encircled his waist.

Thinking about Tamara also brought to mind the day he went to
church with her. She had driven them. Terry wore a shirt and tie borrowed from Cap. Tamara wore heels and looked gorgeous. His dread
of that morning threatened to paralyze him, and Tamara had to cajole
him from the car. They arrived late; the choir was already singing and
his mother was already seated.

Terry tried to sit in the very last pew, but Tamara pulled him forward. They compromised on a middle pew. His mother sat four rows
up and to the right of them.

Reverend Saunders stood at the pulpit and thanked the choir.
"Your spirit invigorates my spirit," he said. He started his sermon,
then paused, looking over the congregation. Terry could have sworn
the pastor made eye contact with him. He looked to Tamara, but she

faced ahead. The reverend pushed some papers to the side and leaned forward. He said God had placed something else on his heart that he wanted to speak about that day. He mentioned the death penalty and how the Supreme Court had just that year lifted the ban on capital punishment, and he talked about how many who consider themselves devout Christians are in favor of capital punishment. Saunders said, "Last month, July second, I believe, in the year of our Lord 1976, in *Gregg v. Georgia,* the Supreme Court ruled that Georgia's new guided discretion laws for death penalty cases removes all the bias and discrimination in death sentencing. The judge, you see, simply has to give the right instructions to the jury. We believe that, don't we?" he asked the congregation. "Court said it. We believe it, right?" The congregation had grumbled an answer. "I'm sure other states will change their laws too, and soon the death penalty will be the rule of the land again. So, I looked to the Bible to see how God handled a capital offense."

He said he didn't have to turn too many pages to have his answer. "One brother has slain the other," Saunders said.

Terry's heart jumped. He whispered, "Tam?"

"It is in chapter four of Genesis if you wish to follow along."

Terry heard pages turning all about him, and he imagined the congregation flipping the tissue-thin pages to find a picture of him.

Tamara found a Bible in the cradle on the back of the pew in front of them. She opened it and held it between them, but Terry did not look at it.

Saunders said, "Y'all remember the Martinsville Seven? They were executed, all in the same week, for the rape of a white woman. That wasn't quite an eye for an eye, was it? The punishment didn't quite fit Old Testament criteria, did it? But, I suppose, many Christians believe in the death penalty because murder is such a final thing.

You can't take it back. By that I mean you can't revive the victim. And you can't trade places . . . killer and victim can't switch. Well, Pastor Saunders, how can we make it right, except to kill again? you ask.

"How did our heavenly Father deal with the first capital crime?" Then he told them the familiar story of Cain and Abel. "Let's see what example of how to deal with a capital crime we can take from our heavenly Father."

Terry had wanted to leave, and he would have right then had Tamara not placed her hand in his lap. He looked at it and then at her. Her eyes did not meet his, but she grasped his hand as soon as it touched hers; she anchored him.

TERRY HAD TO take frequent breaks, because the vibration of the little motorcycle shook his organs and made his butt numb. The bike's small tank made frequent stops for gas necessary despite its good gas mileage. In his mind, he toyed with a fantasy in which he would catch up to Tamara. He would pull into a gas station along the way and there she would be.

He got off the wide highway in favor of the smaller two-way roads. He wanted a break from the big semis and constant traffic, even though the chances of actually coming across Tamara would be even more reduced. The back roads into the Kentucky hills coiled, turn followed turn. Small towns were found crammed into the walls of rock, and the same rivers needed crossing a dozen times.

His knees hurt when straightened out, and his shoulders and arms were as sore as if he'd been tossing boulders all day.

By noon, he was back to wearing only one T-shirt. After almost falling asleep on the bike, something he had thought would be impossible, he parked under some trees and sat for a brief while with his back against a wide sycamore. The rest, though fitful, seemed to be enough. He rubbed his eyes and remounted the motorcycle.

He saw families at the rest stops, some climbing wearily or eagerly from their burdened station wagons. Once he saw two little black boys running about their family car. No, it was someone else's car, and their mother, near the end of patience, called them to her with hands on her hips.

TERRY'S MOTHER LONG ago had told him that it had happened to her two or three times: You're sitting in church and the pastor's sermon seems designed specifically for you. He has stabbed right to the core of what was on your heart, and it feels too close to be just coincidence; it feels like God is actually speaking to you from the pulpit. She said she went to church hoping for those moments when the word would come at her in a hoarse, rhythmic shout, through the preacher, directly from God to her.

But she had asked Tamara to bring him to church that day, so Reverend Saunders's sermon may not have been as much God's mysterious ways as it was one of hers.

The pastor's eyes raked the congregation as if he dared each of them to make eye contact. He was saying, "People, please don't get the mark confused. A lot of readers do. They think the mark is a curse, that the mark is an awful thing, like a scarlet letter, or a brand, or prison numbers. They believe, mistakenly, that the mark was designed to bring shame to Cain for what he'd done, public humiliation. But that's not God's way. Let's read carefully here. Cain pleads for his life. He says, Lord, the word is all out in the streets. Everyone knows about the killing! They are going to give me a bad time. Lord, they gonna kick me in four different directions."

There were a few of giggles from the congregation at that.

"'And the Lord,'" Saunders continued, "and I quote, from chapter four, verse fifteen: 'And the Lord said unto him, Therefore whosoever slayeth Cain, vengeance shall be taken on him sevenfold. And the Lord set a mark upon Cain, lest any finding him should kill him.' That mark said, don't mess with my boy Cain. I know he done wrong, but we've already talked it out. Don't slay him. Leave him be. Let him live."

Saunders produced a handkerchief and began wiping his forehead. "That mark was a blessed mark. It was nothing less than a sign of God's mercy and forgiveness. Let him live."

In a singsong cadence, Saunders intoned, "See? Um, God's saying, Iyah understand that he slew his brother. Iyah understand, uh-huh, that he tried to hide it. Um, Iyah understand that he tried to lie to me about it. Oh, Iyah understand it was a horrible thing. Iyah understand that blood crieth to me from the ground!" Abrupt silence from the pulpit.

Saunders made Terry wait. He made the entire church wait on him. He mopped his forehead.

Tamara's hand tightened on Terry's.

From the congregation came a scattering of responsive encouragement.

Softly, Saunders said, "I understand."

Terry had to tilt his face up to prevent the tears from flowing.

"But, but, but . . . but I still have plans for him. Uh-huh. He still can redeem himself. He can still help others. He can repent. He can still grow as a human being. He is still one of Mine. Do you hear?

"Leave him be."

TERRY PASSED THE turn off for Lexington, Kentucky, but then turned back for it. He passed the large stable grounds

surrounding the city, the beautiful white fences, and the horses graz-
ing. He rode the city streets. No one knew him here. He could stay
here. For some reason, he did not think Tamara was in Lexington.
Then he chided himself for even considering that he was on a hunt.
Of course he wasn't, except for himself, and for a place where he could
be himself. He saw that Cincinnati was directly north. He would go
there.

He discovered drafting behind the big rigs protected him from
slamming headlong into the air.

The ride had begun to take on the quality of an adventure at last.
He enjoyed the scenery—the gently rolling hills of central Kentucky
and the deep green of its grass were beautiful. He also enjoyed the
looks he got from travelers on the road as cars passed him and young
children waved from back seats.

Not far from the Ohio border, he saw dark clouds gathering. The
dramatic sky had layers of slate clouds, some lofty and wispy, and others lolling and heavy. He knew he was in for a bad storm.

It felt as if someone were pelting him with pins, and he wondered
if he should pull over. But no shelters presented themselves; no exit
ramps were near nor were there any overpasses. He did not want to
stop anyway. He steeled himself to getting wet and wondered how
the bike would behave on the wet pavement. Then he rode straight
into a downpour. In seconds he was soaked to his underwear. The
water pooled between his legs at his crotch. Soon, his feet were soaked
inside his shoes.

The scariest part was he couldn't see. He had to continuously wipe
at his helmet's visor. His speed slackened. The big rigs, like great
whales, lumbered up on him and passed, engulfing him in their wake.
The giant wheels threw up huge sprays. He felt his little bike wiggle
and fishtail as it was struck by the blasts of water. Skirting the rough

shoulder of the road, he tried to stay as far to his right as he could. In his rearview mirror, he saw the flashing headlights of cars racing up behind him. He became pinned in. A semi threw rooster tails of water from the front as another sprayed him while passing on the left. He was inundated in a sparkling, cascading world. He could not hear anything but the loud sizzle of tires churning water.

As a semi passed, he made the decision to chase after it. He moved up so close to it, the sprays fired mostly over his head. He raced after the behemoth at sixty miles an hour and when it returned to the right lane, Terry turned the throttle full out and zipped by. Immediately, he could see. It was still raining, but this was nothing compared to the wall of water the trucks had been throwing up. He made sure he stayed in front of traffic, and just two miles later he found an exit ramp and a gas station that offered shelter.

The station attendant gestured for him to come inside.

"I'm soaked," Terry said.

"No sweat," the man said. "I ain't mopped the floor yet anyhow."

His bundle was soaked too, so there was no dry shirt to put on. He waited there, standing in a spreading pool, munching on Slim Jims until the sky cleared.

When the sun reappeared, Terry returned to the road. In a matter of minutes, the sun and wind had dried him out.

By evening, he was desperately tired. He had not realized how long-distance riding could wear you down. He circumvented Cincinnati and took a road that would have taken him to Columbus, but he stopped at a roadside rest stop. He walked his bike to a place behind some trees where it would be hard to spot from either the road or the rest facility. He used the bathroom and splashed water in his face. He ate chips and drank soda from a vending machine. He had stopped at a McDonald's hours ago, so he wasn't too hungry. He might have to get used to hunger pangs, though; checking his cash, he saw with alarm how quickly it had dwindled.

He used the duffel for a pillow and slept next to the motorcycle, but the machine and the ground both cooled off in the middle of the night. Terry shivered even though he put on every shirt he had, and he started at any sound he could not account for. At first light, he found himself lying in an earth-hugging mist. Everything looked soft and new. Glad the night was over, he got to his feet, eager to continue his ride.

At a little store, seemingly placed in the middle of nowhere, he bought an egg-salad sandwich, a soda, and a little pecan pie. He gassed up and counted his money. His right hand that had held the throttle open for so many miles ached when opened. Still, he mounted up without hesitation. Instead of heading to Columbus as intended, though, he turned left. The sun was on his back. Everything looked wide open and beautiful. Without consciously coming to a decision, without wonder of any kind, he headed home.

HE TURNED DOWN Evans Avenue and then proceeded to Washington Avenue. He rode in front of the dark brick fortress that was his high school.

"What do we want?"

"Justice."

"When do we want it?"

"Now."

He rode by his parent's house without stopping. He saw the new porch boards that had not been painted. Lawrence and he had ridden their bicycles over the same cracked asphalt he rode over now. That first time the boys had pedaled down Gum Street with its old, sidewalk-busting trees and houses with porches and flower gardens, they were thrilled because the family had just moved into a real house from the projects. They had left all the stigma of living in the projects behind, and the boys felt a tremendous pride in their parents and themselves. "Check out our neighborhood," Lawrence had shouted.

Terry circled back, and this time stopped in front of the house, letting the motorcycle idle. He patted the contents of his jean pockets through the denim and could feel the shape of a house key. He could use it to let himself in and avoid a confrontation at the door. The idea of mounting those steps to stand on that porch scared him. He could feel his body's reaction, a warm flush, a quivering lower lip. He pressed a hand to his mouth. He would knock and they would be there, and then what would he say? Standing right there where it all happened, what would he say?

It was not yet five o'clock and it was possible that his mother was still at the bank. Tamara told him she had gone back to work.

He eased out the clutch and rode away. He rode down Lincoln Avenue, passed the funeral parlor, and the Penny Queen ice-cream stand. He saw the houses of friends and hoped to actually see them, knowing he would not be spotted as he zipped by with a helmet on. As he rode around corner after corner, he remained only a handful of blocks from home. He passed by Liberty Baptist Church and the larger St. Mary's Cathedral across the street.

Before the rest of the service had concluded that day, Terry had pulled Tamara up and was heading for the door. He felt a hundred eyes on him, imagining one set of eyes in particular. Tamara was disappointed that he did not want to stay and talk to his mother. "I do," he said. "Too many people." She took him back to Cap's.

Terry was tired of riding. He could feel the weariness in his arms and his rear end, yet he didn't want to stop.

He wondered what it was like at his parents' home. He imagined it was quiet and that they have developed a routine: His father cleans out his lunch pail first thing, and he looks to see if Terry's mother has set anything in the refrigerator intended for the night's dinner. He turns on the TV. Then Preston Matheus will get the day's newspaper and sit at the kitchen table and wait for his wife to come home. They will cook together. Terry tries to picture them doing this, now that they are the only two living at home.

Terry came to Stanley Hall School, an old school of worn, chalky brick. The school and the yard were empty now. He stopped the motorcycle in front of it and killed the engine. He remembered how Lawrence had once saved him from some boys who wanted to beat him up. The boys claimed he had stolen some of their marbles, but he hadn't. They had just wanted to take Terry's marbles. Terry had not wanted to fight and tried to walk away. The two boys sandwiched him and threatened him loudly enough for others to hear. Then Lawrence was there. The boys explained what was going on and Lawrence said to them, "If he has your marbles you get to beat him up, but if he doesn't, I'm going to kick the shit out of both of you every day for a week." Terry sat astride the motorcycle ignoring the temptation to step off it. He fell in love with Cathy Walton on this very playground, a crush he held on to all the way to high school. But now he could barely hold an image of the girl in mind and a picture of Tamara Groves replaced it.

He flipped out the kick-start, stepped up, and sent it around. He knew where he had to go.

HE KNOCKED AND waited and knocked again before the door opened and a scraggly-looking Cap stared at him, recognized him finally, and stepped aside. "Oh, are you back? Note made it seem like you'd be gone for a good space. I figured you went sniffing after the girl. What happened? She didn't want anything to do with you, so you're back? Went chasing your brother's girl?"

Terry gave Cap a hard look, and Cap looked away. "I didn't go chasing anybody. I just figured it wasn't time to go yet. I . . . um, I wanted to talk to you. Thought we could talk now."

"Yeah? Lynn's gone. Blamed me for you leaving and the girl leaving. Said I didn't have a job. Well, who needs any bitch who don't stick with you durin' the hard times? I'm better off. Jesus, she was a whiner too, wasn't she? You notice that? Bitch, bitch, bitch all the time." Cap turned on the TV. He clicked the dial around with lightning speed. He settled on an *Andy Griffith Show* rerun and settled back into his chair. "Shit. Like jobs grow on trees around here."

Terry could hear the wavering in his own voice as he said, "Sorry about Lynn, Uncle Cap."

"Don't be. And I saved y'alls asses that night. I did."

"Maybe you can call her later . . ."

"They took my gun, by the way. Part of the deal. I defend my house. Stop a kidnapping. And law enforcement confiscates my gun. Now, when Williams and his punks come back, we can spit at them from the window."

Terry stood there.

His uncle looked up at him for the first time. His eyes blinked as if he were looking into bright light. "What do you want from me, Terry? The bike? It's yours. That'll do you?"

"I came to, uh, I wanted to apologize to you, Uncle Cap. For . . . for the story I told. And for that night that should never have happened. I lied and all, but I was scared. I know I shouldn't have." Terry wanted so much to be a man about this.

Cap looked back at the television. Andy Griffith was locking up the town drunk, no, the gag was the drunk locked himself up.

Terry waited.

Cap's mouth opened, but he said nothing. He shrugged and then waved a hand at his nephew that dismissed everything Terry had said or had tried to say. "You lied to everybody, not just me. I mean, I know it wasn't personal just to me, right?"

"I can't apologize to everybody. You're one of the ones I have to apologize to, Cap. I'm sorry."

Cap rubbed his chest. "What you gonna do now?"

"Go see my folks. I'm sorry about Lynn, Cap. If you call her . . ."

Cap scooted forward, took a step to the TV, and turned up the volume.

Terry used the bathroom before he left.

It hurt getting on the bike; his legs, butt, and knees were sore. He had to flip the valve to his reserve tank as he rode away.

twenty-six

Terry rode down Gum Street. The seven-hundred block, the six-hundred block . . . There were boys he knew on the porch of the Hinton's house. They watched him but did not recognize him. He did not acknowledge them. The five hundred block. The Hale's, the McCracken's, the Payne's—he coasted—the Matheuses'. The new boards on the porch still looked raw and they led directly to the door. Terry cut the engine. The little motorcycle had carried him for several hundred miles making a big loop over three states. He imagined the bike breathing hard after its long ride, its gas tank expanding and contracting like lungs.

He pulled off his helmet and absently scratched at the back of his head. He hung the helmet from the handlebars.

His parents' car was in the driveway.

He fished in his jeans and pulled out his door key.

Terry climbed the steps to the house, feeling something climbing in his throat. He refused to consider the side door. He stepped on the raw boards. He looked at the key in his hand, then put it back in his pocket.

"She's Bread's girl."

"I got something for Bread Williams." Lawrence holds up that gun. That gun again.

Lawrence heads down the hall to the front door and Terry follows. "Dad is going to kill you if he finds out you have that."

"And if you tell him, see if I ever drive you anywhere or even talk to you again."

"Let me see it."

"You can see it from there."

"You're going to get in trouble. Big-time."

"Do you know how much of a baby you are?"

"I don't know what you think you're going to do with it. How much did it cost? Tamara Groves ain't worth it; let Bread have her."

"Be cool, T. I ain't gonna hurt anybody. I'm going to make sure they don't fuck with me. Bread always has his damn pack with him. Fuckin' coward don't go anywhere without his boys. He probably takes them with him when he takes Tamara out. He probably takes them with him when he goes to take a dump."

"Let me see it."

"Quit grabbing."

THE SCREEN DOOR was not latched, and Terry opened it. Using his key tempted him again. He had not truly anticipated this moment. He had imagined how they would react but not how he would feel.

"Oh boy," he whispered and blew out a long stream of air. He knocked, yet could barely hear the sound himself. Still, he waited.

"WHO'D YOU GET it from? If you even show Bread that gun, he'll show you five of his."

"Poor Terrell. Lawrence has everything. Terrell don't have squat."

"Let me see it." Terry reaches out.

"Quit."

Both brothers have their hands on it at the same time and only for a moment; it explodes between them.

THE DOOR OPENED with a loud crack like a dry seal being broken.

Terry gasped.

His mother was looking at him. Her hands went up, back down, and then she grabbed for him.

He was in her embrace. He couldn't hold back the tears. He smelled the light flowery scent of her favorite perfume given to her on Mother's Day a year ago. Birthday and Mother's Day had been skipped this year.

"Terrell, Terrell," she said.

Somehow they went inside without her relinquishing her hold on him. And then she abruptly let go and stood back.

"Where have you been? Lynn called saying maybe you'd gone off somewhere."

"No," Terry said, "I just took the long way home."

"Since early yesterday? Where did you go? All on that little motorcycle?"

"Just around. Just for the ride."

"You look so different," she said. "Look how thin you are! How much have you lost?"

Terry shrugged. "Cap doesn't have scales, but I have to put safety pins in my pants."

"I can see your cheekbones. You look a bit like . . . Did you get taller too? And your hair . . ." she said.

Neither of them seemed to know what to do, so they stood there. Terry was suddenly very tired. The ride had been exhausting. He felt as if he'd run the five hundred miles.

"You're back to work. You have your work clothes on."

She looked down at herself as if to verify his statement. "Yes, back to work. I suppose it's for the best. I suppose." She crossed her arms. "The girls at work, they try to be nice . . . I've been back for a week now. Some don't mean to, but . . ." Her voice shrunk until her last few words were inaudible. Then she said, "Saw you at church."

"I need to use the bathroom."

"You hungry?"

"I should be starved, but I'm only a little bit hungry."

"I'll get you something. Bring in your suitcase."

"I left most things over Cap's. Where's . . ."

"Your Dad's working an extra project this week. He works all the time these days. We've had a busy week." Busy week. This used to be her refrain about the whole family, with the boys going off to school or to school activities, her husband and her working, it seemed the four of them were never in a room together at the same time. "I don't know when he'll be home. Guess I'd better fix him something too.

"Call Lynn, tell her you're here."

"She . . . I've already been over there."

His mother made him a sandwich, and he sat alone at the kitchen table and ate. He heard his mother moving around upstairs.

He couldn't finish the sandwich. He looked at the kitchen clock, wondering when his father would be home.

He sat on the couch in the living room. He wanted to say what he had come to say. He wanted to say it first thing and get it over with. He would say it to both of them together. He would say again that he was sorry, and this time he'd ask them to forgive him.

He fell asleep on the couch.

• • •

When he awoke, still feeling groggy and heavy, he heard voices from the kitchen. His father was home. Terry suddenly felt nauseous. During his ride through the flat Ohio landscape, he had chastised himself for the great lie he had told his parents and his hometown. What had I been thinking, he would wonder. But now, hearing the voice of his father just down the hall, only yards away, he understood perfectly.

They were talking about him, of course.

"And he's been riding that little motorcycle outside?"

He could not hear his mother's reply.

"Why did he come now? Did he say why he came now?"

This time he heard his mother say, "Does he need a reason?"

"I'm just trying . . . Was there trouble at Cap and Lynn's? I'm just trying to figure."

He didn't hear his mother's answer and suspected she didn't have one.

"Is he staying? Is he back for good? Or is he visiting and still going to live with Cap?"

"I don't know, Preston."

Heavy footsteps marched toward Terry and he dropped his head back on the sofa's arm rest and closed his eyes.

He could feel his father standing over him. He could smell his clothes—the sweat and the heat and dust. He could hear his father's breathing above him. He felt like a small woodland creature playing possum to the great and curious bear snuffling directly over. Preston stood there for a long time, and Terry wondered if he shouldn't feign awakening, throw his arms wide, and fake a yawn.

Tamara had hooked one of her fingers in his belt loop. That action, that gesture had a profound effect on Terry. He felt like a man when she did that. No, he felt more like he wanted to be a man. He was conscious she was older than he. He wanted to be grown for her, not to be a boy in her eyes or in his own.

They walked along the road to her car.

She'd said, "One of the reasons I wanted to go back to my apartment that day was I had left my money. I wanted the clothes too, but I had saved up money. Now I can get away."

"You're the only friend I have. God, doesn't that sound pitiful!"

"If they're any good, we only need one. You're my one too." Tamara had hugged him.

LATER, TERRY WAS called to dinner. His father sat at the kitchen table and did not get up. They exchanged sheepish greetings.

They ate quietly.

Terry thought it the perfect time to say what he had come to say, but the words would not come out.

His father asked, "Are you done with the community service?"

"Not yet."

"Did you go to summer school, or are you going to have to repeat the whole year?"

"Nah, no sir. But I don't have to repeat the whole thing."

"Well, you could have made it up in summer school, right? Now you're going to be behind. What if they don't offer the courses you need this fall? You'll have to wait until the next spring semester. And, by the time you take Geometry 2 or whatever it might be, you'll probably done forgot what you learned in Geometry 1 last year. This is going to be a mess."

Something in Terry began to evaporate. He looked at his mother, then down at the plate between his elbows. Whatever had gotten him through his parent's front door was trying to abandon him now. Once again, he was a schoolboy, caught with inadequate explanations. "I was busy with the community service."

He knew, then, he could never say what he had wanted to say, to ask for what he had come to know he needed.

His mother said, "He could monitor what he needs to in the fall as a refresher and be ready for next spring."

Terry pushed his mashed potatoes around on his plate. He sensed rather than saw something pass between his parents.

His father stood, shoving his chair back. "Okay, Judith," he said. He left the table with half the food still on his plate.

THEY DID NOT sit together at the kitchen table again. For the next two days his father left for work early and came home late. Terry felt relieved each time the presence of his father was gone from the house.

He spoke a little with his mother. He told her a bit about the doings at Cap's but not about Bread's stalking or Cap's shooting.

He rode his motorcycle around, stopping anywhere he thought might be a decent place to look for a job. Twice he passed friends he knew, but rode by without stopping, and they did not recognize him.

Finally, he got a call back from a restaurant that made pizzas. He would help in the kitchen and bus tables.

On his third night home, Terry and his mother sat in the dark living room with the television light coating them. She sat on the sofa, and he sat on the floor with his back against the sofa.

They watched *Starsky & Hutch,* but Terry paid very little attention to it. His father was upstairs, already asleep.

"Mom," Terry said. "I, um . . ." He glanced back at her, saw the shifting light in her eyes as she looked down at him. He spoke in a rush, "I'm sorry about everything. I know I said it before, but I really am sorry and . . . and I was wondering if you could find it in your heart to forgive me." He turned back toward the television so she could not see the tears welling in his eyes. His vision was blurred.

He waited.

She didn't say a thing.

He couldn't bring himself to turn back around and face her. "Mom?"

He gathered himself to jump up and run from the room.

"That's why you didn't ride away on that motorcycle. That's why you came back," she said. Suddenly her arms were wrapped about his head with a vicelike fierceness. He barely heard her—her encircling arms covered his ears. "You've been forgiven a long time now." And he felt soft pecking kisses, dozens, on the top of his head.

TERRY'S ROOM WAS across from Lawrence's. The door to his brother's room was closed. He realized he was grateful not to have had to pass that door each day this summer. He got a brief glimmer of how things must appear to his mother. A house that had once been loud and raucous, a bustling turnstile, whirling with the ins and outs of two teen boys and their friends, had become an attic door, a cabin in the woods, isolated in the middle of nowhere.

He opened the door to Lawrence's bedroom and went in. Most of Lawrence's things had been boxed. A pyramid of cardboard boxes was stacked against one wall.

A sewing machine and table had been moved in and placed in front of a window.

The packing was far from completed and clothes remained stacked on Lawrence's bed. Terry sat on a corner of the bed and a stack of clothes tumbled over.

Tamara had wanted to conduct a funeral in Lawrence's room. She had been unsatisfied with the funeral Lawrence had been given. They'd isolated themselves in Lawrence's room that day. "I didn't like the funeral. We should hold our own." Her hands flew up between them. She tapped one index finger against the other. "First, we would make it about how he lived, not about how he died."

"Right on."

"And, second, sorry, but anyone who didn't know him could not attend."

Ultimately, though, Terry had walked out on her.

He wished he had completed the funeral with her. Knowing her now as he did, he decided she was probably trying to help him more than help herself even though she had been in just as much pain. The thought of Tamara put a smile on his face.

"You were right about her, brother of mine," he said to the room.

He could have told her a story. Tam had told a story about Lawrence. That was her idea of a funeral—share a good story about the one who's gone. Righteous. A far better idea than going to church with a bunch of impostors who never knew Lawrence.

And there were good stories. There were things he could have told her. How they got up early on Saturday mornings and made pancakes together for the entire family. And how it was Lawrence who'd taught Terry how to ride a bike after his father had thrown up his hands and marched off saying, "Boy's got no equilibrium."

Lawrence had tried to give him tips on how to talk to girls. Those hadn't worked so far.

There was the time Terry had rummaged in the garage to get down an old model train set his father had told him to leave alone. In getting it down he'd knocked over an iron pipe, which fell against his father's car and broke out a taillight.

Terry had hurriedly put the train set back and returned the pipe to its precarious corner. He had been so scared. He told Lawrence, who at first laughed at him.

"You are in big, big trouble. Dad is going to wear you out. Oh, crap, but you are deep in it." But then Lawrence must have seen how frightened his younger brother was, and he put an arm about his shoulder.

Terry had said, "Maybe he won't notice when he leaves, and when he gets home he'll think it happened while he was parked at work or something."

"That's a chickenshit idea. Not gonna work either. Look here. Get all your money together, even your Christmas money. This is an emergency. You tell him you were just hunting around in the garage. You don't have to say what for. We'll order a new taillight and you'll be able to tell him it's paid for and on its way. See, that way you done made up for it even before he can get his belt off."

Terry had to borrow some money from Lawrence, which he paid back by taking all of Lawrence's turns at the lawn mower, but it had worked. Preston had railed, but there was no punishment.

He should have told Tamara that story.

From beneath the fallen pile of T-shirts poked the sleeve of Lawrence's letter jacket. His big brother had lettered in track. Terry remembered seeing him strolling down the crowded hallways of the high school in that jacket.

Terry pushed the other clothes away and held up the jacket. It was a deep crimson with gray leather sleeves. It had a large *B* on the left chest with a golden foot pinned to it.

Lawrence had once caught Terry wearing one of his jackets—not this one, which was special to him, but another one Terry knew his brother cared little about. "There's two things wrong with this picture," Lawrence had said, "You're in my room, one. And you're wearing my jacket, two."

Terry put on the letter jacket. It fit well, just a little loosely.

"If it's something of mine, you just got to have it, don't you? You're always following behind me and getting into my stuff. I swear you only want something because you know it's mine."

"You're right, big brother." Terry traced around the jacket's letter with a finger. "I only want this because it's yours."

twenty-seven

TERRY LAID THE primer on generously and let the sun dry it. He felt a little uneasy being out on the porch. Someone driving by might spot him. "He's back," they would say, "that punk, who almost had the whole city rioting. He's back." But it was a quiet afternoon, and they lived on a quiet street and no one drove or strolled by. Still, he moved from the porch steps, and sat behind one of the porch columns to wait for the primer to dry.

He shook the paint can vigorously and then used a screwdriver to pry open the top.

He started painting the porch boards. He liked doing this. He liked doing something and not thinking. It reminded him of working on the motorcycle at Cap's, or working in the kitchen at the rescue mission.

He heard the grating sound of his father clearing his throat. His dad was looking at him through the front screen door.

Terry nodded to him but continued painting.

"No. Go with the grain," his father said. "I been meaning to get around to that. Have you got another brush?"

Terrell pointed to the extra brush, again without looking up.

Preston stepped out and lowered himself to the porch. His knees creaked. "Damn," he said. He dipped his brush and scraped the excess paint on the inner edge of the can. "Like this. With the grain," he said.

O. H. Bennett is the author of *The Colored Garden,* which *Booklist* called "beautiful and real." A graduate of the George Mason University creative writing program, he lives in northern Virginia.